Zen's mouth landed on Blade's with graceful precision.

He grabbed her arms to push her away. Not expecting a kiss, he'd been blindsided. And when he wanted to shove her off and march out of the room, he suddenly relaxed his grip on her arms and leaned into the kiss.

And then he leaned in a little more.

He pulled her closer, sliding a hand up her back to keep her there. Her mouth fit his like no other woman's had. She felt...not so much right, but rather as if she'd found something and did not want to again lose it. A missing piece to her puzzle? Despite being unable to remember things about herself, she'd certainly not lost the skill of delivering a kiss.

Blade moaned deep in his throat and then opened her mouth with his and slid his tongue inside her heated kiss. She felt impossibly exquisite. She smelled like honey and her body was warm and supple against his. A sweet thing.

And that was the kicker. Her scent did not allude to her identity. What was she? And worse, could whatever she was be bad for him?

Michele Hauf has been writing romance, action-adventure and fantasy stories for more than twenty years. France, musketeers, vampires and faeries feature in her stories. And if she followed the adage "write what you know," all her stories would have snow in them. Fortunately, she steps beyond her comfort zone and writes about countries and creatures she has never seen. Find her on Facebook, Twitter and at michelehauf.com. You can also write to her at PO Box 23, Anoka, MN 55303.

Books by Michele Hauf

HARLEQUIN NOCTURNE

Saint-Pierre Series

Ghost Wolf
Moonlight and Diamonds
The Vampire's Fall

In the Company of Vampires Series

Beautiful Danger
The Vampire Hunter
Beyond the Moon

HQN BOOKS

Her Vampire Husband
Seducing the Vampire
A Vampire for Christmas
"Monsters Don't Do Christmas"

Visit the Author Profile page
at Harlequin.com for more titles.

THE VAMPIRE'S FALL

MICHELE HAUF

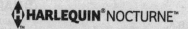

HARLEQUIN® NOCTURNE™

Recycling programs for this product may not exist in your area.

ISBN-13: 978-0-373-00946-6

The Vampire's Fall

Copyright © 2015 by Michele Hauf

Printed in U.S.A.

Dear Reader,

I've written more than twenty stories for Nocturne and I have to say I never get tired of writing about paranormal creatures. I could write vampires and werewolves, faeries and witches, demons and angels, well...forever. And some of my characters live that long! Could you imagine forever? I don't think I can. Some days I think it would be amazing; other days I'm thinking a good century on this earth is more than enough for me. But if I had the added history of having walked through various centuries, perhaps that would make hitting the millennial mark more interesting.

The vampire in *The Vampire's Fall* is not that old. He's one of the four Saint-Pierre brothers. Blade is the quiet one. The mysterious one. The dangerous one. And he's not all vampire—he's got some faery blood (from his mother's side) stirring around inside him. I admit he was a difficult hero to crack open and figure out. I'm still not sure I know much more about him than that he possesses the same desire most of us do—to be loved.

Here's to a long and loving life,

Michele

Chapter 1

It wasn't often Blade Saint-Pierre walked through the Darkwood without a purpose—or a weapon. Tonight he'd craved the exhilaration of awareness that always accompanied such a venture. Instincts on alert and every muscle in his body strung tightly, he closed his wings against his back as, barefoot, he strode toward the clearing that opened to a mossy bed edging a stream.

A dark forest of no return, the massive acreage edged his property. The Darkwood was a no-man's-land that was principally Faery, but as well, a place for all breeds to congregate. It provided respite for those who could not walk amongst humans. A wayside stop for those paranormals traveling this realm that wished to take a breath before meeting the challenge of humans.

No humans dared enter the forest, for rumors told it was haunted and that the former residents of Blade's property—the original 1910 mansion had been razed— had killed themselves after hearing voices tell them to cut out their hearts.

Great rumor, Blade thought. It helped him maintain his privacy. It wasn't at all true. But it worked for him. Though he respected the boundaries of the Darkwood and only entered it with a certain reverence and much caution. Even then, he only stayed so long as his comfort level allowed.

Rumors told that people went into the Darkwood and they never came out. Deer, squirrels and wildlife? They didn't exist within the dark thickness of evil that formed the murky wood.

Blade smirked as a squirrel scampered past him, its goal, the stream. And at that reminder that all was not as it seemed—or was rumored to be—he let down his shoulders and knelt on a mossy stone, pressing his fingers into the thick, verdant frosting. For the moment, he connected with it all. The grass, stones and trees. All creatures small and large whose heartbeats he could sense. The atoms that formed his body were the same atoms that formed nature, the very air, earth and flora.

How blessed was he?

You are alive. You have survived. Move on, yes?

He was trying.

While principally considered vampire, Blade had also his mother's faery genetics coursing within his system. His black wings were not so faery-like, and the leathery edges were serrated and sharp, as if demonic. He didn't mention his faery side to others. It was his dark beast, which craved unnatural tastes, such as demon blood, that others knew about—if they knew at all.

Blade honored all of nature's creatures, including those breeds considered monsters by humans who would believe in myth. And yet, he hated demons. That a part of him looked similar to the creatures disturbed him. His wings shamed him and defined him as different. And different amongst the varied species was not always a saving grace.

Such a difference had attracted cruelty to his life.

He'd kept to himself over the past year. To the point that his brothers and sister had begun to call him a hermit. The quiet one.

He'd always been quiet. More in tune with nature than with what was going on with the human realm. The cruelty that his difference had attracted? He'd suffered torture a year ago. And following that, he had hidden away. Not wanting to show his face, his scars, to anyone. Not wanting to put himself out in a world that could attack at any moment.

For if attacked, he would retaliate.

He didn't wish to harm others. Unless it was necessary.

He'd almost mastered the hermit role until last month when an old man filling his rusty 1970s Ford at the gas station had asked him if he'd any carpentry skills. Reluctantly, Blade had nodded and stepped outside his self-imposed prison of comfort. He'd been helping the elderly with small projects in and about their homes for a couple weeks now, and…it did feel good.

Life was beginning to look up.

At the sound of something heavy lighting onto the moss behind him Blade tilted his head. He smelled no odor out of the usual, yet his skin prickled. He should be able to pick up most scents. He rose to his six-feet-four-inch height, and with a stealthy twist, turned to stare into the cold white irises of a man with equally pale skin.

From the Darkwood? Most likely. The man looked human, save for the diagonal scars over each temple, which resembled gills, but no breath opened and closed the slashes. His brows were as black as his hair and clothing, which blended him into the night. His pale face, neck and hands were the only things remarkable; the pinpoint blue glow that seemed to radiate from around his irises especially stood out on his face.

"Blade Saint-Pierre," the man said in tones that slithered with a sharp silver edge. "I am Sim."

"What are you?" Blade asked, stepping up closer and thrusting back his shoulders. He unfurled his wings and they stretched out boldly behind him.

"Nothing so spectacular as a winged vampire," the man said with a glance to take in the imposing wingspan. "I have an offer for you."

Blade inhaled through his nostrils, frustrated that he couldn't scent the man. Which meant he was not one of the many species he could instinctually sniff out. But for every breed with which he was familiar, there were so many more he could not scent.

The curiosity wasn't demon. That scent always put up Blade's hackles. And that small detail was the only thing that stopped Blade from sweeping forward a wingtip and slashing it across the stranger's long pale neck.

"I can move much faster than your feeble mortal realm allows you," the man warned, seeming to sense Blade's defensive thoughts. "You do not know me, but trust me, you've no reason to fear or consider me enemy. In fact, what I want of you will give you such satisfaction that your faery will delight in the riches."

"I don't need money," Blade countered. "You know nothing about me."

"Not monetary riches but rather such that feeds your very soul. I know you crave demon blood, fanged one."

Blade's fingers twitched for the knife he'd left back

home. He'd not revealed to anyone his insistent craving for demonic blood. It had developed during the torture a year ago. His family members would be appalled to learn of his new habit. For a man without a vast network of friends, their opinion meant everything to him.

He remained before the scentless curiosity, willing to hear him out.

"The demonic ranks are growing in the area," Sim stated, clasping his pale hands before him. "I want you to annihilate them."

Blade chuckled.

"You laugh as defense, vampire. Foolishly so. You have the desire to do as I request. I know you have been humiliated and crushed by the *mimicus* denizen. I offer you the chance to bring them all down. Cleanse this realm of the demons who dare to tread amongst humans before their denizens populate into rages."

A *denizen* was a group of demons, much like a vampire tribe. When their numbers increased or the denizens joined forces they were termed a *rage*, vast quantities of the merciless bastards.

The man was playing it dramatically, and that made Blade wonder if he was mentally unbalanced, or if it was just his manner. It wasn't every day he met a dark stranger in a haunted woods who asked him to slay denizens.

But he did have one thing right—beyond the insistent craving for demon blood, even more fiercely, Blade craved vengeance.

But he was no assassin. Not without good reason.

And he had begun to step toward the light. To do good. He strived to avoid making the same mistake twice.

"No," Blade stated simply. He folded down his wings and took a step back off the mossy rock, putting himself a head below Sim's stance. "The way to redemption is not through violence."

"It doesn't concern you that the demons will soon take over? They will torment humans and paranormals alike."

"Where's your proof? I've lived here all my life. There are demons who live amongst us, sure. But not in numbers so great as a rage."

"You'll simply have to trust I know of what I speak."

"I do not blindly offer something so valuable as my trust." And Blade walked around the man and into the woods. "Get off my property!" he called back.

"The Darkwood belongs to no man." He heard the quiet reply. "You will change your mind. I can wait. But not for long."

Blade started to run. Flapping his wings, he soared up from the ground. He dodged a ghostly wraith that lived within the forest, but which would never leave.

Kill all the demons? Sounded like a dream. But Blade was trying to turn his life around and be less violent. And he could do it.

If he could get beyond the need for revenge.

One week later...

Zenia parked the olive-green Chevy truck at the end of the block where she'd been hit by the bus. Hopping out, she skipped across the grassy road verge to the sidewalk. A wind-strewn newspaper lay on the ground, and she recognized the faded ad she'd seen a week earlier. A pharmaceutical ad touted something called Zenia. A word she'd liked so much she'd taken it as her name. It conveyed mystery. Just like her.

Which was about the only thing she did know about herself. That she was a mystery. The term used to describe her condition was *amnesia*, and she had it. And it had started in this neighborhood.

The street and houses were quaint. A smooth, narrow sidewalk stretched before neat yards, and most of those yards were fenced with white pickets. Bright yellow marigolds, pink-and-white roses and orange zinnias bloomed in profusion. Butterflies and bees fluttered from bloom to bloom.

The bus must have been cruising this quiet neighborhood so slowly that if someone had been hit by it, they wouldn't have sustained a serious injury. And the bus driver may have never noticed the casualty.

Zenia strode down the sidewalk, a long floral skirt flitting between her legs. Her pink T-shirt was encrusted with rhinestones in the shape of a heart. She loved anything that sparkled. That much she did know about herself.

Summer sun warmed her skin and she flipped her long, midback hair over a shoulder. She brushed at an insect that briefly landed on her arm, and took note of the faint design on the inside of her elbow. Barely there, it looked as though someone had taken a white marker and drawn an arabesque. It was also on her other inner elbow, and had faded, but perhaps still needed a few more showers to completely wash away. It resembled the mehndi designs she knew were a Vedic custom in India.

How she knew about that baffled her. She seemed to know quite a bit about many things—except personal details. Had someone drawn these marks on her?

Or perhaps she'd scrawled it during a lazy afternoon doing...what?

She wanted to know what she'd done in life, if only so she could resume doing that for survival. It had been a week since the accident and she had no money, had stolen clothes from a donation box on a street corner, and had only managed a handful of meals by chatting up lone men in the local diners and then dashing before they could ask her out.

And while remembering who she was would be terrific, perhaps she didn't know for a reason?

Weird thoughts. But what else was there to think about?

A lot actually. Everything. From the solid feel of the sidewalk beneath the pink flip-flop sandals she wore to the warmth of the air embracing her shoulders. The sensory details were immense in this world. And it was almost as if she was experiencing touch, sight, smell and sound for the first time. There, a bird chirp sounded like a song she must know the words to, but unfortunately had—like her identity—forgotten.

Forgetting was frustrating. So she had returned, determined to trace her steps to learn where she had come from and what she had been doing before the accident.

Zenia stopped walking. A warm sensation blossomed in her chest. A visceral feeling of memory. She studied the pink, two-story house in front of her. White paint decorated the window frames and front door as if it were a confection under glass at a bakery. It looked familiar.

She walked up to the picket fence and darted her gaze over the yard, which was overgrown with brushy emerald grass and dotted with yellow dandelions. It smelled lush and wild. Didn't look as though anyone lived on this lot. Did *she* live here?

"I walked through this yard," she said with definite knowing.

She turned and eyed the street. The bus stop sign was thirty yards to the left, and the grass around the sign had been worn to dirt where she assumed people waited while sipping their morning coffees. "And there is where I got hit."

Turning and wandering into the yard, she had to lift her skirt so that she didn't get tangled in the long grass. Had she been walking out from behind the house? She could see an open backyard. No trees. And beyond that a field stretched quite a distance before it ended at a forest's dark, jagged tree line.

Paralleling the side of the pink house, she walked around to the back and let out a gasp when someone stepped right in front of her. The woman couldn't be younger than ninety, and her posture curled her spine forward so she had to lift her head to look up at Zenia. She smelled smoky. And a little too ripe for Zenia's heightened senses.

"I'm sorry," Zenia said, stepping back a pace. "I didn't mean to trespass. I'm trying to track down a path I took a week ago. Would it be all right if I walked through your backyard to that field?"

"Never seen you before, young lady. Why would you walk through my yard?"

"I don't know. I've lost my memory. I'm trying to piece things together, and I recall walking from back here. Maybe even through that field. Though I'm not sure why I would be in a field. I won't do any harm to your property. I'll walk straight through and on to the field."

"Very well. You go find yourself. And I'll go, uh… find myself."

The old woman gestured dismissively with a swing of her arm then made a surprisingly hasty retreat into her house through the back door.

"Yes, find myself," Zenia muttered. "But out in a field?"

And the old lady needed to find herself? Curious. But old people were some kind of curiosity, for sure. If not badly in need of a shower.

Zenia strode onward, her sandals stomping down the grass until she landed on the soft black earth of the freshly plowed field. Didn't feel familiar to walk across the uneven surface. Hmm…

"This is the closest I've come to finding myself. I won't give up."

She walked onward.

Blade Saint-Pierre shoved the Craftsman toolbox into his truck box and pushed up the creaky metal gate to close it. He'd helped old man Larson fix the trellis that had come detached from the back of his house. Squirrels had been nibbling at the trusses. Now it was secure and the violet morning glories that reminded Larson of his dead wife, Gloria, showed through his bedroom window.

These neighborly fix-it stops were fast becoming an enjoyable way to spend the day for Blade. It made him feel better to help someone he didn't know. But he was sure it would never counter all the guilt that weighed down his heart. It certainly wouldn't grant him redemption.

But neither would slaying a rage of demons. He hadn't seen the stranger, Sim, since that night in the forest a few days ago. Probably for the better.

Opening the driver's door, he paused to eye the stunning beauty walking down the sidewalk on the opposite side of the street. He'd not seen her in Tangle Lake before. Blade had seen a lot of pretty women pass through this tiny Minnesota town. Most visitors hailed from the big city. Some liked to do an antiques run through the smaller towns along the highway that stretched from the Twin Cities north to the shipping harbor of Duluth.

So he was unusually curious about this beauty who looked as out of place as a demon in a salt factory.

Long red hair spilled down her back. He wouldn't exactly call it red, more like copper that caught the sun in glints much like polished metal. Her skin resembled creamy caramel. A flowery skirt flitted between long legs as she strode the sidewalk, her attention taking in the house fronts and tidy yards. A faded T-shirt with an obvious hole at the back hem topped off the bohemian look. She scampered through an overgrown yard, which Blade wondered if he should offer to mow the lawn. Could be a hazard to an elder person trying to navigate the long grass.

He observed the sexy bohemian chick speak to an elder woman who seemed a bit too spry as she bounced back into her house. Blade could see the old woman's shadow through the front window that wasn't obscured by drapes. He kept her in peripheral vision while he satisfied his need for beauty.

The woman in the skirt scampered toward a dirt

field. Did she have something to do back there? It was a big empty expanse. And across the stretch of black dirt was forest, which, after dozens of acres, backed up to Tangle Lake. Maybe she owned a strip of the black earth and intended to plant a garden? It was a little late in the season for that and she hadn't any gardening tools on her.

An odd commotion inside the house made Blade turn his attention to the front window. The old woman's silhouette was…changing. One moment she stood hunched, her head hanging and shoulders curved forward and down. The next moment, she'd grown another head. And another.

Instincts kicked in and Blade tugged out the silver bowie knife he kept stuffed in his combat boot. He closed the truck door. He knew better than to doubt his instincts.

The silhouettes in the house were now three separate entities, and big, and…

Blade sniffed. A faint trace of sulfur curled into his nostrils.

"Demons," he muttered. "I do hate demons."

Chapter 2

Running along the side of the house, Blade veered around the corner and toward the back door, noting that the woman with the copper hair stood three hundred yards away in the field, her back to him. Unaware of the weirdness brewing within the house. Or so he hoped.

He opened the door and dodged to avoid the slash of obsidian talons. Pulling the door shut behind him, Blade hoped to keep the demons contained. And the beautiful woman safe.

The threesome of demons growled and spat at him, and lunged. Blade leaped to the top of a laundry machine, and jumped, flipping in the air and landing behind the nasty trio. Bowie knife at the ready, he defied them with a come-on gesture of his fingers.

"Are you the rage Sim spoke about?"

In a rare pause from attack, the demons glanced at one another. Black-hooded red eyes blinked. It was obvious they knew nothing about what he'd just asked. And really, a rage of demons would blacken the sky with their numbers. These three were barely a denizen.

"Is the woman one of your own?" he asked. He knew some demons could take on human form, many of them, actually, but he doubted the woman in the field had anything to do with this bunch.

"She is ours," one of them hissed. "Keep away!"

"I don't take orders from demons." He twirled the knife and caught it, blade pointing toward the speaker. "Want to try asking nicely?"

The next hiss was accompanied by burning spittle that sizzled on Blade's wrist. Wrong move.

The best way to kill a demon was with a blast of salt to its black heart. Blade did have a salt knife, but rarely carried it. In lieu of salt, he'd have to do this the old-fashioned way.

Leaping to the left, he feinted right, ducking to avoid attack. With that demon occupied in missing him, Blade slid under a groping talon and stood before Thing #2. He jammed up his knife, catching it deep in the rib cage of the surprised demon. A knife wound wouldn't take out a demon. Unless it was more than a wound, and the weapon had been warded against demons. Dragging the blade upward, he cut open the creature from gut to throat and flung its spasming body aside to scatter in a spray of black ash.

Grabbed by the shoulders, the creature's talons pierced his skin. Blade growled, and slashed blindly, feeling resistance and tasting a spatter of black demon blood. He lashed out his tongue, even as he bent to fling the one on his back toward Thing #3. The taste of blood frenzied his faery's wicked craving. His fangs descended as he snarled. He tightened his grip on the knife.

"Now I'm angry," he muttered.

Standing tall, Blade turned to face the two, who actually cowered at the sight of the vampire with black blood dripping from his mouth.

Charging, he continued his assault. Catching one demon about the neck in a clothesline, the other demon he stabbed with the knife. He gouged his hand upward, tearing the warded steel through the shrieking demon. As the blade tore out of viscera, he curled his hand around to land the other thing through the skull. Both demons scattered in ash behind him.

Blade licked the side of his hand, coated with black blood, and growled in satisfaction. Nasty stuff, but it hit him with a jolt of power and comforting darkness. And that was an irresistible high. Mmm... He could feel it move down his throat. Delicious strength shimmered in his muscles. His wings trembled for release, to allow the wicked blood to course through their very structure like cocaine to an addict's soul.

"Hello?"

Kicked back to reality by the female call from outside the back door, Blade shook his head and stopped his wings before they could unfurl. Right. *Keep your head, buddy.* He shoved the knife down the side of his boot and stepped out the door and marched across the unkempt backyard. The woman in the long skirt strolled toward him, oblivious to what had just gone down inside the pink house.

Demons didn't follow humans around. Not that he was aware of. And the woman had purposely gone to this one; he had seen her speak with it. Had she known it was demon? And if so, what was out in the field that the demon had directed her to?

Blade wiped the blood from his mouth and retracted his fangs. The woman's face brightened as she neared, and she lifted her long skirt to run toward him. "Hello! Do you live in the house? I didn't find what I thought I would find—"

Blade grabbed her by the upper arms and growled. "What are you?"

The man's grip was too firm, Zenia thought. He actually looked angry, his dark brows narrowed, and the sun shone on his hair, bluing it around the one eye that was visible. A fathomless, gray eye. He had seen tribulation. Zenia knew that with certainty, as she knew so many odd facts.

And he was sexy. Devastatingly so. His broad chest stretched a charcoal-gray T-shirt in ripples, and thick veins corded his massive biceps. Combine his remarkable physique with a handsome face and he was the complete package.

Yet he did not relent his strong grip. Zenia struggled and finally managed to squirm out of his pinching grasp.

"What am I?" she asked, stepping back a few paces from him. "What do you mean? I'm a woman. A human. You think I'm some kind of alien?" She looked over his shoulder and noted the back door of the woman's house hung open. "I should go up and close that door for her. She probably forgot. She's old—"

"Don't go near the house." He gripped her by the arm, and again Zenia shoved his chest and struggled. She stumbled in the long grass and he helped her to stand. It was all she could do to step away from him without falling again.

"Who are you?" she demanded with an impertinent lift of chin. "You don't live here. If you did, you might have taken care of the yard for your grandmother, or whoever she is to you."

"She's not my—" The man gestured a wide splay of fingers toward the street. "I was working across the street and saw you two talking. I just— I don't need to explain myself. I asked first. Who, and what in particular, are you?"

Zenia crossed her arms and looked the man up and down. Dressed all in dark clothing from his loosely laced Dr. Martens to the black jeans and gray T-shirt, his muscled arms gave her pause, as did his broad chest. But the long black hair with a weirdly blue sheen to it screamed goth. Goths were skinny and morose. This man's physique said, *I work out*—a lot.

"Well," she provided, "I'm certainly not an alien." Of that she was aware.

The nerve of the man. He hadn't even offered a friendly how do you do. Perhaps this neighborhood wasn't as friendly as she'd originally thought. And for as much as she enjoyed the view of him, she did know not to trust a complete stranger.

Zenia marched past him and up toward the house. He passed her and slammed the door shut, stepping before it as if to guard the contents. His anger was so palpable she felt shivers trace her arms. But it wasn't warning enough to make her run away from the guy.

"I didn't find anything here," she offered, hoping to appeal to his compassionate side. If such a thing existed. "This is where I came walking out and into the street before I lost my memory. I feel as though I was walking in from that field, but I haven't a clue what I was doing out there. It's just a bunch of dirt."

"What the hell are you talking about, lady?"

"I, uh…" She raked her fingers through her long hair and splayed out her hand uncertainly before her. When she noted the cream-colored markings inside her elbow, she slapped a palm over them and offered with a shrug, "I have amnesia."

This time when he raised his hand, perhaps to clutch her again, she flinched. That paused him. He put up both palms facing her, placatingly. And Zenia sensed whatever it was that had made him so tense and angry settled. Just a teensy bit.

"I'm sorry," he said. "I shouldn't have grabbed you like that. There was a commotion in the house while you were wandering in the field. I don't think you should go inside."

"What's wrong with the old lady?" Zenia bobbed on her toes in an attempt to see over his broad shoulder and through the window near the back door. "Is she okay?"

He narrowed his gaze on her so intently that she felt as if he'd physically touched her. Over the heart. And she suddenly wanted to know that touch for real. She'd not been touched by a man before. Maybe. She couldn't remember if she had. Oh, woe, if she had not.

"She's…been better," he offered.

Arms sliding defensively across her chest, she studied his eyes again. Both of them now, for his hair blew away from his face. A curious gray and some fleck of brighter color. Violet? They had softened, though she could see the sharpness in them as if a cut to her hope for his kindness.

When he asked, "Did the Darkwood denizen send you?" her mouth fell open.

Because Zenia knew what a denizen was. Yet that

knowledge startled her. Why did she know the word for a group or gathering of demons?

Because there are demons in this world. As well as angels, vampires, witches and other things most didn't believe in.

Did she believe in them? No, such things were mythology. Fantasy bred into wild stories designed to entertain the masses. Which made this guy, as handsome as he was, some kind of wacko.

"I am not a demon."

She turned to march around the side of the house. She wasn't going to find what she was looking for here. And most especially, she did not want to deal with a crazy man. Even if he was the most remarkable specimen of male she'd seen. Ever.

A hand grabbed her by the arm, halting her near the picket fence that hugged in the front yard. "Yet you are familiar with the terminology?"

She shrugged. Annoyance felt new to her, and she didn't like the feeling so she tried to look beyond it. Was his hair so black it gleamed blue? When the sun shone on it, it appeared blue. Kinda cool. She wondered if it was as soft as it looked.

Oh, Zenia, do not let his good looks distract you!

"I know a lot of things," she offered when he gave no sign to leave her alone. "Except who I am."

"So then how can you be sure you are not a demon?"

Zenia slammed her hands to her hips. "Are you for real? Demons are myth, buddy. Stories. Fantasy. I think it's time I got some facts from you. Who are you?"

"Blade Saint-Pierre." His shoulders stretched back proudly, yet his eyes remained dark. Uncertain? "I live on the outskirts of Tangle Lake. I was helping Mr. Larson across the street fix his trellis." She followed his gesture to the yellow rambler across the street and spied the climbing purple flowers on the side of the house. "And who are you? Oh, wait, you don't remember."

"Zenia," she offered with a lift of her chin. "It's the name I'm using until I learn my real name. And I'm quite sure you and your weird fantasy ideas will be of no help to that quest, so if you'll leave me alone, I'll be on my way. Do not follow me!"

Stalking away from the man's accusing stature, she strode through the long grass toward the sidewalk. Her truck was parked down the block. Feet shuffling quickly, she landed on the sidewalk and did not look back. A weird feeling that she was rushing forward, walking toward knowledge, flittered into her brain, and as quickly, fluttered back out.

And yet…it had been a *familiar* feeling. She'd felt the very same when she'd been walking this sidewalk previously. Before the bus had changed her destiny.

Destiny?

Hmm… It felt right to think that. At least, nothing in her being screamed, *No, you're on the wrong path.* Interesting. Maybe she had gathered a bit of her memory by retreading her footsteps? Albeit, memory she didn't know how to decipher. A quest for knowledge? It meant nothing to her.

The man followed so close behind her she could hear the trod of his boots on the concrete sidewalk. His name was Blade? Interesting name. Sharp and dangerous. It certainly matched his demeanor.

And he was stalking her.

"I have a weapon!" she called out, and scrambled for the truck keys in her skirt pocket.

"I'm not going to hurt you," he said firmly.

"Says the serial killer before he dumps the girl in the pit," she called over her shoulder.

Where had she mined such macabre information? It was frustrating to Zenia that she knew things—weird, odd things—and yet, knew nothing about herself.

"A knowledge walk?" she whispered as she neared the truck. Her stalker's black truck was parked across the street from it. The truck bed was loaded with lumber and tools. So he'd been telling the truth about helping the old man. He earned trust points for doing a kind thing. Right?

"I need to make sure you are safe," Blade said as he strode beside her, intent on not leaving her alone. "If you're not from around here, and you don't remember anything, you could be in trouble."

"I appreciate that," she said, still walking. "Really. Kindness of strangers, and all that. But I don't know what I have to worry about. Wait. The old lady. I should have checked on her."

"She's...fine."

"You said that with a pause. As if maybe she's not fine. As if maybe you've just murdered her."

He managed to overtake her rapid steps and stop before her on the sidewalk, planting his boots and slamming his fists akimbo. "Will you quit with the serial killer bit? I didn't kill...the old lady. She wasn't in the house when I went in there. I promise. There were others inside. Others who mentioned you."

"Me? Really?" She turned at the hip to eye the pink house, then swung back to Blade. She had to tilt her head to meet his gaze; he was a tall one. "Who were they? They must know me. Maybe they can tell me who I am."

"They were demons."

He said it without a smirk or a wink. And that pulled the cord on Zenia's freak-out alarm.

She shoved the guy away and ran toward her truck. Keys in hands, she opened the door, slid in and started the ignition. She'd be damned if she was going to talk to him one moment longer and risk his kind of crazy.

"Demons?" she muttered. "Talk about attracting a weirdo. I'll have to return later, after he's gone. If someone in that house knows about me…"

She shifted into gear, and rolled quickly by him. He waved, but it was more of a dismissive gesture. In the rearview mirror, she saw him get in his truck and turn it around on the narrow street. She quickly turned at the intersection, hoping to lose him.

"Demons," she whispered again. "Can't be. No. I won't believe it. He's a crazy madman that I was lucky to get away from him. This is bad." She pressed a palm against the thumping heartbeats under her rib cage. "Really bad. Now I've got to shake a serial killer. I don't want to die. I can't die. I don't even know what name they'd put on the tombstone."

The image of a fresh grave made her miss the next stop sign. A shout alerted her to the pair of teenaged girls who had stepped off the curb, and now shook their fists at the truck.

"Oops. Sorry! Concentrate, Zenia. You don't want to be arrested for murder."

She glanced in the rearview mirror. The big black truck still followed.

"But who might be more guilty of such a heinous crime?" she muttered to herself.

He'd said there were others in the house who had asked after her. What had happened to the old woman?

Chapter 3

She was the prettiest woman in Tangle Lake. Demons wanted her. And she had amnesia.

Blade had discreetly followed Zenia to the Blue Bass, a dive bar nestled at the edge of town. So the tail hadn't been as discreet as he'd hoped. Not easy to be covert in a small town with only two main streets. It was nearing eight in the evening and he suspected she had tried to give him the slip, but again, one of the hazards of a small town was lack of privacy.

Normally, he was not a curious man. That was his brother Trouble's mien. But it wasn't every day he watched a sexy woman tread about in a dirt field, and then had to slay demons to keep them from going after her.

He wanted to know where the demons had come from and why. And if she thought to use an amnesia defense to cover her knowledge then she'd better think again. She had to be hiding something. If a person had amnesia, shouldn't they not operate a motor vehicle, avoid drinking in a bar and most likely be lying in the hospital?

Yeah, she was definitely pulling something over on him. Yet if there was a slight chance she was on the up and up, he sensed she wasn't safe.

He entered the bar, and stood by the door to take in the yawn of an establishment paneled in rough-cut timbers and decorated with fishing rods, neon beer signs and the mascot stuffed bass with the milky white eyes. At the bar, Zenia ordered a beer. She didn't fit in this redneck outpost. She looked more like a wine kind of gal.

Currently, she held her own against Brock Olafson, the town asshole. The guy had been divorced twice, owned a tanning bed—which explained his weird orange leathery skin—and never slowed his Hummer for a stop sign unless he sighted a black-and-white nearby.

Asshole was trying to pick up the pretty woman. Blade's fingers had curled into fists the moment Brock sat down next to her. He held his jaw soft, not tense. Years of practice had allowed him to remain calm while holding within the roiling need to attack. It was never wise to attack. At least, not with human witnesses.

On the other hand, if a man opened the door of a house and was greeted by three demons, by all means, attack.

Brock slid his hand up the back of Zenia's T-shirt. She slapped at him and shifted over to the next bar stool. Blade could hear her politely say, "Leave me alone. I just want to finish this drink in peace."

"I'll buy you another," Brock said, shoving thick fingers over his short blond crew cut.

Before the asshole could slide onto the vacant bar stool, Blade pushed his palm onto the bar between the two of them. The bartender nodded at Blade and poured him a shot of Krupnik, a honey-sweet vodka the owner kept in stock for him.

Brock stepped away from the bar, muttering something about weirdos under his breath, but Blade kept an awareness of the man's location in his peripheral vision as he tilted back the shot.

"Despite his rudeness, he did pin you correctly," Zenia said and sipped her beer.

"How's that?"

"You're a weirdo. And I'll ask you to leave me alone just like I did the other guy."

"Sorry," he said, and pushed the shot glass forward. "Did I interrupt something promising?"

She snickered and when she looked at him, he was momentarily fixed to her green eyes. She was so exotic and colorful, this memory-less woman who didn't seem to belong, no matter the setting. And she smelled like the long grass and flowers he'd followed her through but an hour earlier. Blade lost track of Brock.

"Thanks," she said. "But you can leave now."

He sat on a bar stool and propped his elbows before him. "I'm not a weirdo," he offered.

"You accused me, a person you don't even know, of being a demon. Your hair is blue. You look like a goth. And you followed me here like some kind of serial—er, stalker. In my book that's considered weird."

The bartender poured another shot for Blade. He swallowed the vodka with a wince. Good stuff. He had a difficult time getting drunk. Blame it on his genetics. Being vampire and faery did come in handy when he wanted to hold his liquor. The only time he got drunk was when drinking from someone who had consumed whiskey. Whiskey-spiked blood always went straight to his head.

"It's black," he offered regarding his hair. "The neon light from that sign over the bar makes it blue."

"If that's your story. But I did see it in the sunlight. It's blue."

It wasn't. Well, it sort of was. It was the faery in him. It sheened his black hair blue. It was a damned sight better than the pink that donned his sister, Daisy Blu's, head.

"And yours is copper," he offered. "Like a precious metal that someone steals to hock for as much cash as they can manage. It suits you. Looks great with your skin tone. Sorry." He shoved the empty shot glass toward the bartender. "I don't say things like that to women—"

"You mean compliment them? Are you flirting with me? Trying to pick up a demon?"

She was going to work that one until he surrendered. So he would. But only because she was pretty.

"Listen, can we start over? I'm Blade." He offered his hand to her and she stared at it. "I live about ten miles out of town near the Darkwood."

"That sounds…dark." She smirked and he wondered if she might be a little tipsy. But when she took his hand and shook it, he felt a good firm clasp warm his fingers. "Zenia. No last name. At least, not that I recall. I live nowhere, or probably somewhere. But you know, Amnesia Chick."

"So, Zenia, who is only recently Zenia, what's up with that? Did you used to be Martha or Gertrude?"

This time she laughed out loud. Blade heard Brock's huff on the other side of the pool table. The asshole tossed a dart at the board nailed on the wall—and missed.

When Zenia looked at him now he decided she was assessing him. A better risk than Brock? He should hope so. And then, he knew he was not.

"For all I know, I probably could have been Gertrude," she said.

"You don't look like a Gertie. The hair is all wrong. Gertrude likes curls and something shorter. Maybe even a blue rinse."

"You could be right. Okay, so weirdness aside, I like you, Blade." Her long dark lashes fluttered with a look over his face. "I'll reserve judgment on your weirdness quotient until I get to know you better."

He was about to say that she would be better off not liking him, but instead he simply smiled. A rare thing for him. Just ask any of his brothers or sister. The dark silent one put people off with his stoic expression. And for good reason.

He'd learned that keeping his head down was best for all. And yet, his surprising curiosity for this woman demanded satisfaction.

"No memory?" he asked. "How did that happen? Or do you know?"

"I think I only lost personal stuff. I know things. It's as if I know crazy stuff like Russia's population is almost one hundred and fifty million. The main ingredient in miso soup is dashi. And it would take the average person about eighteen months to traverse the wall of China. But I don't know my name, who I am or where I came from. That's why I'm here in Tangle Lake. I was hit by a bus in front of that old woman's house."

Blade was about to order another shot when he paused. "Seriously? Hit by a bus?"

"Yes. I was walking out of a yard—probably that old woman's yard—and onto the street, and—bam! No memory of my life after that."

"So you woke up in the hospital? They must have taken you to Unity. Closest hospital from here."

"No. I, uh, stood up and walked away." She offered a sheepish shrug. "Never saw a doctor."

Blade put up two fingers when the bartender tilted the vodka bottle over his glass. This information was worthy of a double shot.

"It's been a week," she said. "I thought about going to the police, but—I don't know, something inside me said they wouldn't be able to help. So I hitched a ride into the Twin Cities and have been staying at homeless shelters, trying to make some cash to survive. A girl's gotta eat, you know?"

"They have homes to stay in for people who have amnesia. Maybe." What did he know? "If they don't exist, they should. You should see a doctor."

"I'm fine." She bent her head and brushed aside her hair with a curl of delicate fingers over her ear. "I know it sounds weird, but I think the bus sort of…nudged me to pursue a different life. When it hit me, I was flung against the street pole and banged my head. Had a bruise right here." She tapped her temple. "But that faded within a few hours."

A hit that could take away one's memory had to have left a big bruise. Blade had a hard time believing it had faded so quickly. There wasn't a mar on her skin. Another reason to doubt her story. And she could be allied with demons. What game was she playing?

"So here I am." She narrowed her gaze on him. "Do *you* know me?"

He had to chuckle at that hopeful question. "Never seen you before."

"I had to ask. I'm not sure if I'm from Tangle Lake.

Everywhere I've been no one seems to recognize me. Friendliest person so far has been that asshole behind us tossing the darts."

"Name's Brock Olafson, and you should stay away from him if you value your safety."

"Thanks. I got that 'stay away' feeling from him." She sipped the beer and wiped off the foam moustache. "I thought visiting the scene of the accident would make something click in my brain, you know?"

"Well, if you want me to hit you upside the head…?"

"Does that work? The knowledge I have on that is it's mainly been used in children's cartoons and tear-jerker love stories."

"I was kidding. So were you hoping asshole would pay your tab?"

"I, er…" She shrugged and focused on her drink.

Blade tugged out his wallet and laid enough cash on the bar to cover his and her tab. "On me," he said. "If you don't have memory, you must not have a job."

"Nope. Not that I know of. There could be a cubicle that's empty right now. Is the whole office wondering where I am? Do I have a big project due any day now?"

She didn't look like a cubicle drone, but Blade couldn't decide what kind of work she might have done. Her exotic coloring and flowing clothes hinted at a bohemian nature. And those sorts were usually musicians and artists. Maybe?

Why not go to the police? Her story just didn't jibe.

"If I can ask, how do you survive?"

"I spent a couple days hawking raspberries at a farm stand just off Highway 35 and earned enough to eat on. And I have the truck."

"You remembered you own a truck?"

"Uh, no. It was running and no one was using it, so…" She winced and tilted back another swallow of beer.

She'd stolen a truck. Blade was impressed. Pretty *and* devious. The woman had survival skills, that was for sure.

But she'd been hit by a bus and had stood up and walked away? Was she something beyond human? If her story was the truth, she had to be. He didn't scent his own species on her. He could also scent when werewolves or demons were around. Faeries were a challenge.

He got nothing from her. Just plain human. A human who had attracted a shifter demon who had claimed she was their own.

"You're not afraid the cops will remind you that you don't own a truck?"

"I'm not sure what fear is, actually." She offered her hand again to shake. "I should get going. I'm tired. It was nice to talk to a kind person for a while. Blade Saint-Pierre, right? Maybe we'll run into each other again?"

"I'm in town a lot." He almost offered his services if she needed anything, but…he'd learned his lesson with pretty women. They were nice to look at, touch and make love to. But getting to know them and caring about them? Wrong, just wrong. "See you, Zenia."

She strolled out of the bar with a wave to him. And Blade remained to keep an eye on Brock.

A knock on the truck window woke Zenia from the first tendrils of sleep. She sat up on the front seat, knocked her foot on the steering wheel, swore and spied the dark-haired man peering in at her.

"Blade."

After talking with him in the Blue Bass she'd assessed that he was a nice guy who had the compassion to worry about a complete stranger. But here he was again. And her heartbeats picked up pace. What made her believe she had any skill at reading another person's intent? As she'd once suspected, had she gained a stalker?

She sat up to open the door, but paused. It was close to midnight. She had parked in an empty parking lot beneath a streetlight. A city park paralleled the lot, but no residential houses or businesses were nearby. It had seemed a quiet place to sleep through the night, but now her caution rose.

He hadn't tried to touch her, as had the other creep in the bar. But something about this man was dark. Mysterious. And now the hairs on her arms prickled.

She turned the key backward to the accessories position, then lowered the window down two inches. "Yes?"

"You sleeping in your truck?"

She nodded. Wished she had an iron pipe, or even a wood bat.

"This is going to sound strange," he said. "It might even put up your weirdo alarms again."

"I haven't completely lowered them, so give it a shot."

"You're welcome to park on my land tonight. Uh, it might be safer. Unless you don't mind taking your chances with Brock." He turned and cast his gaze across the parking lot.

Zenia followed his gaze and there, across the street

from the lot, idled a big yellow Hummer rimmed in chrome. She couldn't see inside the cab, save for the glimmer of burning cigarette embers.

"Is that the guy from the bar?"

Blade nodded. "I've been watching him watching you for about an hour."

Zenia clutched her arms over her chest. "You've been watching me a lot today."

"Sorry. Seems as though you need it. This is not what I normally do. I mean—"

"Stalk women?"

He nodded and shrugged. It was a sheepish kind of move that settled her worries. She wanted to trust him. She would allow herself to trust him.

"Where do you live?" she asked.

"Ten miles north of Tangle Lake. It's secluded. Brock won't follow you there because he's afraid of me. We had…an altercation a few months back. But then, if you follow me, you do risk leaving the safety of town."

Yikes. When he put it that way. And yet, as strange as Blade was, Zenia sensed the other option would see her struggling with the man across the street not long after Blade left.

"Maybe," she said.

"I'm heading back to my truck. You can follow me if you want to. The drive is down a long forested road, just so you know. You can park in my driveway. Lock your doors. I won't bother you. You have my word."

"I don't know if your word is good."

"That you don't."

Was it fair or even rational to give him points for honesty?

"So you think you need to protect me from demons or something?"

"Beyond the very human Brock?" He shrugged. "You never know." Blade shoved his hands into his front pockets. "Your choice, Zen."

And he strode off toward the truck that Zenia now saw was parked down the street. A bowlegged stride moved him swiftly, as if a shadow in the night.

Zenia scrambled into the driver's seat and turned on the ignition. When Blade's headlights blinked on and slowly drove past the other man's truck, she made a snap decision and shifted the truck into gear.

Chapter 4

Zenia woke with her name zinging between her ears. Except it wasn't the way she had chosen it. Blade had called her Zen last night. She liked it. It sounded like the man had made the name his possession when he'd said it. And that didn't bother her at all.

But did she feel Zen right now? Hard to tell. She wasn't sure what to feel. She was a woman out of place. Did she have a place to return? Was there a house or an apartment waiting for her to push a key into the lock and resume her life? She hadn't a key, a purse or any identifying materials on her after the bus had hit her.

Only that weird tin circle.

She glanced at the flimsy circle she'd hung around the rearview mirror. She'd been clutching it after coming to a stand against the street pole. In that moment, she'd almost tossed it aside, but she'd felt an intuition to keep it. For some reason. Curious.

Had it anything to do with the destiny she felt she tread? For the undeniable feeling that contacting the police would not be wise? Was it a true feeling or was it that she thought she should have a goal or reason for existing so *destiny* was a good fill-in-the-blank answer?

Sitting up, she pulled her knees to her chest and

bowed her head to work out the kinks from sleeping across the stick shift. A knock on the driver's window startled her. A swath of dark hair reminded her that she'd had the audacity to follow a complete stranger out to his property last night. She'd parked at the end of the driveway closest to the highway just in case she'd needed to make a quick getaway. He'd been good to his word. Hadn't bothered her.

Until now.

Zen hit the window control and lowered the glass. The scent of steaming coffee wafted into the truck interior. Never had anything smelled so good.

Blade handed in a black mug. Steam rose from the liquid surface. "Just brewed it. Extradark. Hope you take it that way."

She'd take any offering of food or drink no matter the strength or weakness. Thank goodness he'd paid for her beer last night. That left her twenty dollars in her pocket—left over from selling raspberries—and a half-full gas tank. It was terrible not to know who she was. But not having the funds to rent a room or pay for a hot meal? She would have to look into that home for amnesiacs he'd mentioned if she didn't figure her life out, and fast.

"Thank you." She sipped the brew. It kicked her. Hard. "Whew!"

"It's called Death Brew for a reason," Blade offered. "Have a good night's sleep?"

She shrugged. No one named Brock had tried to break in and attack her, so she figured that was as good as it got.

"Here's the deal," Blade said. "I'm heading into town in an hour. Got some work to do for a couple of nuns.

If you want, you're welcome to use my shower before I leave."

"Really?" She hadn't showered in days. Had begun to wonder if her hair would ever see a comb again. "I'd like that."

"Cool. Just me and Oogie live out here in the barn. If my cat likes you, I like you."

"Then here's hoping I pass the cat test."

The eerie, hairless black cat hissed and arched its back as Zenia landed at the top of the stairs leading to the loft level of the big barn. The lower level was a wide-open garage littered with vehicles in all states of repair. This was the living quarters. Vast and open, it felt modern and airy, not at all barnlike.

Blade, who had led her up the stairs and directed her to the left for the bathroom, peered out from around the stainless-steel fridge at his cat, which was poised on the back of a green-and-blue-plaid couch. Blade glanced at Zenia, who had frozen at the top of the stairs, clinging to the backpack strap she'd tossed over her shoulder. Then he eyed the cat, who had arched up its back so high Zenia thought it might fold in half.

"Guess I failed the cat test," she offered.

"Oogie?" Blade knelt and called to the cat. "What's wrong, buddy?" He tilted his head at her and she felt as if his look peeled back her layers and zoomed right to her oozy core.

If only it were so easy to learn who she was.

"Who *are* you?" he asked. Yet again.

And yet again, she had no clear answer.

The cat leaped into his arms, and the man stood,

stroking its wrinkled suede-like head. "Oogie likes everyone."

"Obviously I'm not everyone. And that's the big question, isn't it?" She rubbed her arms, though she wasn't cold, just frustrated. And it had taken a cat to nail that frustration to the wall. "Who am I?"

The cat hissed at her.

Zenia flinched. "Uh, do you want me to leave?"

"No. Shower's that way." He nodded toward the hallway. "Oogie and I will talk. You have to walk through the bedroom," he called as Zenia made her way down a short hallway. "You'll see the bathroom door once you get in there."

Overlooking the cat's defensive reaction, she glided into a dark room that was lit by the sunlight beaming through a window set into the slanted roof.

Her gaze swept over the unmade bed. Black rumpled bed sheets. Cozy, in a manly way. Beneath her flip-flops, the floorboards were wide unbleached timber, as were the walls and slanted ceiling. Overall, a darkly clean, yet rustic decor. Just like the man.

And yet, he'd sweetly cuddled that ugly cat. Surprising to see such a big, intimidating man handle a tiny beast so gently.

Veering into the attached bathroom, Zenia was thankful it wasn't all black. In fact, bright white tiles decorated the floor and walls, and though small, the gleaming shower looked inviting through the clear glass door.

She closed the bathroom door and set down the backpack. She'd raided a clothing donation box one night and found a sack of folded clothes that didn't smell. Freshly washed? She could hope. And they'd fit, so she'd taken the whole bag and the canvas backpack that had been stuffed under a pile of smelly gym shoes.

Stripping off her clothes, she caught her reflection in the small shaving mirror above the sink. It was too small to see her whole face so she bobbed to get a view of her condition. Her hair begged a good combing and dark shadows curved under her eyes. She so needed a good night's sleep and…to know.

"Who are you?" she repeated Blade's question to her reflection. "And why the hell were you able to walk away after being hit by a freakin' bus?"

She'd sensed his utter astonishment when she'd told him that. At the time she hadn't thought anything of it. Could have been the adrenaline racing through her system. Shouldn't she have a broken bone or even come away with a bruise or gash? She'd not even bled!

But instead of panicking, she'd been thankful. And that was about all she could do, wasn't it? Live day to day, grateful that she had clothing and a vehicle.

Stepping into the shower, she adjusted the water temperature and said thanks for the kindness of strangers. And then she had the thought that she should have locked the bathroom door behind her.

Blade stood outside the bathroom door, his fingers glancing over the clear glass knob. On his bed sat his pet of thirteen years, the feline's hairless black ears tilted backward and gold eyes wide. Oogie generally liked people. Though, he did tend to get his hackles up when demons were around. Full-blooded demons. Recognizing the *mimicus* breed of demon that could mimic other species had given Oogie trouble.

Don't think about her. Just forget.

Forgetting was what he most wanted to do. But the memory of her had etched itself into his soul. And no amount of charity work was going to rub it away. Not even moving a heavy stone fountain into a garden for a couple of retired nuns.

Blade shrugged at Oogie. "What do you think?"

Oogie's ratlike tail flicked with annoyance.

"She seems harmless. She doesn't even know who she is."

Which didn't necessarily render her harmless. She could have forgotten she was some kind of assassin. Or maybe she was a real good liar.

He was jumping to wild conclusions. Zen was simply a pretty woman who had had a bit of bad luck. With a bus. And demons. Though she seemed genuinely unaware of the demonic trouble.

A stolen truck and no home or belongings? Had to be tough. She couldn't sleep in her truck every night. But he wasn't prepared to offer her a place to bunk down, either.

That way lay madness. Been there, done that. Wasn't about to wear the T-shirt.

But she was a curiosity to him. And her looks were exotically appealing. She couldn't be from around here, Land of Ten Thousand Lakes with hoards of Scandinavians who were whiter than white and had the tendency to mutter *uff-da* to express everything from annoyance to excitement.

Maybe she hailed from the more culturally varied Twin Cities? Had to. She could be a professional, or even a model or an actress.

Why not go to the police? They must have a way of searching for a person without a name but rather a picture. If she was a registered driver her license would be on file. Name learned. Problem solved.

For the most part. Simply learning her real name wouldn't automatically restore her memory. Had to be tough not remembering a thing. She could have family. Friends. A husband.

Blade made a note to check her finger for a wedding band. He didn't want to step on another man's territory. Not that he was stepping. No, he was just helping a needy soul. It's what he did, apparently.

"Come on, Oogie. We can't sit out here like a couple of stalkers."

The maxi dress with bright yellow-and-blue horizontal zigzags was a bit loud, but it felt comfortable and wasn't too low cut. She did have nice, full breasts though, so revealing a little cleavage wasn't going to kill her.

Zenia fluffed out her wet hair, and then borrowed Blade's comb, which lay on the edge of the white porcelain vanity. A search in the small cupboard beneath the sink didn't spy any hair products. And she didn't want to check the drawers in the bedroom. Who knew if Oogie, the attack cat, might come after her?

After hanging the towel she had used to dry over the shower door, she shoved her dirty clothes in the backpack and headed down the hallway. Lured by the delicious scent of pancakes and maple syrup, she got right up to the kitchen counter, dropped the backpack, then veered toward the double cathedral windows at the end of the living area.

The old barn had obviously been restored and the windows added. They looked as though they belonged

in Notre-Dame in Paris. And for some reason, she felt
as though she'd been in the French city, though briefly;
long enough to claim familiarity with the medieval cathedral. No color filled the glass sections that gently
curved to a peak at their pinnacles. It gave the windows
a clean, modern look. Very suitable for a man's home. In
a barn. It was an interesting choice, but again, seemed
to match Blade's no-frills, rough demeanor.

"They are so beautiful," she said of the windows,
then flinched when she heard the hiss behind her.

"Oogie!" Blade tossed a red stuffed mouse down
the stairs that led to the garage below. "Go play with
your mouse."

The cat cast her a discerning look, then dashed off.

"I'm sorry," Zenia said. "I don't know why that thing
doesn't like me."

"Oogie is a cat, not a thing."

"Yeah, but it looks like a rat. Why doesn't it have
any hair?"

"He's a Sphynx."

"Oh, right. I know those breeds are hairless and require special care. Does he wear a sweater in the winter?"

"Actually, he does have one with a skull and cross-
bones on the back. Got a problem with that?"

She approached the kitchen counter and slid onto
a stool. "No. Sorry, I seem to offend at every turn. I
should leave. You've been more than kind."

"Not until you eat." He placed a plate stacked with
pancakes before her. Beside that sat a coffee cup steaming with dark brew. "You like maple syrup?"

"I...don't know."

"Right." He tapped his temple. "But you do know about Sphynx cats. Interesting."

She dug into the pancakes. Mercy, but it had been days since she'd eaten a decent meal and not a candy bar or bag of Doritos that she'd gotten out of a vending machine. Her aching stomach growled with glee.

"So your bedroom is all black," she stated between bites. Ah, hot food. And it smelled so good. And tasted even better.

Blade stood across from her by the stove, arms crossed and one hand wielding a spatula. He was noticeably not eating. "That it is."

"And you're all into the dark look yourself. Is that called goth?"

He made show of looking down the front of his black T-shirt, stretched tightly across muscled biceps, black jeans and, well, his feet were bare. "For a chick who's lost her memory, you're very judgmental."

"And you are being sarcastic. I do know what sarcasm is."

"Good for you. I'm not a goth. I'm just Blade. You find everything you needed in the bathroom?"

She touched her hair. "I borrowed your comb. I hope that was okay. You can't imagine how good it feels to be showered and reasonably groomed. My hair must have looked horrible before."

"It's gorgeous," he said quickly. And then he turned and made a show of checking that the griddle was turned off, mumbling as he did so, "I mean, it's fine."

Zenia brushed the wet locks over her shoulder, but couldn't hide what felt like a blush. "So what do you do, Blade? You said you were running into town? To your job?"

"I do some fix-it work for the locals here and there. Got a quick job for a couple of retired nuns who are designing a water garden in their backyard. And I work with my brother, Stryke. He's, er...leader of a...group."

She sipped the hot coffee carefully, trying to figure out what he wasn't willing to say. A group? Of what? People? For what reason? But she wouldn't ask. Whatever he wanted to present to her, she'd take, and anything he didn't want her to know was fine, too.

Should she be more curious? She had enough problems of her own to worry about. And she wanted to move over to his good side, maybe even befriend him. She could use a friend. Where were her friends? Were they worried about her? Had they called the police?

"Stryke is building a compound for...his work," Blade offered. "I'm his second-in-command. It's family stuff."

"Sounds important. Do you think I have friends?"

The man shrugged. "Not sure. But you're not wearing a ring."

She studied her hands. The fingers were long and slender. "I must not wear jewelry." That seemed sad. One should never forego a chance to sparkle. "I should have a couple of rings. I like sparkly things. Why did you notice the absence of a ring?"

"It's nothing," he said again, taking great interest in the griddle.

"These pancakes are delicious," she said. "I'm trying not to devour them, but it's not working."

"Devour all you want. Griddle is still hot. I can make up more fast."

"No, I think five is more than enough. Though, I will

take a refill on the coffee. I figure it's the last good meal I'll have for a while. Aren't you going to eat?"

"I did when you were in the shower. So you're sleeping in your truck and I'm going to assume you don't have a lot of cash."

"Twenty bucks." She shrugged. "I'll figure something out."

"There's an inn at the edge of town where you could stay. Family owned. I don't think it's expensive. It's got a big red cock out front."

Zenia sputtered on a sip of coffee. "A what?"

His smile was slow but genuine and it warmed her all over to finally see some levity from him. His eyes were all kinds of sexy now.

"The inn is called The Red Rooster. There's a giant iron rooster sculpture on the front lawn."

"I see." But looking for an actual red cock may have proved more interesting. "How much you think they charge a night?"

Blade opened a drawer beside him, took out a roll of bills and set it on the counter before Zenia. "That should help you out a bit."

A bit? Her jaw dropped open. The tightly wound block of greens looked as though it could bankroll an entire building project.

"Oh, no, I can't." But she couldn't stop from grabbing it and testing the weight of the roll. They were hundred dollar bills. And there had to be a couple dozen of them rolled up. "This is… No. I don't know how I'd ever pay that back. I'm good with sleeping in the truck and eating Doritos. I like the cool-ranch ones."

"It's a gift. I can afford it."

"You don't even know me."

"That's the best kind of gift. It makes me feel good to give. Maybe it will even tilt me out of the guilt column I've been stuck in. Will you let me have that good feeling?"

"I uh…" She set the roll beside the plate. It would certainly come in handy and definitely pay for a month or more at a cheap inn or hotel. And she could really use a hot shower every day. And maybe even new clothes. And some sparkly rings for her fingers.

The guilt column? What had the man to feel guilty about?

It was none of her business. If he was trying to buy some redemption or whatever, far be it from her to get judgmental, as he'd suggested earlier.

"Okay," she said. "But what will I owe you? Besides all this cash?"

"You think I expect something from you for that money?"

"You're a man. If I know anything about men it is that they generally do not give things to others without expecting something in return. And you, being handsome and single, and me being, well—whatever and whoever I am—maybe you want *something* from me."

"Something." He leaned forward onto the counter on his elbows and his hair fell over one eye. He rapped the counter. Considering what his terms would be?

"I don't want to give you sex," she suddenly felt the need to say. "I mean, I don't know you very well. So if that's the condition, then I'll leave without this." She pushed the roll toward him.

"If I'd wanted to have sex with you, Zen, it would have happened last night."

"Oh."

So that meant he wasn't interested in having sex with her? Because the guy was ten kinds of handsome. And— didn't he find her attractive?

Why that thought? She wasn't curious about having sex with him.

Maybe a little. Oh, mercy, to imagine that blue hair falling over her face as he kissed her and those rigid abs brushing across her stomach...

"I want to help you out and make sure you're safe."

As he seemed to do with the locals. Helping nuns? Despite his dark-and-dangerous appearance, the man must be a pussycat at heart.

"Okay." She clasped the money roll. "Can we be friends?"

Blade abruptly straightened and crossed his arms again. "I don't do the friend thing with women very well."

"I see." A wad of cash and a don't-let-the-door-hit-you-on-the-way-out. Never mind the guilt column, this guy was still occupying the weird column. "So this is it, then? I indulge in your tasty pancakes and then take the money and run?"

"Yep."

Her heart fell, but she kept her shoulders straight and didn't show her disappointment. "That's cool. I've overstayed my welcome as it is. Got some memory tracking to do." She grabbed her backpack and stuffed the money in it. Holding out her hand, she shook his. "Thanks for everything, Blade. Blessings to you."

"Stay away from Brock Olafson," he called as she headed down the stairs.

She would. But it was too bad Blade didn't want to be friends. She could really use a friend right now. This being-on-her-own thing was for the birds. Whoever she was, she was probably a person who thrived on the connection with others.

Which was why it felt as if she was walking away from the best thing to ever happen to her as she took the stairs downward.

Chapter 5

"Uh, Blade?"

A wave of relief fell over Blade when he heard Zen calling from the bottom of the stairs. She hadn't left.

And what was that about? He didn't care if she left and never returned. He'd told her he didn't want to be friends. Had given her enough cash to survive a few months on her own. Add another tally in his charity column. End of story.

"There's a police car at the end of the driveway," Zen called up. "The officer is looking over my truck."

"Ah, hell. They must have gotten a stolen vehicle report. Get back up here. I'll go out and talk to him."

He passed her on the stairs. The skim of her hair across his biceps felt like silk on his skin. He wanted to feel it brush his lips, to draw in her scent and—

Blade forced his thoughts back to the dire situation. "What's out in the truck that belongs to you?"

"Nothing. All I own is in my backpack," she said, patting the backpack she held before her. "Not as if any of this stuff is mine. Fingerprints?"

"Yeah, well, maybe that would be a good thing? If they traced your prints there could be a chance you'd know who you are."

She shook her head and studied her fingertips. "Not sure about that. I don't want to go to jail. I was just borrowing the truck. You think they'd believe that?"

"Nope. Stay. I'll handle this."

She nodded and he waited for her to reach the top step of the stairs before heading outside.

Earl Smith was a local cop who knew his family. Of course, Smith didn't know the Saint-Pierres were werewolves, vampires and faeries. He thought they were just regular folk that tried to fit in, save when Trouble got rowdy and a bar owner called to have the police escort him home. Blade was sure Trouble knew all the officers and deputies within a thirty-mile range by first name and badge number.

"You're at the wrong place, Earl," Blade said to the lanky man who was probably twice his age and half his weight. "Trouble lives east of town."

"You know where this truck came from, Saint-Pierre?"

Fortunately Zen hadn't driven all the way up to the barn, and had parked near the end of the short drive.

"Wasn't here last night when I got home. First time I've been outside today, Earl." Blade rubbed his jaw and walked up to peer into the cab of the truck. As Zen had said, it didn't appear as if any personal belongings had been left inside. The key was in the ignition. "Hell, I didn't even hear it drive up." He laid a hand over the hood. "Engine's not hot. Must have been here awhile. Who's it belong to?"

"It was stolen from a parking lot in Fridley about a week ago. Got a tip from Brock Olafson—we have breakfast at the Panera every now and then—that I should probably check your place."

"That's odd. How would Brock know about a truck I've never seen before? Maybe he had something to do with it being here."

"I, uh, hmm…"

While Earl gave that one a good think, Blade glanced up toward the kitchen window. Zen's face ducked out of sight.

"I don't know what to say, Earl. You know I wouldn't do such a thing as steal a truck. I have enough of my own in the garage."

The officer straightened and hooked his thumbs at his belt loops. "Mind if I take a look?"

"Inside the garage? Sure thing."

Blade led him toward the barn where the entire ground floor had been converted into a garage for his fix-it projects. Best thing to do was play along. He'd not asked for this trouble, but for some reason, he was damned good at extricating himself from sticky situations.

It was a talent he'd gladly surrender if only everyone would leave him in peace.

By the time Blade returned to the loft, Zen had watched a tow truck haul away the vehicle she had borrowed. Okay, stolen. The keys had been in the ignition. How else to get around while she was trying to figure herself out and had no cash whatsoever?

Was that it? Had she been a thief before losing her memory and the criminal act was so ingrained that stealing a truck hadn't given her a moment of guilt?

Blade topped the stairs and veered toward the kitchen, where the coffee machine blinked in wait. He inserted a coffee pod and leaned over the machine, his back to her. Zen could sense his irritation. He was still barefoot. Her worry vanished as she studied his feet. They were sexy. Seriously. Those dark jeans slouched over his feet, the hems torn and worn from treading without shoes. It was so animal, in a sensual, easygoing kind of way.

And he had once again saved her butt, this time by diverting the police from her. Because there was just something about not going to the police that made sense. And she was going to call that intuition about the life she couldn't remember.

"Sorry," Zen offered. "Guess I'm not making a fast getaway now like I had planned. Are you in trouble?"

"No. But the local police will certainly be keeping an eye on me for a while. Earl left convinced it was a joyrider who had abandoned the truck here. Why they hadn't driven it into the woods and trashed it was beyond Earl, but he'll dust for prints. I told him to keep me in the loop if he gets an identification."

"Thanks. I think. If they come up with my prints, will they arrest me?"

"Probably." He removed the full mug and turned to face her, sipping slowly. "And why not go to the police?"

She shrugged. "Doesn't feel right. Not part of the destiny."

He raised an eyebrow.

Zen shrugged again. Because really, the words had just come out; she didn't have a clear reason for them. "Don't ask me to explain."

"Uh-huh." He tilted down a few sips of the hot brew. "If you say so."

"So it's as easy as that?" Zen asked. "I tell you not

to ask questions and you don't. Whew. You must have a heck of a closet filled with your own skeletons."

He smirked and approached her, laying his hand over her heart. Zen flinched but didn't want to pull away from the surprising touch of his big warm hand over her breast.

"What are you—" It didn't matter what he was doing. She just didn't want him to ever stop.

"Your heart is racing," he said.

"Well, duh. A handsome man is touching my boob."

He flinched away at that statement. Shook his head. "Sorry. Just wanted to know if you were for real."

"I am real. I'm standing right here. What doesn't look and feel real to you?"

"The whole not-knowing-things part. You can tell a lot about a person by measuring their heartbeats. Just thought I'd give it a try."

With a nod he turned and pulled out another coffee pod and set it in the machine to brew.

"All righty, then." Zen sat at the counter, more confused about the man than ever. So her heartbeats were fast. To be expected.

And what did she have to do to get him to touch her like that again?

There was something about this woman that was accepting and open, Blade thought. But also too damned curious. Dare he tell her what he'd encountered inside the house while she had been wandering about the field? That would then lead to a discussion on how he was familiar with demons, and...

Destiny?

There was certainly something *other* about her. But

Blade wouldn't necessarily label it destiny. Whatever that meant. When he'd laid his hand over her heart it had felt sure and strong—and fast. His sensory perception of other paranormal beings was excellent. Vampires he could tell by touch. Vamps gave off the shimmer, a knowing tingle. Werewolves were a scent thing. And faeries were a more difficult tell, even though faery blood ran through his veins, but some were just…bright. And that wasn't a glow but rather a feeling he got.

As for witches, he felt a twinge in his spine when near them. Demons gave off a sulfurous scent and they generally had a difficult time hiding their red eyes.

He met Zen's eyes as she sipped the coffee. Hers were blue.

"Yesterday they were green," he said suddenly, leaning forward to closely inspect her irises.

"What?" She met his gaze, and then shook her head. "Listen, after your emphatic statement that we could never be friends, I find your gazing longingly into my eyes a little befuddling, not to mention the free feel you just took."

"They've changed color."

"What? My eyes? No, they're still—" She touched her cheek below her eye. "I guess I've never given them a good look in the mirror."

"Yesterday the color resembled emeralds. Today they are azure. Not red."

"You're hanging on to that theory, eh? Demons have red eyes. Or so the mythology states as much."

"Zen." Blade set his coffee mug on the counter and leaned forward. "That old lady back at the house where I met you? She wasn't old or even a lady."

"Sure she was. I spoke to her. Told her I was there to

find myself. Though she did say something odd about finding herself. If she wasn't an old woman, then what was she?"

"What you saw and spoke to was her human facade. I saw her shift into three demons. And then I slayed them."

Tapping her fingernails against her mug, Zen surprised him in that she didn't protest or stand up and dash off. The woman was reading him, delving into his words to glean their integrity. Trustworthy? Always. Upstanding? Rarely.

"What kind of demons?" she finally asked.

"I don't know." He narrowed his gaze on her. She wasn't running. And asking questions was a good thing. Right? "The standard nasty-assed terrors that disperse into black dust when I draw my blade down their sternums."

Zen clutched her chest and made a gagging face. "And you think *I'm* one of them?"

"No. Maybe."

She gaped at him.

"I don't know. But I do believe they were after you. When I was in the house, one of them said something like 'she's ours.' You're really cool with this conversation? Because most humans would not be."

"I haven't decided yet. I know demons exist. In mythology. As do bazillions of other breeds and species. But they are fiction, Blade. You do know that, right?"

He sighed. The conversation about paranormals was never easy, and he didn't have it with humans unless it was absolutely necessary. Something about Zen made him believe this was a necessary conversation, so he decided to jump in with both feet and hope she didn't freak.

"Demons are real, Zen. As are all other creatures of myth you believe are fiction. If you don't have your memory, what makes you think your beliefs are real? That they have merit? Maybe you only think you don't believe in mythological beings?"

She opened her mouth to say something, then paused. He had even confused himself with that question.

"I know some things," she insisted. "As you seem to believe you know things. So I'll play along. Say demons do exist. And you, apparently, are aware they exist. What does that make you? Are you some kind of creature, Blade?"

The million-dollar question. And she couldn't hide the smirk of laughter that niggled at the corner of her mouth. But he wasn't going to lie to her. Because to shuffle around the truth wouldn't get him anywhere. And after slaying three demons he felt as though he'd become involved in something. A something that demanded he pay attention for Zen's sake.

"Vampire." He sipped the coffee and set it down. He ran his fingers through his hair and offered a tiny smile. He wouldn't mention his faery half. That would only complicate matters.

He waited for Zen to digest his confession, and expected a calm reaction, as she'd displayed thus far. So when she stood abruptly and grabbed her backpack, nearly knocking the coffee cup off the counter in the process, he knew he'd gone too far.

"Quit playing with me," she said. "I need help and I need answers. Not some idiot who thinks he can one-up the town asshole. Brock may have been the better choice last night."

And she marched away from him and down the stairs.

Blade leaned over the sink and watched through the small window as she stopped halfway down his gravel driveway. She realized she no longer had a vehicle. The town was ten miles south. Would she make the walk? In a long dress?

Or would she come back inside and ask for his help? She hadn't asked for his help thus far. And yet, he had willingly offered, and had gone above and beyond by giving her the roll of cash.

What was with that?

Normally Blade Saint-Pierre stood off and to the side, in the shadows. He didn't call attention to himself. He didn't like confrontations. Nor did he engage in small talk and friendships. It was easier that way. The unseen were not challenged, or tortured.

Too late for that, eh?

Yet he wanted her to see him for reasons that baffled. Of course, asking her to believe he was a vampire was out there, even for the smartest and most open-minded of humans.

After shuffling down the stairs, he headed out to his truck—he did have the appointment with the nuns— and smiled to himself. Zen would have a much longer walk than she anticipated.

He was following her, so Zenia picked up her pace, determined to make it to town before he could stop and once again offer her help. She didn't need help from a wacked crazy who believed himself a vampire. What role-playing nightmare had he gotten lost in? Didn't boys generally give up that stuff when they left their teens?

But it was a long walk. And he must be driving five miles an hour. Superobvious follow. Yet when his truck pulled in front of her to make a right turn, and his passenger-side window rolled down, it took all her strength not to rush up to the truck door and see what the handsome man had to say.

Arms crossed and posture stiff, Zenia stood at the road's gravel edge. The sun was high and she guessed it would be a hot one today. She wondered if her skin burned easily. She didn't want to make the long trek into town on foot. But she had reached her limit with trusting this guy. Handsome did not win over crazy. Usually.

Maybe?

Blade leaned across the seat and called, "Tangle Lake is in the other direction!"

Zenia steeled herself against turning and looking back the way she'd walked. "I knew that," she said.

He tilted his head, as if to ask, "Really?"

"Fine." She marched toward the truck. "You win."

He popped the door lock open and she stepped up inside, setting her backpack on the floor. The tin circle poked out of the unzipped top.

"What's that?" he asked with an urgency that again alerted her that this guy wasn't all there in the head.

She tugged the pack onto her lap and pushed the circle inside, zipping it securely. "It's mine. Now, would you mind giving me a ride to the big cock? Or whatever it is you called it? And I recall you had mentioned something about helping a couple of nuns. You must have an appointment to get to, so the sooner you drive me into town, the faster we can both be done with each other."

"The big cock it is." Blade shifted into gear. He drove a few miles before turning the radio down to a whisper. "It's called The Red Rooster Inn."

"Whatever," she managed with as little interest as possible.

"I gave Beckett Severo a call while I was following you down the road. He's my sister's husband. Owns an auto-body shop. He has a sweet little Mini Cooper he can let me buy cheap. He's going to wash it and give the interior a good cleaning, then he'll call me when it's ready. Work for you?"

"What color is it?" she asked, only because she suddenly felt as if he was making all the decisions for her, and she needed to wrangle some control.

"Red?"

"Like a demon's eyes?"

"Yes, like a demon's eyes. Believe me, Zen. I'm not making this stuff up."

"Really? I want to believe you, but…" She sighed and tilted her head against the window. All out of argument. And so desperate for some small grace. "All right. Let me try out belief for a minute. You're a vampire? With fangs?"

"Got the fangs. I need warm blood to survive. Every few weeks. Though I prefer it more often."

He winked at her and it was all she could do not to drop her jaw in horror. He'd just confessed to drinking blood! And the truck was going the speed limit. If she opened the door and jumped now, could she get up and walk away as easily as she had after the bus incident?

But deep within, Zenia felt this man meant only good toward her. If he had a strange belief about his origins then she should allow him that. But that allowance should be countered with a healthy dose of caution on her part.

The giant red iron rooster swept by on her right as Blade pulled into the inn's parking lot. Zen wanted to dash out of the truck and run as far away as possible. She wasn't about to stay where he knew where to find her.

And yet. It was his kind eyes. And he had given her a huge roll of cash. And made arrangements for her to use a car. Balancing his crazy with his kindness was actually leveling out the scale.

So Zenia said something that surprised herself. "Come in with me."

"Why?"

"We need to talk."

He winced.

Yeah, so she'd just given him a standard girlfriend line. Poor guy. But she needed to get on the same page with him.

"I don't believe you're so lacking in curiosity that you can simply drive away, are you?"

He considered the subtle challenge. Twisting the key in the ignition, the truck settled to quiet.

After checking in, Zen filed down the narrow hallway with Blade in tow. Her room was small and fashioned with timber furnishings that sported green-and-red-plaid fabric on the chair and bedspread. Sure was a lot of plaid in this neck of the woods, she noted. She tossed the backpack on the bed, directed Blade to make them coffee and excused herself to the bathroom.

The blue-and-yellow dress was loud. She did need to pick up some new things. Something a little less crazy cat lady and a bit more sensual. Because she knew she was attractive, and Blade's admiring gaze hadn't gone unnoticed. Nor had his attractiveness gone unnoticed.

She wondered if he would flinch if she tried to touch his soft hair. She sensed that would be his first reaction. And then she wanted to test that theory because pushing him to his unknown boundaries felt important to her. To see if he could stand up to any challenge.

Because if pushed maybe he'd reveal his lies. That perhaps he clung to the fantasy of being a strange creature for reasons that helped him survive in this world. Or maybe it was simply that he watched too many movies. Believed women would go for the brooding vampire act. Ugh.

She tilted her head aside, her reflection tracing a finger down her neck. A vampire. Did he want to bite her? What would that feel like? *Orgasmic*, her knowledge provided on a whisper. And what was orgasmic? Had she ever had the experience of sex?

She didn't know. And that frustrated immensely.

She hadn't learned anything about herself out in the field yesterday. And maybe she had. Demons had been after her? Incredulous. She should have stopped to say goodbye to the old lady.

Why was he making up such an elaborate ruse? For what reason the lie? No, he was being truthful. And to test that theory she'd have to see proof.

"Fangs," she muttered.

And once he had to confess to a lack of such telling signs of vampirism, then she could move forward. Both of them could.

Nodding once, she turned off the bathroom light and found Blade waiting with two cups of coffee in hand.

"Dark?" she asked.

"As black as I could get it."

She glanced to the backpack. It was unopened. He hadn't snooped. Not that she had anything to hide. Just a bunch of stolen charity clothing and that weird tin circle. And her roll of cash. His cash. Yet she didn't feel as if she owed him for that generous gift. Was it because she couldn't recall if she was the sort of person who had guilt?

Sitting on the bed, she shuffled closer toward the head by the pillows when Blade sat not three feet from her. Inviting him in may have been a stupid idea. She'd hoped it a means to allow him to confess. Did the victim invite the serial killer in so easily?

"I need some proof," she said. "That you are what you say you are."

"Will that make you believe?"

"Of course." Or it would make him believe. One way or another, this was going to get settled.

"So you are not a woman of faith?"

"I don't know." She tapped her head. "Not all there, remember?"

"What kind of proof are you asking for?"

She set the coffee mug on the wood bedside table that looked as though it had been carved from an oak stump. "Whatever kind you're willing to offer."

She didn't want him to be crazy. She really did not.

Sliding closer on the bed, she raised her hand to touch his hair, then decided against it. "Fangs?"

"If that's what you need? I can do that."

Blade tilted his head back and closed his eyes. And when he rolled his head around, his nose drew along her cheek. Her skin tingled at the barely there touch. It seemed as if he was scenting her. And when the tip of his nose dusted her earlobe she felt her nipples tighten and couldn't decide whether to delight or be afraid of that feeling. Curling her fingers, she closed her eyes as a mix of anxiety and breathless anticipation stirred in her core.

A sharpness slid along her neck. Zen gasped in a breath. What the—? Blade's hand grabbed her by the chin, forcing her to look at him. His mouth was barely parted, yet bright white fangs jutted over his lower lip.

"Holy... How did you put those in so fast?"

"I didn't put them in. They are my teeth." A wide grin revealed his fangs rising to sit even with his upper teeth, and then again, they descended into the long, pointed, gleaming weapons. "You wanted proof."

"But... That means..." He was telling the truth? That was incredible. Impossible. Freaky. Real? "Oh, mercy."

Zen raced for the bathroom and closed the door behind her.

After a few seconds a rap sounded on the wood door. "Zen?"

"I'm good!" she called. "Just need a few minutes to process."

Chapter 6

Zenia leaned forward onto the vanity, peering at her eyes reflected in the mirror. What she saw there was not fear but uncertainty.

"He's a vampire. Those fangs were real."

She hissed out a breath and her shoulders sank. The man was really a vampire. Because his teeth had not been fake. No cheesy white plastic dentures. He'd lowered and raised them as she had watched.

So here she stood. Processing. And to do so, had locked herself in the bathroom to put herself away from the creature on the other side of the flimsy wood door. Who could probably knock it down if he wanted to and suck out all her blood before she could manage to scream for help.

She shook her head. "Don't let your imagination make this into something weird. Weird? Ha! The man is a vampire. Which means the mythology is real. And what makes me think all I know is real anyway?"

Of course, if vampires were real that also opened the door to other creepy critters being as real. Werewolves, ghosts and demons?

"He killed demons. There were real demons in that

pink house. He was telling me the truth. And they'd mentioned me? What is going on?"

She'd fallen into some kind of creature feature. And while she should do the smart thing and run like hell, she couldn't resist a peek down the dark stairway.

"He's been nice to me so far," she reasoned with her reflection. "I can trust him." A nod confirmed her decision.

And so she turned the knob and walked out into the room. Blade leaned against the wall, arms crossed over his chest. Head bowed, his hair was tinted blue, no denying that. Was that indicative of his vampire nature?

Wow. Just wow.

"Are you going to bite me?" she asked calmly.

He smirked and shook his head. "No."

"Why don't you want to bite me?"

Now he laughed. "In the course of two questions you went from curiosity to fang junkie."

"Fang junkie?"

"Women and men who seek the vampire's bite. It gives them an orgasmic high. Sort of a thank-you for giving blood."

Zen blew out a breath. Shook her head. She'd asked for proof. And he'd given it to her in spades. The guy was a vampire. And the more she considered it, his fangs were actually kind of cool.

She walked up to him. "Let me see them again."

With a shrug, he opened his mouth to reveal the fangs. She touched the tip of a fang and he flinched away.

"What's wrong?"

"Women don't generally touch," he said defensively.

"I'm sorry. They are interesting to me. Don't you ever poke yourself in the lip?"

He smirked, again revealing the gorgeous fangs. "I've been living with them awhile."

"Since birth?"

"No, since my teen years. We vamps don't come into the blood hunger until puberty. A vampire baby is just wrong."

"I imagine so." Frowning, Zen ran the idea of a fanged baby drinking blood from its mother's nipple through her thoughts. Yeah, that was wrong in too many ways to consider. "Wow. So you are really a vampire."

"And you are having a tough time with this."

"No. Not anymore. I did some processing in the bathroom. Had a pep talk with my crazy ole self. So the myths are real? And you don't seem a danger to me."

"I have no reason to harm you, Zen. Believe me."

"I am inclined to trust you. You've shown me nothing but kindness thus far. Will you tell me about being a vampire? That'll help me to further process. You said you drink blood every few weeks? Is it a sexual thing?"

"You just ask whatever is on your mind, don't you?"

"Are you offended by my questions? You should be pleased I'm not screaming and whittling a stake."

"I am. Although the adrenaline that comes up when a person screams does season the blood nicely." He paused. Gauging her reaction? Likely.

Zen didn't feel disgust. She'd accepted that vampires existed. Now she needed to learn how and why.

"And so you know," he added, "it would take a damn long time to whittle a stake. Use an ax to hone a point on a thick wood dowel. It will go faster."

"Did you just tell me how to kill you?"

"I did. Feel better?"

"It's not as though I need to feel better about your condition—"

"It's not a condition. It is what I am."

"Okay. I understand. Blood is your means to survival?"

"Yes. I like drinking blood and it is a sensual experience if I'm having sex with the person when I bite them. But I can take someone in a dark club or back alley without it turning me on. My bite leaves the victim in a state of bliss. As I've said, a reward for giving blood."

"Do you ever, uh—" Zen ran her fingers along the plaid bedspread "—kill?"

His fangs retracted, and she missed them immediately. "When drinking blood? No."

That he'd categorized that question bothered her. "So you have killed at other times? Of course, the demons yesterday." She had no choice now but to believe they had been real.

He suddenly took her by the wrist and lifted her arm to hold her elbow toward the sunlight beaming through the window. "Those markings are faint but remarkable. Do you know what they mean?"

The man had deftly avoided the question about killing. She'd give him that. He had killed. Many times. She simply knew it. Perhaps he'd been protecting another damsel in distress from demons?

"I'm guessing it was something I drew on my skin before the accident," she offered. "Should fade away with a few more showers."

"Has it faded since you've noticed it?"

"No. I guess not."

"It doesn't look like ink or even one of those white tattoos that are so popular nowadays."

"Demonic?" she tossed out teasingly. She regretted it immediately. Demons were serious and real. What kind of nightmare had she fallen into?

"I don't know what it is," Blade said. "One of my brothers is full faery. He has pale violet markings on his skin. But the patterns don't look similar. Aren't you curious?"

"I am, but it's not as if I have any idea where to begin learning about such a thing. A faery brother? That's fascinating. How does that work exactly?"

"It's a long story. My family is a mix of races."

Nodding, she rubbed the inside of her elbow to distract herself from the need to delve into his family history. He'd been kind in answering her questions so far. She didn't want to press her luck. "How do I learn more about these markings?"

"There's a witch in Minneapolis. She might have a clue."

"Witches. Of course." And so many other species she would likely learn about the longer she hung around Blade. The idea of gaining such knowledge compelled her. If she couldn't learn about herself then she may as well gather info about the secret world that existed around her. "You know all the exciting people, eh?"

"Do you want me to take you to her?"

"I sense you are more eager to learn about these markings than I am. Digging up proof I'm not an evil demon?"

"I hate demons," Blade stated plainly. He paced to the window. His frame stiffened, shoulders tilting back and fingers curling into loose fists. Zen could palpably feel his cool anger. He was a man who didn't like to speak about himself, but he didn't have to. His emotions showed in his tightly strung physicality.

"Would you hate me if I were demon?" she asked.

He turned a glance over his shoulder. "I don't know what to think of you."

"Well, I think very highly of you, just so you know."

"Despite my being vampire?"

"Your race or species, or whatever you call it, matters little. It's you, the man, whom I make my judgment on."

"Not a lot of people in this world who can be so open-minded."

Zen smirked. "And look at me, not so much open-minded as absent of some of my mind."

His smile was an unexpected surprise. "You'll remember who you are."

"I hope so." She sat on the bed. "And then I wonder if it really matters. I don't know, I guess if I do have a family or job I would like to learn about that. Do you think vampires can get amnesia?"

He lifted a brow.

"They can?"

"There was a vampire who lived in the area, decades ago, who lost his memory. He got it back. We're very similar to humans, Zen."

"Except that part about needing human blood to survive."

"There is that."

"Would you, uh…bite me if I asked?"

"No."

"Why not? You said it wouldn't kill me. What if I wanted to experience the pleasure you said the bite gives a victim?"

"You're moving too fast, Zen. We haven't even gone on a date."

"Oh. Right. Sorry. But if we can't be friends, I don't hold out much hope for a date."

"Dates are…"

"Not your thing. I get it. Tall, dark, brooding guy has a lot of issues and I should just shut up and be thankful he wants to help me. Hmm, but what if having a friend was part of the help I needed?"

"I don't know what you are."

She shrugged. "Does it matter?"

"It does. Instincts tell me you're not human. And there are certain species within this realm that I can't drink from."

"Really?"

He nodded. "Faery ichor is addictive to a vampire. And demon blood is just— It won't kill me, but I… Well, it's not important. Angel blood will kill me, though."

"I'm pretty sure I'm not an angel. I haven't any wings."

"I don't know much about angels. Those markings on your arm make me wonder if you're faery. You'd be able to bring your wings out if you were aware of them."

Wings? Bonus!

Zen closed her eyes and focused on the space between her shoulder blades and up and down her spine. She imagined wings popping out. Hey, if the man was a vampire, anything was possible.

"What are you doing?" he asked.

She opened one eye. "Trying to bring out my wings. I don't feel anything. Not even a flutter. Nope. I don't think so. Though it would be cool if I had faery dust. I like sparkly things."

His smile was always such a welcome change from stoicism that this time she stood and walked right up to him, lured by the seductive promise of his lips. She slid her hands up the front of his shirt and touched the tips of his long hair. It was soft, as she'd suspected. And then she tilted up on to her tiptoes and kissed him.

Chapter 7

Zen's mouth landed on Blade's with graceful precision. He grabbed her arms to push her away. Not expecting a kiss, he'd been blindsided. And when he wanted to shove her off and march out of the room, he suddenly relaxed his grip on her arms and leaned into the kiss.

And then he leaned in a little more.

He pulled her closer, sliding a hand up her back to keep her there. Her mouth fit his like no other woman's had. She felt…not so much right, but rather as if she'd found something and did not want to again lose it. A missing piece to her puzzle? Despite being unable to remember things about herself, she'd certainly not lost the skill of delivering a kiss.

He moaned deep in his throat and then opened her mouth with his and slid his tongue inside her heated kiss. She tasted like coffee. She felt impossibly exquisite. She smelled like honey and her body was warm and supple against his. A sweet thing.

And that was the kicker. Her scent did not allude to her identity. What *was* she? And worse, could whatever she was be bad for him?

Forcing himself to pull away from the kiss, he held her at a distance even as she leaned forward, attempting to ply him with another kiss. "What was that for?" he asked on a raspy tone.

"I had the compulsion to kiss you. You taste great. And your fangs didn't get in the way. Cool," she said with more enthusiasm than she probably should have. "Did I do it right? I mean, I'm not sure if I've kissed a man before."

"It was nice. Er, I mean... Yeah, it was okay."

"Okay? Hmm, that implies I need more practice."

The second kiss was firmer, more demanding, and was filled with an eagerness that rippled through Blade's system and hardened his cock. And then it jabbed at his vampiric need for a deeper, more intimate, connection. His fangs wanted down, and he fought against it.

He'd meant it when he'd said he would not bite her. Not when he didn't know what the hell she was.

Practice? This chick was an expert kisser.

"Zen, stop." He shrugged her off and backed toward the bed, but realized he was trapped unless he scrambled over the bed and out the door. "I can't do this. I—I don't do this."

"You don't do what? Kiss women? Are you gay? Stupid me. I don't have the gaydar that I know some do."

"I am not gay. Though, I wouldn't confine my sexual choices to women, either. I just don't do...this." *And leave it at that. Please.*

"Oh. You mean like the physical-contact thing? Or the emotion thing?"

"I think we've chatted enough for today."

"You mean kissed?"

He nodded. "Whatever you want to call it. Just drop it, will you?"

"If you insist. But you did share with me, so I guess that was my return share."

A kiss in exchange for a confession to vampirism. Worked for him. Until it did not. Blade did not want to get involved with a pretty woman in need of saving. He just. Did. Not. He either made love to them or rescued them. There was to be no in-between. Not anymore.

"Will you get me that car?" she asked sweetly. "The town is small but it's easier to get around in a vehicle."

He swung around the side of the bed, but the door was so far away, and did he really want to run out like a scared boy who'd just gotten his first kiss?

"Of course. And I want to take you to the witch. But I have to stop by the nuns' place today."

"Did you miss that appointment?"

"No, I told them I'd swing by when I was in town. Didn't specify a time."

"If I have a car I can run around on my own. I wouldn't need your help."

He wasn't sure if he should applaud that or lament not having a damsel to save. Because then his only other option would be to make love to her.

"I don't mind helping you, Zen. We'll get you figured out."

"You really think I could be something *not* human?"

"It's a possibility. It would help if I had some notion of what you are…"

Getting an idea, he bent and tugged out the knife from his boot. Turning to Zen, he held up the big bowie knife that had saved his ass on more than a few occasions. Her eyes widened. Her *gold* eyes.

Lowering the knife to his side, he leaned forward to peer at the irises. They changed color often.

"What? You looking for the best place to jab that big blade? I just start trusting you and then you go and freak me out of that trust, over and over—"

"They're gold now."

"My eyes? They were sort of a muddy green when I was in the bathroom processing things." She blinked. Rubbed an eyelid. "So what does that have to do with you bringing out the big bad weapon?"

"Nothing at all. And maybe everything." Jaw tensing, he weighed his options. The easiest choice was going to once again tug her out of trust and push her toward freak mode. "I want to make a small cut in your skin to see your blood." He grabbed her hand, holding her palm upward. "Will you let me?"

"Once again, you're making me think Brock was the better bet."

He frowned at her.

"Is this a vampire thing?"

"No. I have three brothers and one sister. One of my brothers is full-blood faery. He bleeds ichor. Ichor is clear and sparkles. Not red."

His blood was red, and yet—she didn't need to know that it had a tendency to sparkle, as well.

"So you think if you cut me…" She squeezed her fingers a couple times. A nervous reaction. Then she closed her eyes, squeezed them tightly and nodded. "Okay. I've processed. Go for it."

He wasn't going to argue and give her a chance to reconsider.

Blade dragged the tip of his blade in an inch-long cut down the center of her palm. She didn't make a peep. Points for bravery. Blue blood seeped out and dribbled toward his hand. He panicked and dropped her hand.

And even as he backed away, the blood spilling from her palm changed color. Black droplets hit the worn beige carpeting.

Zen studied her hand and then the floor. "It changed color. And it's not red. Wow. I—don't think I'm human," she said with wonder. "How strange is that? I think I just passed you on the weirdness scale. But what bleeds blue?"

Heart falling in his chest, Blade stumbled backward, landing on the bed. "Angels."

The man sitting on the bed growled at her. And then he revealed a flash of fang. It was a combative display, and Zen didn't like it. Not coming from the man whom she trusted to help her learn about herself. And then she did not trust him.

And then she got over her freak-out to trust him again.

It was exhausting trusting this man.

But the display of fangs cautioned her that she knew little about him. And he could be very dangerous.

So back to not so much trust.

"Are you serious?" she asked with a gesture toward his fangs. "Don't go all warrior on me, Blade. Settle down. This is news to me. I'm an angel? I can't be." She thrust out her palm. It no longer bled, and had completely healed. "What the—? Do it again."

He held up his hands in protest, the knife in one of them and shook his head. "I'm not touching angel blood."

"I am not an angel. I mean…I don't feel angelic." She patted her chest, ran her hands over her hips. "What do angels feel like?"

"I don't know what you are, Zen. Angel is a guess."

"Right, but then my blood turned black. What does that mean?"

"Demons bleed black."

She gaped at him.

"That must have been your denizen back at the house."

"I am not part of a denizen."

"You have amnesia, so that argument is invalid."

Slamming her hands to her hips, Zen pinned the man with her best snappish look. Tossing the truth at her wasn't going to win him any points. All she wanted to do was move back to the window and resume their kiss. That perfect, delicious, erotic kiss. It had shimmered through her insides, warming in its wake, and had made her feel—things she wasn't sure she'd ever felt before.

But the evidence was not something she could ignore. Her blood wasn't red. That ruled out human. Right? For all the mythological knowledge she held in her brain, she could confirm that, yes, angels were the only creatures that bled blue. And quite a few things bled black, though the majority were demonic.

Maybe she was angel *and* demon? Was that possible? She didn't know. She'd only just begun to believe in creatures beyond humanity. She didn't feel particularly angelic. Where were her wings?

"This is," she started, "surprising. I need to process this." She inspected her palm. "Look."

Blade leaned over, without touching, though his hair did skim her wrist. "It's healed. You are not human by a long shot."

"We should talk to the witch."

"I'll give her a call."

"Blade." She grabbed his hand as he stood and fished out his cell phone. "Thank you."

He shrugged and pulled out of her grip.

"I know you think it's something you're doing, like helping the elderly. But you could have left me in that parking lot last night. And you could just walk away now. The door is right there. I won't protest if you leave. Too much. I mean, I *am* all alone. But you know, I've managed to survive this long. A week. I could probably manage awhile longer."

Now his body changed from the stiff defensive posture, his shoulders relaxing. He touched the ends of her hair. "You need my help. That's something I'm willing to give."

"Great. Let's seal that with a kiss." She tilted up on her toes, but he stopped her with a hand to her shoulder.

"The two of us kissing? I'm not cool with that."

"Why—"

His hand between them frustrated her. "No questions. Deal?"

If she didn't agree, he might take her invitation to walk out the door. But if she agreed, did that mean she'd never taste his kiss again? It seemed a ridiculous sacrifice in exchange for some information about herself. She had some ideas. Angel?

But not knowing would keep him from kissing her again for sure. So she'd choose the lesser of the two evils.

"Deal."

Blade hadn't forgotten about the nuns. He told Zen he'd give her a call when he was finished and they could go see the witch. She said she planned to do some shopping—which he didn't argue, as that dress was… loud—so he said he'd look for her at the local strip mall later in the evening. He estimated a whole afternoon of work.

The nuns had been sitting out in the backyard sipping lemonade when he'd arrived. Thrilled at his arrival, they had helped him haul heavy stones around the fountain. A couple of workhorses. And their jokes had been surprisingly ribald. He'd ensured the water flowed and the fountain was secured to the concrete base with a couple heavy-duty bolts. When all was finished, he refused their offer to pay and promised he'd return with further landscaping assistance in a few days after the plants had arrived.

It was seven-thirty in the evening when he drove by the strip mall and spied Zen. Blade had told her he would park in the back lot. The lot butted up against an abandoned sewing-needle factory. The brick walls were crumbling, but he liked the decay. And the quiet.

Leaning against the pickup truck bed, he confirmed by phone call with Dez Merovich it was okay to stop by tonight. She was a nearly millennium-old witch who, a few years ago, had cured his brother Stryke of the silver poisoning he'd received after a hunter's arrow had cut him while in wolf shape. She also studied diabology. If anyone would have some answers for Zen, Blade suspected it could be Dez.

And while waiting, Beck called. The Mini Cooper was ready. He could take it off Beck's hands for three grand. A pittance if it would enable Zen to find her feet and survive on her own. The price tag wouldn't even dent his finances.

Was he going out of his way to help this chick to

achieve his own redemption? The gods knew he was desperately in need of forgiveness. Or better yet, forgetting. He'd take Zen's amnesia from her if it were possible. A woman had died because of his indiscretions.

Could helping Zen find out who she was erase his sins?

All Blade wanted was to feel the weight of that horrible disaster lift from his shoulders. He'd wear the scars to remind him of it forever. The mental place he went to when Octavia's memory popped up threatened to bring him down so deep he'd never rise. It was why he kept to himself. Safer for him and those innocents with whom he came in contact.

Was Zenia an innocent? If she was an angel, he didn't know what to think. Same if she was demon. Either way, she was not a species he wanted to get involved with. He'd learned his lesson.

He had.

So when the taste of her kiss shimmered onto his tongue, he couldn't decide whether to savor it or grab the water bottle he kept in the truck cab and wash it away.

I am all alone. She'd said it with desperation, and he hadn't felt as if it had been a ploy.

He knew that desperate feeling. Sometimes being the loner wasn't what his soul desired. And that was why he couldn't walk away from Zen now.

A woman's scream alerted him. At the end of the alleyway he saw the silhouettes. Zen stood holding armloads of shopping bags. A tall, broad-shouldered man wielded a circular blade that he swung toward the hapless female.

Chapter 8

In a matter of two seconds Blade assessed and reacted. The attacker was big, but so was Blade. The enemy had a weapon, and Blade had the bowie knife. The alley was secluded. For the moment. He couldn't know how long before Zen's scream would bring curious onlookers. This matter needed to be dealt with. Fast.

So he shifted into his most powerful form.

With a warning growl, his wings emerged and his shirt tore across his biceps and abs. When in faery form his muscles tightened and grew more defined and powerful. Everything about his vampire was heightened, as well. His fangs slid down, pinprick sharp and longer than usual. Scents grew stronger and the air vibrated against his skin. He could navigate by sensation with his eyes closed and in the blackest cavern if need be.

He kept his eyes open and raced toward the intruder and Zen.

The attacker swung his weapon toward Blade, who caught the man by the forearm. The weapon clattered to the ground and Zen grabbed for it. At the sight of the circular weapon, Blade did not sink his fangs into the man's biceps. An angel halo? Which would make this guy an angel.

The last thing a vampire wanted to do was suck angel blood. That was the way to certain death.

The man swung Blade around and his spine hit the brick wall, wings folding about his shoulders in defense. The attacker's grasp was supernaturally strong, and he closed his fingers about Blade's throat. Blade slashed a wing forward, the edges of the black-and-silver appendage razor sharp and cutting through his opponent's cheek. Blue blood oozed from the cut.

Just as Blade felt a bone crack in his neck vertebra, the man—angel—suddenly gleamed bright white. His eyes glowed all colors. His mouth gaped. Then he dispersed in a cloud of crystal dust, dropping on the ground between Blade and Zen.

Zen held the circular weapon, dripping with blue angel blood. "Holy crap, that was awesome!"

Blade immediately shifted back to his vampire form, tucking his wings in and insinuating them into his system. His neck had cocked at an uncomfortable angle, and he jammed the heel of his palm against his vertebrae to shove them back into position. That smarted, and took his senses from him. Landing on his knees before the pile of crystal ash, he was aware of his torn jeans. Didn't matter. Zen was safe.

"That was interesting," Zen announced with more glee than a woman who had almost died at an angel's hands should have.

"You just killed an angel."

"I know! This thing rocks. I picked it up from the ground when he dropped it. It's just like mine."

"Yours?" He gasped and looked up at her. Did she beam unnaturally? Her smile was effusive. Not at all like someone who had just killed. And those marks inside her elbows seemed to glow. "What do you mean it's like yours?"

She flipped the halo over and over then made to put it over her head.

"No!" Blade blurted out and stood. He put up placating hands. "Don't do that."

She cringed and lowered the halo. "Uh, sorry?"

"If there is any chance you might be angel, if you put a halo in its rightful place—above your head—you will turn human."

"Oh. Okay. I think I need to process that."

"Yeah, you do that. Maybe I should hang on to that for you?"

She clasped it to her chest possessively. Okay, maybe not. He wasn't too keen on touching the blue blood tracing the circular metal anyway.

"So!" Her eyes wandered down his form and lingered at his crotch, where he felt a draft due to his ripped jeans. "You're going to need some new pants. The store just closed, but maybe there's a Target at the edge of town?"

"Zen!"

"Oh." She waved the angel halo before her. "I suppose you can have it. Mine is in my backpack. So this blood is blue." She inspected the bladed edge of the halo. "I didn't think it would be so easy to kill an angel. What's up with that?"

"It's the halo. It can be used as a weapon against the divine."

"I'd hardly call someone who had the intent of killing me divine."

"Neither would I."

She wiped the blood across her skirt, then thrust it toward him. "Here."

He accepted the cleaned halo, putting it around his wrist for the moment, and grabbed her shopping bags by the handles and strode toward the truck. "You get what you need?" Seriously? He'd just asked about her shopping trip instead of the obvious, like how was she able to kill a freaking angel?

"Yes!" She scrambled after him. "But, oh, there was this tiara. It was part of a display. It sparkled madly. They wouldn't sell it to me. It was just rhinestones, but it was so pretty—"

"Zen."

"What?"

"We need to get out of here before someone comes. But before we do…" He opened the truck door and dumped one of the shopping bags out, littering the floor with frilly clothing, and handed it to her. "Go scoop up the angel dust. We can give it to Dez in repayment for any info she might give us."

"Cool. I love the sparkly stuff." She gestured to his shoulder. "Nice wings, by the way."

"I am so out of my element with your easy acceptance of me," he admitted.

"Yeah?" Her eyes glided down to his crotch. "You're easy on the eyes, no matter what your form. I'll be right back."

"Hurry!"

He slid into the driver's seat and pulled a shirt from her bag over his lap. He hadn't a clean shirt to pull on to cover his back and prevent her from seeing the scars. Maybe she wouldn't notice.

Hell, she'd notice. The woman's eyes had practically licked every part of him just now.

Shaking his head and trying not to smile, Blade focused on the serious stuff. He'd shifted into faery shape in the middle of the city. Not something he'd ever done before. Too risky. Yet when weighing the risk against Zen's death, it hadn't required thought.

And yet, she had made the killing strike. The woman was utterly remarkable. And that was not a good thing. Because the more she fascinated him, the harder it would be to stand back and not get emotionally involved.

The passenger door opened and Zen stepped up into the truck. "Got it! And there was this." She held up a soft red feather as long as an ostrich plume but with tighter barbs.

"We'll show it to Dez. First I want to swing by my place and put some clothes on."

"Good plan. I don't really understand why your clothes are all ripped and…" Her eyes landed on his bare chest. "Missing."

Blade bowed his head to catch her gaze.

Zen shook her head as if to jar herself out of the stare. "Right. So vampires have wings?"

"Uh, not full-blood vamps."

"You're not full blood? What does that make you?"

No avoiding this conversation because the woman was persistent. He shifted into gear and headed north toward home. "I told you one of my brothers is faery."

"That you did. Can I assume one of your parents is faery?"

"My mother. And I got some of her sidhe mojo. Sidhe

is the universal term for faeries. I consider myself vamp, but I have the faery wings, so there you go."

"I'm surprised."

"Why?"

"That you can be more than one thing."

He found her gaze in the rearview mirror. "If you know so much about the world, you must be aware that the humans carry a mix of many heritages in their DNA. Look at you. Your skin color is light brown and your eyes are bright and your hair is almost red. Whatever you are, I'd guess you have a mixture of races in you."

"So? Oh."

"So that would imply I am allowed a mix of as many different breeds."

"Fair enough. And when you saw the big bad guy standing over me, you determined your faery had the best chance against whatever it was and you reacted. Good call."

"Lot of good it did. You were the one who killed the angel."

"I did, didn't I? Felt kind of empowering." She flexed her skinny biceps, and when she noted his frown, added, "You held him in place for me."

"I can live with that." And despite himself, he laughed at that one, and drove onward.

Yep, this woman was going to try his every staunch effort to never get involved again.

Chapter 9

Blade pulled on a change of clothing and tossed his torn jeans into a sack he kept to collect the damaged stuff. His mother was able to fix some, and with the unpatchable things, she made quilts. With five shape-shifting children, she had a lot of torn clothing to work with. Yes, his faery mother was into making quilts. For the grandchildren, she'd say with a wink.

Stryke was the only Saint-Pierre sibling who had a child on the way. His wife, Blyss, was due next month. Blade wasn't ready to be a father, nor was his brother Trouble. He wasn't sure about Kelyn's designs on family. The youngest was a hard one to figure.

Zen had changed in his bathroom and emerged in slim-fitted purple jeans and a blousy white top with multicolored embroidery around the neckline, which further attested to her bohemian nature. On her feet sparkled rhinestone-encrusted sandals. She spun before him and he nodded his approval, which made her beam.

And Blade found himself turning away to hide his own beaming smile. He could get over the fact that a woman had been the successor in that struggle in the alley. But he didn't want to dismiss the bright and sexy appeal of her. Ever. Because how often did a man get to appreciate the bright and sexy?

The twosome hopped in his truck and headed to Minneapolis. The sun yet lingered on the horizon and painted the sky orange and crimson. Rush-hour traffic had subsided. And the city lights had blinked on. Forty-five minutes later, he parked before the Washington Street high-rise nestled on the bank of the Mississippi River, and Dez buzzed them in to her penthouse loft.

Dez was married to the phoenix vampire Ivan Drake, who sat on The Council, which oversaw the paranormal nations. Blade recalled his grandfather Creed mentioning that Dez had been French royalty over nine hundred years ago, an illegitimate daughter of a Merovingian king.

Cool.

He enjoyed listening to his grandfather's tales of life in medieval times and walking through the centuries. To have lived in a simpler world appealed to Blade. Though, he knew no time was simpler, only that it had less technology. And he wasn't sure he could give up the coffeemaker for swords and bucket-topped boots.

The door opened and a cheerful greeting from a slender woman with chestnut hair and clad in a black T-shirt and a long floaty white skirt encouraged Blade to cross the threshold and shake the woman's hand.

"Thank you for seeing us, Dez," he said. He shivered then as a sort of electrical vibe ran down his spine. It was that witch radar he had. But it felt like something stronger.

"The wards," Dez offered in explanation. "I softened them for your entry. And who is this?"

Zen stepped forward and peered through the threshold.

"This is Zen. She's lost her memory and we're trying to remember her past. Uh, and figure out *what* she is. She's had demons and angels after her."

"And you have interesting blood. Or so Blade has told me," Dez said, gesturing Zen enter.

When she attempted to cross the threshold, Zen was repulsed across the hallway. She hit the wall so hard, the sheetrock cracked. Tiny dust particles settled onto her shoulders.

Blade rushed to her side but she shook it off. "I'm good. Whew! What was that?"

"I've warded against all species," Dez said. Arms crossed, the witch stepped out into the hallway and peered down into Zen's eyes. "I'm sorry, but I never take them down completely. It's not wise. I lowered the vampire and sidhe wards for Blade, but you are something else entirely, aren't you, my exotic one?"

"That's what we were hoping you could help us with," Blade said.

"Do you mind if I place my hands on your head?" Dez asked Zen.

"Go ahead. Work your witch magic."

The witch pressed her hands aside Zen's temples and placed her thumbs low, near the corners of her eyes. Closing her eyes, Dez bowed her head toward Zen's in a silent communion.

Blade stepped back and leaned against the open door frame. He wasn't sure how witches worked, and didn't have curiosity about it. That the wards had repelled Zen so violently, and yet she seemed to have brushed it off did make him wonder. Whatever she was, the woman was strong.

But not strong enough to have avoided getting amnesia from an apparent bump on the head. Interesting. If she were an angel, shouldn't she be able to endure a much greater blow? *Could* angels get amnesia? He knew nothing about them. With hope, Dez could fill him in on that, as well.

With a heavy exhale Dez stepped back from Zen and looked about as if she were emerging from a long sleep. Zen opened her eyes and Blade saw they were now pink. He'd never seen that color iris on anyone before.

"What?" Zen asked them both.

"Your eyes are pink," he offered. "What does that mean, Dez?"

The witch swept a palm up her arm as if cold. "I honestly don't know. I can't get a read on her. She's... not anything. Specifically."

Zen quirked a brow. "Well, I have to be something. Human?"

"Oh, no," Dez said quickly. "I can feel power rushing through you. It is immense. Supernatural. You can't feel it?"

Zen shrugged. "I did kill an angel an hour ago. That wasn't due to strength, but rather the halo I'd picked up from the ground."

Dez cast a wondering glance at Blade. He nodded. "We had an altercation before coming here. An angel tried to kill her."

Dez had no reply, but now she did shiver, rubbing a palm up one of her arms.

"I cut her palm and she healed instantly," Blade offered. "She also bleeds blue, but then it quickly changes to black."

"Yes, so you said. And an angel after you? Your arm," Dez noted. "Can I see?"

Zen held up her arm, the inside of her elbow exposed so Dez could study the markings. The witch looked them over carefully, her long fingers tracing the air above her arm, but did not touch Zen's skin.

"They look sidhe in nature," she said carefully.

Blade studied the markings over Dez's shoulder. "They don't look anything like Kelyn's markings."

"The breeds of sidhe are vast, Blade. Some have markings to denote tribes or birthright. Others are completely without such notable skin designs. If I knew any more about Faery and its occupants I'd be a far wiser woman. I regret that Faery is not one of my more studied banks of knowledge."

"If Zen has sidhe markings, then why are demons and angels after her?"

"You're sure it was an angel? It's not often they fall to this realm."

Blade unhooked the circular weapon from the back of his leather belt and handed it to Dez. She didn't take it, but nodded knowingly.

"Well, well," she said. "A halo. The angel had that on him?"

"Yes. It's the one Zen used to slay it. One slice took him out and reduced him to angel dust."

"Interesting. And remarkable. I need some tea. Yes, a lot of tea." Dez strode back inside the loft, and Blade followed.

Then he remembered and looked back at Zen, who stood just outside the threshold, clutching her backpack.

He had the notion that she was like one of the oddball kids that never got invited to the cool kids' table.

"I can wait out here," Zen said. "I'm fine."

"Dez? Can you let down your wards so Zen can enter?"

"I haven't a clue what ward that would be. And I refuse to drop them all. Not wise in my profession. I'm sorry, Zen. I'll leave the door open."

"No problem." Zen squatted against the wall.

At that moment she looked…lost. Her pink eyes fluttered a glance across the threshold and she wrapped her arms about her chest.

Blade resisted reaching out to her. The urge to pull her against him and offer reassurance surfaced. Because it felt right. Connection tended to soften fears and worries. He knew that. He wasn't a hermit who denied himself touch or communication with others.

But it was easier to not offer that comfort, to keep up the shield around his heart. He wore the scars from caring too much about a woman—scars he'd deftly hidden from Zen when he'd taken her home to change. He wouldn't so easily embrace another helpless female again. But he would stand before her with weapons in hand and a fierce determination to protect. That part was easy.

"Won't be long," he muttered, and walked inside.

The south wall of the loft featured floor-to-ceiling windows and overlooked the Mississippi. Pale floorboards and white furnishings gave the area a clean feeling. Didn't look like a witch's home, but then, Blade decided pentagrams and hex bags were just movie lies. The real witches blended into society and took advantage of their surroundings to create the illusion of being merely human.

"Ivan is in Berlin," Dez said as she put a pot of water on the stove. "You'll have to say hello for me to your grandfather Creed next time you see him."

"I will." He sat before the kitchen table where he could keep Zen in sight through the open doorway. She gave him a little wave and he winked at her. To Dez he asked, "You think she's faery?"

"I suspect she isn't anything right now." Dez leaned a hip against the end of the white marble kitchen counter, positioning herself between Blade and the door. "I'm still considering the part where you encountered an angel with its halo. They don't normally have their halos when they come to this realm. When they fall from Above the halo falls away. The angel then seeks a muse—one specific female born for him—to mate with and ultimately give birth to Nephilim. If the angel ever does find its halo, it can be used to restore its earth-bound soul, and thus the angel becomes mortal. Perhaps it was another angel's halo?"

Blade shrugged. "Could be." He set the halo on the table. It was thin and clattered like cheap tin. At first glance, not a quality weapon, but to use it was another story. One slice down the angel's back had taken it out. He was going to hang on to this thing. "Zen has one, as well."

"What?" Dez turned to the doorway and Zen nodded in confirmation.

"It's in my backpack." She lifted the canvas pack from the floor. "Do you want me to show you?"

"No," Dez said hastily. "I don't like that power being in my home. The one Blade holds makes me nervous enough. It's only the angel dust that would truly interest me."

Zen pulled out a crunchy pink paper shopping bag from her pack and shoved it toward the threshold. Dez looked to Blade.

"The remains of the angel she slayed," he confirmed.

The witch took the bag and inspected the contents. "The feather, as well. It contains most powerful magic. I can use this."

"It's yours," Blade said. "For talking with us."

"Bless you."

The teapot whistled and Dez poured three cups. She stepped over the threshold and handed a cup to Zen, then returned to sit across from Blade. For a woman who had walked through nine centuries she looked no older than midthirties, and reminded Blade of a classic movie star with her perfect hair, smooth complexion and elegant moves.

He couldn't imagine living so long. If life intended to toss emotional challenges at him just for living he wasn't sure he wanted any more than the usual human's lifetime.

Then again, he never backed down from any challenge. Bring it all on. What didn't kill him only made him stronger.

"So when an angel falls," he said, "it immediately begins searching for its muse?"

"If it's the type of angel who has a muse," Dez explained. "But first and foremost the angel walks the world. It's a knowledge walk. They can walk the world in a day, crossing oceans and passing through cities at a speed that renders them imperceptible to all around.

They glean facts and information about their surroundings. It's how they insinuate themselves into this realm."

Blade narrowed his gaze on Zen. "For a chick who lost her memory, she keeps saying she knows so much."

"I do," Zen provided. "I don't know why, but I do."

"If she was walking the world…" He considered the possibilities. "Maybe when she was passing through Tangle Lake, the bus hit her and jarred her out of that knowledge walk."

Zen tilted her head in wonder.

It was just a guess, but it made sense. But that implied she truly was an angel. He wasn't buying that just yet. Because the part where her blue blood turned black remained suspicious.

"I suspect—" Dez sipped, lingering over the lavender steam that wafted from the delicate porcelain "—she's in the process of becoming. The halo…" Dez turned and studied Zen. "Did you bring the halo you claim as your own with you to this realm, Zen?"

"I don't know. When I came to after the bus hit me, it was in my hand. I've kept it with me. Figured whatever it was, I must have valued it to have held it through such an experience."

"So you could have either found it, or…come to this realm with it in your possession. Which doesn't make sense. It would have fallen away from you had you actually fallen."

"*If* she was an angel," Blade said.

"Exactly. Yet I get an odd sidhe vibe from her. You do know that betwixt Above and Beneath lies Faery?"

Blade pushed the tea away. The sweet smell wasn't for him and it actually made his eyelids heavy, as if he needed sleep. He'd heard about the location of Faery from his mother many times. It was imperceptible from the mortal realm and often overlapped less-populated areas of this realm. "So?"

"So." Dez set her teacup on the porcelain plate with a clink. "Besides the existence of a specific demon race who possess angelic origins, there is also a race of sidhe who originated as angels. They fall and get caught on this realm and become sidhe."

"If that were Zen's case, then why would angels *and* demons be after her?"

"That I don't know. I'm sorry I can't be of more help." Dez turned her shoulder so her back was to the doorway. She spoke quietly. "I know about your trouble with demons. If she happens to be demon, then…what?"

Blade had briefly considered the implications. If Zen was demon then his faery could be a danger to her. That was, if he bit her and his ichor-tainted saliva got into her bloodstream. So he wouldn't bite her. Because one way or another, that bite would kill one or the both of them.

He shook his head and huffed out an exhale. The witch's expectant gaze brought up his defenses as if an invisible shield. He was finished talking.

"If you wish to help her, perhaps she should know about you," Dez insisted. "All of you."

"I don't see how that will help matters."

"It's your choice." Dez raised her voice so Zen could hear. "Perhaps your best source of knowledge might be Michael Donovan. He's a halo hunter. Knows a lot about angels. And I'm sure he'd pay a fine price for that halo."

Blade gripped the weapon. "If angels are after Zen, the halo hunter will have to pry it out of my cold, dead hands."

The witch touched him lightly on the wrist. "Don't

lose yourself in this one," she warned. "You already feel as though you've lost so much, but there is yet much of you that remains. It is the bold warrior within, Blade Saint-Pierre. Be bold, be bold, be not too bold."

He didn't know what the hell that meant, but he wasn't in the mood for exploring his unlost parts with Zen sitting so close.

"Thanks, Dez." He shook her hand, then grabbed the halo and headed toward the door. "How can I find this halo hunter?"

"I'll give him a call, see if he's in the States. He travels the world in search of halos. I'll let you know what I find out. As for you, Zen…" Dez approached the doorway. "Trust this man. But don't ask too much of him."

Blade straightened at that odd warning. "She can ask me anything. If I'm capable, I'll do it."

The look Dez gave him was more sad than warning. He shook it off and strode down the hallway, leaving Zen to follow after she'd thanked the witch.

Zen followed Blade down the six flights of stairs— he'd avoided the elevator—and out to his truck. He had left the witch's place in a hurry, and she suspected it was because the witch had asked him to tell her his truth. Much as they'd thought they'd been talking quietly, Zen had heard.

Did Blade have something against demons? Well, sure, he'd said as much. But it must be bad if it had shut him up so quickly. And if the witch had warned him that it was something he should reveal to her? Hmm…

She rubbed her inner elbow, wondering about the markings. Blade had fired up the engine and waited behind the wheel. Sidhe markings? *Could* she be faery?

Didn't feel right. Though what *right* should feel like was beyond her. The most right thing she'd experienced since losing her memory had been standing in Blade's arms, falling into his kiss. And he didn't want any more of that romantic nonsense.

Zen sighed. All she really needed was a friend, and she wasn't going to get that from Blade, either. He was a challenging bit of mystery and darkness. But he was her only hope. Because if she was involved in all this paranormal hoodoo, a vampire would probably be her best bet at keeping her in the loop.

And did she want to be in that loop? When she thought about it she realized she did, and it didn't bother her as much as she thought it should. Consorting with vampires and witches? She, possibly an angel or even demon or faery? She could deal.

Really, she could. She just needed to process.

And she carried an angel's halo in her backpack. That was beyond cool. Unless it was hers. Because that would mean she was, or had been, an angel.

Why hadn't the halo fallen away from her when she'd fallen to earth, as Dez had suggested should have been the case? And had she really been on a walk around the world to gain knowledge?

"I do know stuff," she murmured. "Weird, odd stuff." All but the important stuff.

She didn't feel particularly angelic. The tug of wings between her shoulder blades was remarkably absent. And she'd already tried to pop out her faery wings. But what did an angel feel like? She had easily defeated the angel in the alley, but only because he'd been occupied with trying to choke the life out of Blade.

There were so many questions, and she was beginning to feel overwhelmed. The hot tub in her room at the inn sounded like a terrific escape from it all.

Once outside, the half-moon sat in the pale night sky, which was decorated with wisps of gray clouds. Opening the truck door, Zen climbed up and buckled in and Blade took off before she even got the door closed.

"You don't have to tell me what the witch asked you to reveal," she offered when they veered onto the freeway that would take them back to Tangle Lake.

"There's nothing to tell. You already know I don't like demons."

"All righty, then. For now, I'm going to stand on the side of not liking angels. One did try to kill you after all. I didn't see the demons who were after me at the old lady's house so I'll reserve judgment on that species."

"It's a free world. You can do what you want to, think how you wish."

"I think I'm hungry. Would you mind pulling through a fast-food drive-through on the way? I'll buy."

The expected smile did move his mouth the tiniest bit. Because really? It was his cash.

Zen sat back, satisfied she may have softened his hard exterior just for a moment.

They sat on the grass below the red rooster statue before the inn. As vampire, Blade was not a voracious eater, yet he'd downed two hamburgers in the time Zen had finished a cheeseburger. The faery in him needed sustenance. A hearty meal usually dampened his vampire's urges, as well. The vamp in him got nauseated to consider drinking blood after a greasy meal.

The struggle within was always a kick. Blade had mastered it. Mostly. But the times his faery ruled without discretion—well, as he'd told Zen, there was nothing to tell.

"Doesn't halo hunting sound like a fascinating job?" Zen asked as she sipped from the milk carton and crumbled up her paper wrapper and napkin. "I wonder what breed he is?"

"Halo hunters are usually human. I hope Dez can contact the guy."

"You're really interested in helping me."

"I've said as much."

"And yet, you push me away at every opportunity when we are just beginning to connect." She tapped the toe of her sandal against his boot. "What does it take to crack your armor, big guy?"

"I'm not wearing armor. And do we need a connection to find your memory?"

"I don't know. I feel as though if we're spending time together, conversation and general niceties toward one another would be, well, nice."

"We are conversing right now."

"Indeed we are. And yet I'm not allowed to befriend you. Or kiss you. So many rules for a man of so few words."

Blade grabbed the paper bag and crumbled it. "You were headed inside?"

"Right. I guess that's my cue to leave. Thanks again, Blade. For everything. But I can't promise I'm not going to try to crack that icy exterior of yours. I'm alone on a raft floating in the middle of a big ocean. I need contact. Connection. Someone to anchor me."

She leaned over and quickly kissed him on the cheek. "And touch. Good night."

She grabbed the paper bag and tossed it in the garbage can on her way toward the hotel lobby.

Blade touched his cheek where the brief warmth of her touch lingered. His fangs descended. Despite the hearty meal, his vampire insisted on blood. Something to quell the ache deep inside him.

And yet, the hunger he felt was a familiar one. One that called for demon blood. He'd tasted it once. Craved it again.

And Zen may very well have that wicked black treat gushing through her veins. Was that the only reason he was attracted to her? Hell, he was attracted to her, no denying it.

He just hoped it was for a better reason than to feed his craving.

Chapter 10

Blade handed the lumber deliveryman the signed bill of lading and waved him off as he drove down the long gravel road away from the designated compound grounds. His younger brother Stryke was building a compound for his newly formed pack. Blade was tossing around the idea of being his brother's scion, or second-in-command.

He'd not accepted the offer when Stryke had made it last winter. He'd simply said he'd think about it. Because for as much as a loner he was—and he liked it—family was everything to him. And if he could stand by Stryke's side and help him to build a solid pack, then he was all for that.

But the pack building was going slowly. And that suited Blade fine. He still needed time. And things were working that way for him because Stryke wanted to select the pack members carefully. Yet also he wanted to expand beyond the family pack in which the brothers had grown up. He wanted to diversify, and if the prospective pack wolves were married to other breeds, they were more than welcome.

Hell, having a vampire as scion was radical.

Blade was behind Stryke's diversification goals 100

percent. Except when it came to demons. He would stand firm on his suggestion that no demons were allowed in the pack.

His brother strode across the cleared building site, rolled plans in hand, and slapped Blade across the back. "You're up bright and early, Dracula."

Stryke was the only one Blade would allow to remain standing after such a tease. It had started when they were teens and Stryke had seen the movie on a late-night creature feature. Only then had Stryke begun to understand that his brother was different from him. Now, if Trouble used the moniker Blade would deliver him a swift fist to the jaw. And Trouble would love it. And then they'd fight. And then Stryke would have to break it up. And Kelyn would stand off to the side snickering.

Brothers. Can't live with 'em, but sure as hell couldn't survive without 'em.

"Had some things to do," Blade said. "And it's going to rain today so I always get out early when I can avoid the sun. I signed for the lumber. When does the construction crew begin?"

"Next week. I wanted to get everything shipped to the site and ready to go. Let's go in and have some coffee."

"You don't do coffee."

"Yeah, but Blyss does. She likes it as dark as Beneath, just like you."

Blade strode beside his brother up to the cabin-like house where Stryke had settled in with his Parisian wife. Yep, Stryke had gone all the way to Europe to find his werewolf wife. Thing was, she hadn't wanted to be a werewolf, and had taken pills to suppress her wolf, until she'd met Stryke, and he'd brought out the wild in her.

A very pregnant, gorgeous woman with long black hair stood in the doorway wearing a terrycloth robe and pink slippers that sported tufts of pink fuzzy stuff on the toes. She was 100 percent feminine and always smelled like candy. Trouble, who picked up a lot of French words from Grandpa Creed, said she had je ne sais quoi.

"Blade!"

He kissed Blyss on both cheeks—the French way—and startled when her belly nudged his hip. "What was that?"

"I don't know." Blyss ran her palm over her belly. "I'm hoping it's a girl, but she kicks like a boy, *oui*?"

"Feels like there's a little bit of Trouble in there," Blade teased, with a wink to his brother.

"Blyss, give this guy some coffee before his jokes kill us all."

She poured a cup for Blade and herself, then kissed Stryke and excused herself with a wink over her shoulder at her husband.

"I haven't forgotten our date tonight, glamour girl," Stryke called after his wife. "A hot tub and massage." Stryke met Blade's wonky gaze. "What? Can't a man be in love?"

"My condolences," Blade offered.

"Love will find you again some day," Stryke said, "and when you least expect it."

"I didn't come here to discuss something as stupid as love. Have you any knowledge about angels?"

Stryke whistled and sat on the stool next to Blade. The two men wrapped fingers around their mugs—

Stryke drank chai, as coffee gave him the jitters—and gazed out the picture window over the kitchen counter that revealed the razed building plot framed by mature oak trees.

"Angels," Stryke muttered. "What the hell have you gotten your hands into now, big bro?"

"I met a woman the other night."

"Really?" Stryke turned completely toward him.

Blade did not miss his brother's inquisitive raise of brow. "It's not what you think."

"What do you think I think?"

He wasn't going to say it. His brothers knew how he operated. He saw a pretty woman, he took her home and had sex with her—and usually a bite—then never saw her again. It was safest that way. For his damaged heart.

"She's in trouble, Stryke. Lost her memory. So she's in town to try to piece things together. In the past few days I've killed three demons and one angel, all of them in pursuit of her. And Dez doesn't know what she is."

Stryke set down his mug. "The witch doesn't know? That's strange."

"And she's got one of these." Blade laid the halo he'd decided to carry on him at all times on the counter.

"What is this?" Stryke picked it up to inspect. He ran his thumb along the edge and blood oozed from the fine slice in his skin. "Ouch! Doesn't look as sharp as it is."

"It's a halo. From the angel I killed. Or rather, Zen killed it while I distracted the bastard."

"I'm not following. I know you're into the calm, meditative stuff, but when did you start practicing Zen?"

"Zen is the chick's name. And I don't want her to be demon. Or for that matter, an angel."

There, he'd said it. And he knew exactly what Stryke

was thinking. So let him assume the pretty chick with the copper hair and ever-changing irises meant something to him. She didn't. Hell, he hardly knew her. She couldn't mean a thing to him. Yet.

"Sorry, brother. I would have sent you to Dez for answers, but looks as though you've already tried that. Does Zen have wings? If she's got a halo that's a pretty big mark in the angel column. Don't angels have multicolored eyes?"

Blade knew that about angels. Only, he'd always thought that meant all colors at once. Not ever changing as Zen's eyes had displayed. "Shit. And her blood is blue, but then turns black."

"Some kind of angel-demon mix? Blade."

He shrugged off his brother's hand from his shoulder. Stryke was the one he and his other brothers always went to when they needed to talk because he listened and didn't judge and always seemed to offer some wise words. But he didn't want the emotional, reassuring touch today. It would mess with his determination to stand aside unaffected.

"Whatever she is," he muttered, "I won't let this one bring me down."

"It's always the ones you most want to avoid that you really need in your life, bro. Trust me on that one." He smirked and sipped his chai.

Stryke also had a weird way of extolling advice in cryptic form. Blade decided not to question. He could handle this one.

And he would.

The long floral skirt with pink flowers on a white background felt sexy and looked great paired with the white T-shirt. A few cheap rhinestone rings twinkled on her fingers and a necklace flashed more bling as the sunlight landed on the stones. Zen slipped on the rhinestone-bedazzled sandals and twirled before the bathroom mirror. Felt good to have some things that fit her and which hadn't come from a smelly donation box.

And she owned a comb now! So she pulled her thick copper hair up into a blowsy bun and stabbed a few hair sticks in it. It worked for her. Before dashing out, she leaned forward, peering into her eyes.

"Blue," she said and then wrinkled her nose. "They really do change colors. Beats contact lenses, I guess."

But what she knew about angels was that their eyes were like kaleidoscopes, all colors at once.

"I can't be," she said. "Don't feel as though I've ever had wings."

The witch had suggested she could be sidhe. Again, where were her wings?

Though the halo was an interesting clue. She stuffed it in her backpack and headed toward the lobby, intent on getting some breakfast at the Panera down the road. The afternoon goal was to find the library and look up the newspapers from a week ago, see if they had reported the accident.

"Ma'am!"

She turned before pushing the glass door open and spied the inn receptionist dangling a key chain. "This was left for you by a handsome man."

"Handsome man?" She took the key. The Mini Cooper logo was emblazoned on the black rubber fob.

"Guy had long bluish hair. He said you'd find the car in the parking lot. Is he your boyfriend?"

"Uh, no. Why do you ask?"

"Don't you want him to be? He's hot. All those muscles bulging under his shirt. He stood there like some kind of warrior."

Zen searched her knowledge for the slang explanation of hot as related to a man, and had to agree. "He is, but he doesn't believe in friends."

"*Uff-da*, you're going to have to change his mind about that one, sweetie. Have a nice day!"

"Thanks. You, too."

Outside, the sun warmed her cheeks and the back of her neck. A breeze tickled the skirt fabric between her calves as she aimed for the little red car. It was an older model and the paint was matte instead of glossy. A dent creased the back quarter panel, and the silver trim was pitted in a few places. Overall, it looked roadworthy.

And she wasn't going to look a gift cow, er—she couldn't recall the proper animal for that one, so she dismissed the thought.

Sliding in and discovering it was a stick shift, Zen wondered if she could manage it. The truck had been an automatic. Just shift into gear, press on the accelerator and go.

Pulling the halo out of her backpack and hanging it from the rearview mirror as a sort of good-luck charm, she shifted and put her foot on the gas. And the car sputtered to a clunking stop.

A rap on the driver's window alerted her to the man who stood outside. Zen rolled down her window without thinking. "I'm not sure how to drive this—"

He shoved a neon green flyer inside the car. "Party tonight! Only the coolest are invited."

She took the paper and glanced over it. "You don't even know me. How do you know I'm cool?"

Tall and blond, he looked Nordic, and Zen guessed him for a skier with his long lean lines and the athletic wear. Yet a beard didn't hide the tattoos climbing up his neck. "It's a guess," he said. "You like to dance?"

She considered the question. "I'm not sure."

"Come on, everyone likes to dance. We'll see you tonight, sure? It's just out of town. A map is on the back of the flyer. Come alone. There will be plenty of guys there to hook up with."

"I don't think I need to hook up."

"That's cool. Like I said, dance! It's going to be a blast."

"A blast sounds…like a blast."

"You betcha."

And he strode off across the lot, looking back a few times over his shoulder at the Mini Cooper.

Zen studied the flyer. The picture depicted a mansion more resembling a spooky Halloween haunt than a dance club. The guy hadn't known who she was. And he would have said something if he had, right?

"Come alone?" she muttered.

She wasn't sure if she should be creeped out by the invite or excited for the prospects. She couldn't remember when she'd last had a blast. Certainly it must be overdue.

Hookups? Obviously she would get nowhere with Blade romantically. But did she need romance right now?

"A little dancing never hurt anyone."

She set the flyer aside. She'd think about it.

Now to figure how to operate this vehicle.

No incident report was listed in the *Tangle Lake Tattler*, the local paper that was issued each Monday. The newspaper featured local news, which tended to be on the homey side. Mavis Butler had won best quilt design in the United States for the third year running. Red MacPherson was having a sale on taxidermy for the critters, including wolves.

Zen wondered what the local werewolves thought about that. And then she had to grin at her knowledge. How quickly she'd accepted that the realm of the paranormal existed.

She wondered if others were in the know. Probably not. If so, she would have never doubted Blade's confession in the first place.

She thanked the librarian for the use of the microfiche and headed back to the car, which she had finally figured how to operate after three dry starts in the inn parking lot.

Had the bus driver even been aware he or she had hit a person? Should she have stayed on the scene after being hit? Probably. But at the time she had felt like getting out of there, not causing a scene. Staying away from notice.

Weird to think that now. What instinctual part of her had reacted that way? Almost protectively of her origins. Whatever those origins were. An angel who had fallen to the mortal realm and wanted to keep her secret? Or a demon who perhaps couldn't shift to demonic form now because of the bump to her head.

Was her amnesia something that had resulted from her angelic fall?

Would certainly explain why angels are after me. But why demons?

While in the library she should have checked out the mythology section. Any details about the various species she could learn would be helpful. And yet, if she simply thought about it, mined the weirdly vast knowledge she seemed to possess, she knew a few things.

Angels did indeed fall, and most often it was to find their muse and procreate. Nephilim were the result. Nasty things, for sure.

Demons were a vast species, and while many occupied the mortal realm, many more lived in Daemonia. Zen wasn't sure what Daemonia was. Something similar to Hell or Beneath?

Faeries were few and far between on the mortal realm, most choosing to live in Faery. They were a hard bunch to figure, and she hadn't any more knowledge on them.

Witches were of all sorts and some were the Light and others the Dark. Warlocks were witches who had committed a grave transgression against their own.

"Wow," she muttered. "I really do have a lot of information in this noggin. I just need to think about something and it comes to me. Maybe a little mindless entertainment tonight will put my brain in a new place. I wonder if Blade would like to go along with me?"

At the very least, she could ask him about the club. Get his two cents on it. He didn't seem the club type. Definitely not the free-for-all dance type. He was more the blade-swinging warrior.

Which, she didn't mind at all.

Realizing she didn't have his phone number—and why should she, she didn't own a phone—Zen decided to drive over to Blade's place.

Chapter 11

"**I** don't do clubs."

Blade couldn't guess why Zen chuckled at his statement, but she did as she wandered over to the window and pressed a palm to it. The sun beaming across her hair lighted her as if…she was an angel.

He shook off the image of her floating in the air with a glowing halo suspended above her head. If she was angel then why had her blood turned from blue to black?

"But you've been there before?" she asked over a shoulder.

"I haven't heard of that club. Must be new. You think it's wise to go to a nightclub by yourself? Even if you didn't have demons and angels on your ass, a single woman alone in a bar…"

"You think I can't handle myself?"

"I'll go with you."

Her nod said so much more than just an acceptance of his offer. Women and their secretive ways. He'd never been curious about them, until it was too late.

"What's the nod for?" he asked, strolling over to stand beside her. Outside, the rain was trying hard to become a downpour but the sun kept interrupting.

"I knew you'd go along with me."

Did she, now? "You know nothing about me, Zen."

"And as much as I'd like to change that, you do have your rules." She turned and tapped his chest. "No friends. Don't get too close. Don't touch. That kiss must have had you reeling."

"I kiss women all the time."

Her arched brow made another statement that he didn't want to be curious about—but was.

"Now what?" he asked.

"So you're a love-'em-and-leave-'em kind of guy? How's that working out for you, Stoic Warrior Dude?"

"Actually, quite well. And it's none of your business, is it?"

"Of course not." She flounced toward the couch. A bohemian goddess with added glints of sparkle today. "I think the club is going to be just what I need tonight."

"And what exactly do you need?"

Did he want to know? If she was looking to hook up that was her own business. Then again, he did want to know. Everything.

Zen plopped onto the big plaid couch, picked up the backpack and pulled her legs up to tuck her feet under her thighs. Tendrils of her hair spilled forward over the soft cleavage her low-cut T-shirt revealed. "Maybe I need connection."

So she did want to hook up.

Blade gripped his hands into fists. She looked so comfortable sorting through the backpack. As if she belonged there, on his couch. In his life. But that was wrong—hell. It was getting tiresome making up excuses to protect himself. He wasn't the guy who tossed out excuses as if they were ammo to blockade emotional shrapnel. If something bothered him he took a stand and showed it his teeth.

And right now Zen's earlier teasing bothered him. He should ask her to leave. Make it easy on them both. Because his life wasn't an easy fit for any woman.

"Let me show you something." She patted the couch beside her. Waited for him with those dazzling pale green eyes.

Why did her eyes have to constantly change color? It was a warning. He sensed it. And yet, the multicolored irises fascinated him. Did they change with her moods? Like those rings the giggling girls used to wear in high school? He'd have to take a survey of her eye color as compared to her mood.

Right now her green eyes indicated a—hmm—flirtatious mood. If he read her correctly.

He sat three feet away from Zen on the couch. "You know, the longer you stay the longer Oogie has to hide out in my bedroom."

"It's not my problem the cat doesn't like me. And he's a cat. Aren't they the supreme I-don't-give-a-shit of all creatures? He can deal."

Oogie probably could deal. From under the bed. Poor guy. Did the cat sense Zen's otherness? He had to. So why couldn't Blade get a fix on her nature?

Zen scooted closer and handed him a postcard.

"What's this?"

"I got it a couple days after the accident."

"Got it?" He studied the image of a painting in vibrant greens and blues.

"Stole it," she corrected. "I didn't have any money then and that picture spoke to me."

The computer-generated image depicted an angel

with wings of binary code, white hair and kaleidoscope eyes. The attribution was to a New York artist who was now living in Italy.

"An angel," he said, and gave her back the card.

"Weird, huh?"

"Maybe. Maybe it means you used to be a klepto."

"Do kleptos take trucks?"

"Probably not. They're usually into the small stuff."

"Thought so." She slid her hand into his. "I want to try something with you."

He knew what was coming. But he didn't dash. A gorgeous woman sitting next to him, casting him the big green eyes and a curious smile? He could handle anything she wanted to *try*.

Leaning in, Zen's eyes took in his face, roving from his hair, to nose, down to his mouth. Her tongue dashed her upper lip. She smelled fresh, summery, like the grass on a rainy summer evening. But he couldn't get a read on her. "Does me being this close bother you?" she asked. Emerald eyes danced over his face, teasing him—no, defying him to meet her boldly sensual challenge.

He shook his head.

"But you'd rather I was sitting over there, two cushions away from you."

Enough. She thought to tease him? He'd show her the man he really was.

Blade threaded his fingers up through her silky copper hair and pulled her in for a kiss. Her body melded against his, and before he knew it, she had straddled him and was taking as much as giving. Now her scent drifted into his senses, summery sweet and addictive. His vampiric instincts matched pulse beats with the blood coursing beneath her skin. His fangs tingled, but he had this.

Too dangerous to bite.

Clasping her hip, he eased her down onto his lap so her breasts hugged his chest. He dipped his mouth to kiss her where the low-cut T-shirt revealed the beckoning crease between her generous breasts. Holding her, a woman intent on seducing him, stirred up desires that he wanted to satisfy. Often.

"Oh, I like it when you kiss me there," she said on a sultry sigh.

Her hair spilled over his face, a faery flutter. He kissed her breast through the T-shirt, and thumbed the nipple that had perked up beneath. "I like it, too. But this—"

"Don't say you don't want to do this. Just let me have this moment, Blade. You think I've done this before? I don't know if I have."

"You've kissed a man before. You're good at it."

"Yeah? Well, I don't remember, so help me to at least get back that memory. Or better yet. Make new ones."

She pushed him and he fell backward onto the plaid cushions, pulling her down along with him.

Kissing him deeply, Zen took control. She had kissed men. No virgin kissed like this, so aggressively. So curiously. And Blade was inclined to let her continue. To see how far she would take it. Because if she was unsure or inexperienced, sooner rather than later she'd come up short and have to stop. And then he'd have a new wonder about her beyond that of what species she could possibly be.

"Will you take off your shirt?" she asked, kissing down his chin and to his neck.

The vampire within him stirred as her firm kisses neared his carotid artery. The sensual touch was like an electric shock to his system, but in a good, erotic way.

He pulled off his T-shirt and tossed it behind the couch. Zen's hands played over his pecs and abs. The warmth of her was ridiculous, the firm, exploratory touches stirring up sensation, and he hissed with pleasure.

Her eyes sparkled like the rhinestones at her neck as she admired his torso. "You are ripped. But you don't lift weights, do you?"

"Not unless it's to toss them out of my way."

"It's a vampire thing, then? Or maybe faery? Do you ever have sex with women when you have shifted to faery like when you brought your wings out last night?"

He wasn't going to answer that. She was too curious, and moving too fast regarding those kinds of questions.

"Let's just kiss," he suggested and teased the ends of her hair between his fingers. "All of me, vampire and faery, likes it when you press your breasts against my chest and push your tongue into my mouth."

"Mmm...I can do that." She lay down on top of him, twining a leg between his, and then kissed him deeply, toying with his tongue, and licking his lips and teeth. "What does your vampire like?"

She wasn't going to give it up.

"Not important right now."

"Your faery?"

"Zen. Do you want to talk or make out?"

She paused, her hands holding her away from his chest, as she seemed to be considering the two options he'd given her. He threaded his fingers up into her hair and tugged gently. "Come here. Let's make Oogie jealous."

The cat had crept out from the bedroom and now, perched like a gargoyle on the kitchen counter, was watching. He hadn't hissed yet, so Blade was counting that as a favorable sign.

Zen's hands slid down his sides and her fingers tucked into his jeans. He followed her straying mouth, seeking the lush kiss, the wetness of her lips, the heat of her, but when she landed his neck with a teasing nip, he grabbed her by the neck. A little less than gently.

"Too much for you?" she challenged boldly.

The tease of her catching her lower lip with her teeth made his erection throb. The woman had no idea what she played with. And he wasn't about to let this liaison go bad. As in, turn bloody.

Reaching for the hem of her shirt, he tugged it up over her breasts and was nicely surprised she wore no bra underneath. He cupped her breasts and sat up, guiding her onto her back against the couch arm so he could kiss and suckle at her nipples.

She wrapped her legs about his torso. Squeezing a nipple with his fingers elicited a delicious moan from her. "You like that, too?"

"Oh, yes, please. This is better than sleeping in a truck. Better than wearing used clothes. Better than killing an angel."

The remark struck Blade, and he paused, lips about her nipple. Prepared to walk away, to put his brain back in the right place, and not indulge in his desires…

The tickle of her fingernail along his waistband, above where his cock strained against the tough denim, obliterated the need to retreat. He'd give her one more chance.

Feasting upon her skin, he savored and licked and suckled her nipples, her generously curved breasts and down her rib cage. And then back up to linger between the cozy snug of her breasts. Between them he pressed his cheek and closed his eyes. Nice here. Her body heat brewed her summery scent to a heady perfume that he wanted to soak in, get lost in.

When was the last time he'd simply held a woman and admired her softness and scent? *You remember.* But he was this close to forgetting. He needed the distraction of Zen. He needed this sensual venture.

Lost in her, he didn't realize when Zen had unbuttoned his jeans. Her finger brushed the head of his cock, eliciting a shock of desire that radiated through his system. His fangs reacted of their own volition, descending.

Blade pressed his mouth against her neck.

Chapter 12

Zen felt the sharp prick of Blade's fangs against her neck. She didn't flinch. So he'd changed his mind? *Yes.* The fangs nudging against her skin heightened the erotic appeal of his hands gliding over her breasts. She wanted to feel him sink deep into her. To know the rapture of a vampire's bite.

But when she slid her hand behind his head and pulled him closer, he suddenly jerked away. Standing above her, arms splaying and a wild look in his eyes, she watched as his fangs retracted, moving up to sit in line with his other teeth. His pecs flexed. And his opened jeans revealed a thatch of dark hair below the rows of tight abdomen muscles.

"A bite would feel so good," she pleaded. "I want to give it a try. Please?"

"Are you crazy?" He pulled his hair behind his head and then dropped it, fisting the air forcefully. "I can't believe I let this go so far."

"Blade, it's okay. I'm not afraid of your bite."

"Really? Well, that's great for you. Not so great for me. Do you remember what I told you happens when a vampire bites an angel? Shit." He picked up his shirt and then tossed hers onto her chest. "Put that on. Please."

"What happens— Ooh." She winced. "I'm sorry. I forgot. Angel blood makes vampires explode. That's what you said, right? But we don't actually know what I am."

"Exactly. And you were cool with me taking that chance? Nice."

He strode into the kitchen and opened the fridge. Tilting back a bottle of water, his anger vibes were tangible from the couch where Zen pulled on her shirt.

"Way to end a perfectly good make-out session, Zen," she muttered. But stupid of her to have expected the bite when it could have harmed him. Wrong decision. Made in the heat of the moment. Because she was all about new experiences. Especially the ones that made her feel good. She'd have to watch herself. "I should probably leave."

"Don't let the door hit you on the way out."

Zen cast Blade a pleading gaze as she passed him, but he didn't meet her eyes. What a cruel thing to say. Was he so mad that he couldn't understand she was new at this? That she had been following her instincts and emotions instead of logic?

Apparently. He didn't look at her, even though she waited before the stairs, just out of his eyesight.

"The invite to accompany me to the club is rescinded," she said. "If you don't like me, just say so. I can do the memory search myself. Thanks for all your help. I'll find some way to repay you and get the car back to you as soon as possible."

Grabbing her backpack, she marched down the stairs and realized, as she charged outside toward the Mini Cooper, that she had let anger get the better of her. She had no reason to not appreciate the man for all the wonderful things he had done for her. He'd given her a freakin' car.

And he had been right. She shouldn't have expected him to bite her. Not when neither of them knew what she was. He could have risked death if she really was an angel.

"I'm certainly no angel," she muttered as she slid into the car and fired up the ignition. "Angels aren't so cruel to kind souls."

Three hours later, after the sun had set and Zen had found the road leading to the club, she couldn't lament the car's sudden decision to sputter to a halt halfway there, stranding her in the middle of nowhere. The road was paralleled by tall birch trees and the night was dark thanks to the shimmer of moon she couldn't see beyond the tree line.

"Out of gas. Figures. Thanks, karma. I'll try harder next time. I won't be so selfish when it comes to making out with a man."

And she'd never again ask a vampire for a bite. At least, not until she knew what she was. Did she have deadly blue angel blood coursing through her veins? If so, seemed as if she should also have some kind of superpowers. What could angels do? She felt like a normal woman.

A normal woman who didn't know who she was.

A normal woman who just wanted some touch time with one very sexy man. A man who needed time to take things slowly. To gradually work up to closer. He was sexually skittish, which was an odd thing considering his incredible physicality and heart-racing allure.

"Guess I haven't a clue about men," she muttered.

Getting out of the tiny car and gazing up and down the dark road, she wondered which was a shorter walk: toward the club or back to town. Sitting on the hood of the car, she leaned back against the windshield and stared up at the row of stars framed by the treetops.

"Is there a reason I'm not supposed to know?" she asked the heavens. "Am I supposed to go on with life and take what comes to me? If so, I don't get the attacks. Do they want me dead or do they just want to mess with me? And what about the halo?"

She turned and spied the halo hanging on the rearview mirror. "Am I some kind of warrior? But for what reason? Shouldn't a warrior know what she's to fight? Or defend?"

The sudden spatter of raindrops on the hood and her head was not the answer she'd hoped for.

"Terrific. Guess karma wasn't quite finished with me, eh?"

Headlights appeared down the road and Zen hopped off the hood. Maybe she could hitch a ride to the club. Because tonight was for setting her worries aside. She didn't want to think about what she didn't know. And she figured a distraction from the things she did know about, like Blade and his amazing kisses, was necessary.

So when she recognized the big black truck as Blade's, Zen could but shake her head. "Oh, karma, you sneak."

The passenger window rolled down and a man she did not know popped his head out. He had thick short black hair, and a rugged facial structure. He winked at her. "Hey, sweetie, it's raining."

No kidding.

Zen gave him a curious lift of her brow. Hands on her hips, she peered past him to Blade who sat behind the steering wheel. "You don't have anything better to do than follow me around?"

The vampire shrugged. "What makes you think I was following you? My brother and I are headed to the club. You having problems with the Mini? Beck promised me the car was in fine condition."

"Oh, it is. Apparently the ability to remember to put gas in the tank was also wiped from my memory. Maybe I could hitch a ride with you to the club?"

"This the one you told me about?" the man in the passenger seat asked Blade.

Blade nodded.

The passenger door opened and the man hopped out. Clad in black leather pants and a leather vest, but no shirt underneath, he had a remarkable physique. "I'm Trouble," he offered and took her hand to help her up into the truck.

"I bet you are," Zen said as his dark eyes took her in. He hopped in beside her and closed the door. "Brothers?"

"I'm the eldest," Trouble offered as Blade silently drove onward. "Did you lock up your car?"

"Yes, and I have all my valuables here in my backpack. It's not really my car. Blade bought it."

"Yeah, I know he did. Beck told me," Trouble said to Blade, who apparently had not filled his brother in on his recent charity work. "I hear you're a fine bit of interesting," he said to her. "Lost your mind?"

"I have possession of my mind. It's just my memories that are playing hard to get at the moment."

"Sounds as though you like to play easy, actually."

"Trouble," Blade cautioned.

"Sorry, Zen. Just stupid guy talk. You know. Or do you know? Probably you don't. So you were planning to go clubbing all by your lonesome? Looking to hook up?"

"Why is everyone so concerned about me hooking up? I just wanted to dance and forget about things."

"Forget even more?"

"No, I—"

"Trouble, give it a rest," Blade insisted. "She's looking for a night out by herself. Leave it at that."

A bump in the road settled Zen's thigh against Blade's. He didn't move away and the connection felt like the most amazing kind of fire. *Burn me*, she wanted to plead of him. She sensed he had driven this way in search of her. And the fact he'd brought along his brother indicated that, if found, he didn't want to be alone with her.

"So are you a mix of breeds, as well?" she asked Trouble. "Like your brother?"

"Hell no. I am one hundred percent werewolf."

"And damned cocky about it, too," Blade muttered.

"So Blade says you could be an angel or maybe a demon," Trouble stated.

"Or who knows," Zen added. "Maybe even faery." Though, at the moment, she was doubtful for all of the above. She felt so normal. On the other hand, what was normal?

"Really? Our brother Kelyn is faery," Trouble offered. "Stryke is full wolf like me. And our sister, Daisy Blu—ah, you don't need the family history. Blade tells me a bus hit you. And you walked away from it?"

"I guess so."

"That makes you one hell of a woman. Good catch, Blade. Whoa."

The truck's headlights beamed onto a grassy parking lot that was lined with a few dozen cars that were getting pummeled by the summer rain. But they wouldn't have noticed without the headlights. There was no outside lighting in the lot. And a huge mansion that looked like something out of a gothic horror show lurked on the horizon. In the darkness, Zen could only make out a scatter of people-shaped shadows walking toward it.

"This is a nightclub?" she asked. "I thought clubs were all flashy and uh…not haunted. Does it look haunted to you? It does to me."

"Ah, ghosts won't hurt you," Trouble joked and nudged her elbow with his. "I don't recall hearing about an old mansion out this way. You, Blade?"

"Nope." He rolled down the window but didn't open the door. "You smell anything off?"

The eldest brother opened his door and leaned out. Crickets chirped and the wind bristled through the leaves. Zen picked up the scent of dirt and the usual fresh ozone tang from the rain.

"Nothing," Trouble offered. "Kind of odd, but maybe it's supposed to have the creepy vibe. Like one of those goth clubs. You sure you want to go dancing that badly, Miss Zen of the Missing Memories?"

"Oh, come on, you guys, it's just atmosphere. I'm going up. You don't have to stay." She slid out on Trouble's side behind him and walked around on the squishy grass to the front of the truck. "Thanks for the ride, Blade. Sorry to bother you again."

He remained behind the driver's wheel, but nodded once.

Sensing he wasn't going to link arms with her and escort her inside, she turned and wandered through the parked cars until she landed on a cobbled sidewalk. Sort of Dorothy's brick road, but all in black. She didn't want to turn around to check if the brothers were watching her. She hoped they were. Because she suddenly felt very alone. And wet.

And maybe a little unsafe. But no fear.

"Not yet," she muttered as she gained a group of people who nodded and chattered.

The air was noticeably cooler, and she rubbed her hands up and down her arms as, at the back of the group, she followed them up a fieldstone stairway littered with red rose petals.

They were really working the goth atmosphere. But she did like the rose petals. As they neared the front of the mansion the doors swung inward. Myriad candelabras lit the interior and loud thumping music tunneled out. One of the women in the group giggled and grabbed another woman's hand. They skipped through the doors and starting dancing before they even hit the dance floor.

Zen wandered in slowly, shook off the wet from her arms and noticed the tall dark man who stood to her left, his arms crossed high over his chest. He nodded and bowed toward her, but didn't speak.

"Hey." She gave him a little wave. "Just here to dance. No hookups for this girl."

No response.

"Good to meet you, too."

The music had a lively beat. It coaxed her inward, and she didn't resist.

Time to get her wild on.

* * *

"She's got an exotic look to her," Trouble said as the brothers strode up the black-bricked walk. The rain had settled to a light sprinkle. "I can see why you like her."

"I don't like her. I'm just keeping an eye on her."

"Right. Because getting all up in that sexy hair and body would just be wrong. I know how you are about falling in love, bro. That's cool. But I also know you can get a woman in your bed if you want one."

"Maybe I don't want this one."

"Why? Because you don't know what she is? What if she's an angel? That'd be cool."

"Trouble, shut up. We're going to keep an eye on her, and then give her a ride home. That's it."

"Fine. But my eyes will be straying to all the ladies in the house."

"Go ahead and hook up. Zen doesn't need two baby-sitters."

"Then why'd you ask me along?"

"I have a funny feeling about this club."

Blade stopped before the stone stairway. The night hung heavy and wet, not a breeze in the air. The black mansion loomed amidst the gray shadowed surroundings. It was as if he'd walked onto a Tim Burton set. Head tilted, he sniffed the air. Trouble sniffed, as well. When the brothers met gazes, they shook their heads.

"Demons." Blade said.

"Shit."

Chapter 13

Blade charged up the stairs before the mansion. With every step he took the demon scent grew stronger. At his side, Trouble growled, and he sensed his brother's need to shift. Trouble was a smash-and-bang kind of guy. He reacted before looking. And that reaction was always accompanied by fists.

Blade preferred the stealthier approach. But he already sensed that what lay behind the tall black doors was not going to be the party either of them had expected.

"You said that some stranger invited her here?" Trouble asked.

"Yeah. Stopped her in the parking lot and told her about the club."

"Think the invite came from a demon?"

"I'm betting on it. Zen has no sense of the paranormal. She couldn't have known." He clamped a hand on his brother's shoulder. "We go in and look around. Don't start beating in skulls until we're sure there's clear danger. Got that?"

Trouble strode up to the door, clenching his fists at his sides.

"Trouble."

"Yeah, yeah." He bounced from foot to foot, a boxer

move he employed whenever he was pumped for a fight. "Wait for danger. Do we need some kind of bat signal, too, boss?"

His brother's cocky attitude could never annoy him. Trouble was what he was. All wolf, and itching for a fight. Always.

Blade pushed the doors open and strode in, but was stopped by a wall of a man with arms crossed high over his chest. Leather and silver studs wrapped his biceps and his block of a body.

"No admittance," the wall said in a gravelly voice.

"We're looking for a friend," Trouble said. "She just walked in. Tall, copper hair, flowers on her skirt?"

The wall's eyes glowed red.

"She doesn't belong here," Blade tried. He sniffed, but the air was tainted with incense or some odd, sweet scent. "We'll just find her and leave. No trouble, eh?"

"She's exactly where she needs to be," the wall said.

"So you have seen her. And you're stopping us from going in to find her?"

The wall nodded.

"She's in danger," Blade said.

The wall shook its head. Neon club lights glinted in the curl of silver spikes that stuck out along his earlobes.

"Yeah, I think she is."

Swinging the angel halo before him, Blade caught the wall across the chest, cutting through leather, chains and skin and bone. The beast let out a yowl before disintegrating into obsidian ash indicative of the demonic nature.

"Wait for danger?" Trouble said. "Right. You just wanted to be the first one to draw demon blood. I'll give you that, bro. You're owed, that's for sure. *Now* can I bash in some heads?"

"Whatever gets your rocks off, Trouble. What's that?"

Blade pushed toward the edge of the dance floor, where, peopled with hundreds, the flashing glass floor opened in the center. A bright red oval or some kind of portal loomed amidst the dancers. They danced around it but not closer than twenty feet in all directions.

And standing before the weird portal was Zen, looking upon it as if it were a marvel. She reached out to touch...

"Zen, no!"

Blade charged through the crowd, but as he did, every head turned to growl and gnash at him. Human faces shifted to demon. Scales, horns and red eyes replaced the human glamour. Talons clawed at his arms and hair. Sulfur formed a sickening miasma in the air.

Slashing the halo took out two who stood between Blade and Zen. He leaped over the demon ash and managed to grab her before she could step into the glowing portal.

Stumbling against his body, she shook her head and blinked, as if coming out of a trance. "Blade? What are you— Watch out!"

Struck from behind, a demonic talon cut through his shirt and opened his skin in searing pain. Wincing, and swinging around, Blade cut the halo through two demon heads—both attached to the same body. A cloud of demon ash formed and he dodged to avoid inhaling the noxious dust.

Grabbing Zen, he shoved her through the crowd and she landed in Trouble's arms. "Get her out of here!"

Trouble took Zen by the arm.

Blade hadn't time to follow their retreat. A diminutive demon missing a lower jaw jumped onto his chest and when it snarled at him, hot spit spattered across his face. Elbowing the clinging miscreant, he couldn't quite get him off.

"If you're not going to kill me," he muttered to any who would listen, "then I suggest you run."

With that warning, Blade shifted to faery. The demon shrieked and sprang away from him. Faery ichor was poisonous to demons. Blade's bones stretched and muscles pulled to reshape into the powerful winged creature. Wings unfurling, he snapped a flying demon out from above and flung it toward the red glowing portal.

The music thumped hard, pounding in his eardrums. Demons screeched, fleeing the entity that could prove their death.

Trouble appeared before Blade. Black demon blood dripped from his cheek. "Good call, man. Bringing out the big guns. She's safe in the truck. No demons out in the parking lot. Weird. Anyway. Time to party!"

Trouble shifted into a big black werewolf. Two heads taller than his human form, he was half-furred with a head like a wolf and a long toothy maw.

The brothers stood at the center of the dance floor, werewolf shouldered next to vamp-faery, and welcomed the melee that aimed for them. Fangs descending, Blade opened his mouth. He had craved demon blood for months.

Time to party, indeed.

Zen did as Trouble demanded after he'd roughly shoved her into the pickup. *Sit. Do not come out. No matter what.*

Demons had been everywhere inside the club. But they'd initially all appeared human to her. No horns. No glowing red eyes. She was glad to be out of there, and hugged herself as she pulled her legs up and settled into the truck seat. Hitting the door lock provided added security. Felt like it anyway.

And yet, when she had spied the fiery red oval glowing in the middle of the dance floor she had been compelled to walk up to it. It had pulsed. Hummed, actually, a tune that had felt more to her like heartbeats than the raucous dance music that had boomed from the speakers. It had also felt warm, as if it was a sun. Or even a hug. She'd wanted to walk through to see what would happen. To answer the silvery whispers slithering through her veins that had beckoned her forth.

Now, removed from the craziness inside, her senses reset and she wondered: If she had walked through the red glow might she have never returned?

"Oh, no." The marks on the inside of her elbows had brightened to a creamy glow against her light brown skin. And she felt them pulse, and realized that must have been what she'd felt when inside. Was it a calling? From demons?

So what did that mean?

She rubbed her skin. The marks were definitely not something she had put there herself, nor were they going to fade. They glowed. Demonic? Surely there must be someone who could tell her about them. Wasn't there a friendly demon in the area?

Her arm felt warm, and that warmth moved through her blood, softening her muscles and relaxing her tension. And Zen felt…wanted. Needed, actually.

"I should go back inside. They need me."

Just as she opened the truck door, a black wolf raced up to the door and yipped at her. She retreated, and then saw the winged man. His black-and-silver wings were immense, and tipped in deadly points. Demonic in appearance. Yet she knew better. He was vampire with faery blood coursing through his veins.

She glanced toward the mansion. It was dark, as it had been when they'd first arrived. None of the demons had followed their retreat outside.

The wolf propped his front legs on the truck frame and sniffed toward the backpack that was shoved behind the seat. Zen pulled it out and shuffled through it. Men's clothing inside.

"I get it. If you shift back to your human form, you'll be naked." She tossed the backpack out onto the ground.

Blade held vigil twenty feet away, observing the mansion, his wings erect and ready as if he expected the rage of demons within to come at them any moment.

Zen rubbed her arms and shivered. "Blade?"

"Turn away," he said, nodding toward his brother. "He'll shift with you watching, but I'd prefer you not."

She nodded, and shuffled back into the passenger seat, focusing on the mansion. "Right. I won't look." But knowing that the strapping man was shifting, totally naked, just outside the truck, made it very difficult not to twist her head and peek.

Of course, she had no interest in Trouble. It was Blade, who apparently had but to put away his wings to shift back to the regular form, who enticed her. But he no longer stood in view. Had he gone back into the mansion?

The driver's door opened and Blade slid in, sans wings. He wore jeans and no shirt, though he stuffed a wad of gray shirt between his thigh and the seat. Bringing out the wings must be hell on his wardrobe. She didn't even want to consider how many torn seams occurred when shifting to werewolf.

"You okay?" He didn't look at her, but fired up the engine. "Hurry, Trouble!"

The other brother popped in with a pair of jeans on and no shirt. "You are a size smaller than me, bro." He sat awkwardly on the seat, plucking unsuccessfully at the denim wrapping his thigh. "These suckers are tight."

"Be thankful I had an extra pair." He turned the truck around and spun out onto the dark gravel road. "That was a trap, I'm sure of it. Why the hell do demons want you?"

Zen realized he'd asked her that. The tension in the cab was tight, and she felt as if she dangled by her fingers from a tightrope between the two brothers.

"You didn't notice the demons?" Trouble asked as he eased a hand over his crotch.

"Not until you two arrived," she said. "Everyone looked human when I walked in. And I was distracted by the…"

"The portal?" Blade asked.

"You think that's what it was? Where do you think it leads to?"

"Hell if I know. You were going to step into it."

"I was," she said softly, then sank against the seat and pulled up her legs before her chest. She felt so small, being rescued from something that could have been disastrous to both men. They could have been hurt. And she may very well have entered a portal to a place even her curiosity couldn't have fathomed.

She'd sought a night of dancing and mindless fun. Instead, she'd gotten something far more dangerous.

"I'm sorry," she muttered. "I should have stayed at the inn. Or found a quiet place in town to distract me. Like more shopping."

"Not your fault," Blade said briskly. "The guy who told you about the club. He was in on it, I'm sure."

"He said I was cool and only the cool people were invited."

"Ha! Remember when you wanted to be cool in high school?" Trouble asked Blade.

"I was cool."

"No way, man. I was the cool one. The rest of you guys were pussies. But what was that portal thing?" Trouble asked. "And since when do demons gather in Tangle Lake?"

"Since never," Blade said on a hiss. "The last time was…" He shifted roughly, and the truck stirred them into a rumble down the road.

"The last time?" Zen asked.

"Never mind," Blade muttered.

They passed her parked car on the road and Trouble promised he'd drive out with their brother Kelyn and a gas can in the morning. Kelyn could drive the Mini back to the big red cock. He chuckled and rapped his knuckles on the door window.

Zen could but smirk. The brothers did like to work that joke.

"Thank you," she said to Trouble when Blade pulled up to his house and he hopped out.

"You just stay out of demon clubs," Trouble said. "And give my brother a break. He's skittish," he said. "About women and, uh, demons in general."

"Trouble!" Blade growled.

"See ya!" The elder brother winked at Zen and loped off.

Blade pulled away and drove back toward town. He drove past the inn, and Zen didn't bother to ask him why. She recognized the road he was taking. It led to the highway and eventually his place.

He must feel he had to protect her. And in truth, she felt in need of that protection. If he would allow her to stay with him tonight, she would be grateful. Because who knew if she might wake to find a pair of red eyes staring at her?

"Your cat will be pissed," she said after he'd parked and they strode up to the barn.

"He'll survive," Blade offered. "You can sleep in my bed. Oogie and I will take the couch."

"I don't want to put you out. Oh." Even in the darkness, she noticed the cut on his neck. It had scabbed and had probably bled quite a bit for the dried blood crusted on his skin. "Your faery is so valiant. And the wings."

"I'm all vampire even when my wings come out. The faery is sort of…seasoning."

"Okay." Was there something about his faery he didn't like to claim? She wouldn't press.

"I don't like to kill, Zen." And with that he strode inside, leaving the door open for her to enter if she wished.

He'd had to kill to protect her. That had been her fault. It cut into her heart to know she'd been the cause of his angst. Probably even pain. What man could kill so freely and not take some of the consequences of such a terrible act into his soul with every swing of blade or halo?

Squeezing her arm, she remembered the glowing design.

Zen rushed after Blade and only caught up to him at the top of the stairs. "I think you should see this." She thrust out her arms, inner elbows facing upward. "I only noticed it after Trouble brought me out to the truck."

He hissed when he saw the still-glowing marks. "They're getting brighter, more defined."

She nodded. "Do you think they are demon marks?"

"Demonic marks are usually darker. And like I said, they don't look like my brother Kelyn's marks."

"What about you? As part faery, don't you have them?"

"No, just the wings and a touch of ichor in my blood. Do they hurt? Or feel different?"

"They feel kind of good, actually. Makes my blood warm and my whole body sort of relaxes. But as well…" She turned and looked down the stairs. The club was miles away. Yet she could feel the beckon. "I wonder about that portal. It couldn't have been so bad. I was compelled toward it. I feel as if I should have at least peeked through it. Maybe someone inside needed me."

"Needed you?" Blade tilted her chin up with an abrupt move. "That's demon magic luring you toward something you don't want to know about, Zen. Trust me. Nothing good comes from associating with demons."

"Because of the last time they were in Tangle Lake?"

"What? What do you mean?"

"You said something in the truck about the last time demons were in town. When I asked you about it, you dismissed it."

"There's nothing to say." He stroked a thumb over

her arm and the marks actually stopped glowing. "You see that? What's that about?"

"I'm not sure. My skin is cooling fast, too. Huh. Your touch stopped the good feeling. What's this?" She lifted the hem of her T-shirt. Black blood spattered the white fabric.

Blade tilted his head and his hair fell over one eye. And then Zen noticed the fang peeking between his lips. "What's wrong?"

He stepped back, putting up his hands.

"Your vampire," she guessed, "likes demon blood?"

"I'm not talking about this anymore, Zen. You know where the bedroom is. You can use the shower. Pull a shirt out of my drawer to sleep in. I'm racked and need to get some sleep."

"You shower first, then, before I take over the bedroom."

"Fine." He strode past her, whisking up a breeze in his haste that chilled her to the core.

Zen pulled the wet hem away from her skin. He had been eying the blood fiercely. He was closed about so much. It was as if the man wanted to hide things, or even forget things, about himself.

"About demons," she whispered.

Whatever nightmare he fled, she had just led him back toward it.

While Zen was in the shower, Blade picked up the clothes from his bedroom floor and straightened up the room. In the kitchen he pulled out the full trash and he and Oogie went out into the night. He tossed the trash bag in the can outside the barn.

The night was dark for the clouds that shielded the

moon. A scuffle in the grass that edged the Darkwood sent Oogie scrambling inside the barn. Smelled like a fox. Must have been chasing a mouse. That cat was skittish lately.

He turned to go back inside. But when his skin prickled from neck to wrist, he lifted his head and closed his eyes. Spreading his arms and opening his hands, he felt the presence on the air. Someone stood behind him. It was the absence of scent that informed him who that was. "Sim."

"You in now, Saint-Pierre?"

The creature who had asked him to help slay the demons in Tangle Lake. He wasn't sure what Sim was, but that didn't matter. Blade didn't have to think more than a few seconds to give an answer. "Yeah. I'm in."

"Excellent. I see you've already begun. Keep it up. I'll be watching."

"I don't understand. I don't know how you expect that I can take out all—"

Blade turned but no one stood behind him. The crickets chirped. And the red fox ran across the grass with a mouse hanging from its maw.

Zen showered, and after she'd dried off, found a long soft T-shirt in one of the dresser drawers. Swimming in the shirt, she tugged at the hem and climbed into Blade's bed. The well-worn black sheets were cozy. They smelled like him, which was an indefinable woodsy scent with a hard edge of steel. She wanted nothing more than to lay her head on his pillow and inhale his essence. To dream about what the man might be like if only his rules didn't exist to push her away.

After lying there an hour, she realized she couldn't

sleep alone in this dark room with the crickets chirping outside the window he'd left cracked open. She was still unnerved from the club disaster. A trip to the bathroom to splash water on her face, and she returned to pace before the bed. She thought of Blade lying out on the couch with the ugly naked cat sleeping on his chest.

If she sneaked out there and curled up in the chair, would the cat hiss and throw a fuss? She didn't want to be alone. She needed to feel another beating heart in the same room with her. To somehow anesthetize the still pulsing vibrations in her skin that induced images of the weird portal in her thoughts.

And to know Blade was close should a pair of wicked red eyes peek through the window in search of her.

Navigating the darkness proved easy for the lack of furniture in the loft. Zen sneaked through the living room, homing in on the soft snores that came from the couch. Moonlight spilled through the cathedral windows and glistened in Blade's blue hair. A dark blue that was black, but not. Like the folds in azure velvet, she decided. Rich and luxurious. She longed to run her fingers through it and just…fall into him.

The cat crept along the front of the couch like a demon's golem. But it didn't hiss at her. Instead, when she approached, it skedaddled toward the kitchen.

The man didn't have a blanket. The evening was warm. A big fan at the top of the high, curved ceiling rotated slowly. Torso bared, spare moonlight etched his muscles.

Daringly, she lay on the edge of the couch in front of him, using his arm as a pillow. He'd didn't stir, and so she thought she was safe from discovery.

And then he did. His arm moved over her torso and his hand clasped across her stomach, pulling her up against his chest.

Smiling, Zen closed her eyes and drifted to sleep.

Chapter 14

Around two in the morning Blade stirred, his body tilting to turn over, but he sensed a warm presence lay close and under his arm. The wings between his shoulder blades tingled, seeking to unfurl, to feel her skin against the gossamer sheen of them. His entire body shivered, a sexual thrill that shimmied from ears to chest, to cock, to toes.

And then the vampire lifted its head. Her blood scent was exotic, yet dark and perhaps even dangerous. A marked change from when he'd originally scented her as merely human. To bite her would bring immense pleasure, perhaps even a moment of ecstasy. To taste an angel's blood…

Blade pushed down the desire. He wasn't stupid. No moment of pleasure was worth death.

Yawning, he curled his hand tighter, bringing Zen's back close against his bare chest. This felt right, and almost too good to be real. He didn't deserve to touch such innocence.

Yet was she innocent?

With that troubling thought stirring through his muggy brain, he drifted into reverie.

* * *

She slept like a log. Though Blade wasn't exactly sure how logs slept. It was a phrase his father had used often to describe his eldest brother Trouble's sleep habits when they had been kids.

Standing before the stove in comfy loose jeans that hung low on his hips, Blade stirred the scrambled eggs and turned the burner to simmer for the final finishing minutes. He wasn't much of an eater, but when he did consume food he stuck to plants and the occasional egg. Or, okay, burgers fed some weird craving for salt, or something like that.

Glancing to the couch he saw movement. Zen's arms stretched up and she twisted her spine to work out the kinks.

He'd been surprised to wake this morning and find her still snuggled up against him, and had to cautiously work himself out over the back of the couch without waking her. He'd quickly pulled on a shirt to hide his back, while she had continued to snore. So he had stared at her. The T-shirt she wore had ridden up high on her thighs but not high enough to satisfy his curiosity. And then he recalled the weird dream of wanting to have sex with her while his wings were out.

His vampire might be the more sexually voracious of his two halves, as well as wicked and demanding, but his faery was pure pleasure. When his wings were out while having sex every touch was magnified tenfold. And if Zen were faery? The sex could be incredible. Or so he guessed. He'd never been with a faery.

He'd only the pleasure of having sex with his wings out with a woman once. And that had been a brief yet deliriously blissful joining. And to think of her now brought no pleasure whatsoever.

Fuck, he hated demons.

"Hungry?" he asked over a shoulder, and to redirect his darkening thoughts.

Zen sat up, shrugging her fingers through her fluff of copper hair. "Very. That smells great." She scampered across the room.

He dished up eggs and toast for her and then a small portion of fluffy eggs for himself and sat beside her at the kitchen counter. She tilted back a whole glass of orange juice before turning to him and smiling.

"I hope you don't mind me stealing the snuggle last night. Your room was so dark and lonely. Everything is black in there."

"We vampires appreciate the darkness."

"Yeah? But no coffin, eh?"

"A coffin? If you know so much about the world, how come you don't know that vamps and coffins are a fictional trope?"

"Really? Seems like it would be the perfect, snuggly, dark rest."

He hadn't thought much about it. And okay, so he had heard about some vamps who did sleep in coffins. He didn't have claustrophobia, but wedging his wide shoulders into a narrow box and pulling the lid down? Nope.

"I've been sleeping in total darkness since I was a kid. I've known nothing else."

"I wish I could know myself. And then." She set down her fork and turned to really look at him. This morning her eyes were blue. "Maybe it's not so important I remember? Maybe I'm meant to move forward with the knowledge I have."

"Sounds good. In theory. But there's that sticky situation with angels trying to kill you and demons trying to lure you into a vast glowing portal. What was with that?"

"I don't know. I do know I felt compelled to walk toward the glowy circle and the closer I got—let's just say, I'm glad you arrived when you did. You saved my ass once again."

She kissed him then. A sweet kiss to the corner of his mouth that wasn't seductive or teasing, but instead, a simple thank-you. Yet Blade was compelled, as if to a glowing portal, to pull her closer and kiss her deeper. The tingle between his shoulder blades alerted him as it had last night, but he ignored it. And no way would he let his fangs down.

"Mmm, you're a great bit of muscle and blue to wake up to in the morning," she said, and teased the ends of his hair that lay against his biceps. She turned and scooped in more eggs. "Did I dream that you pulled me closer last night?"

"Not sure. I think you were snoring so much there was no room for dreams," he said.

"What? I do not snore."

No, she didn't, but how else to dodge the "pulling her closer" question?

Ah, hell, what should he do about her? He wanted to deny the intimacy that seemed natural for the two of them to share, and at the same time he *had* just kissed her. And he'd liked it. And he wasn't going to regret it, either.

To kiss her or to push her away? Life would have been a whole lot easier had he never seen those demons in the house across from Mr. Larson's lot.

"What's your plan for today?" he asked. "Luring more demons to you?"

"If I knew how and why that happened, I'd avoid it, believe me. I shouldn't have gone into the club alone. That was stupid. I was just…"

Feeling rejected by him after their weird embrace and then his pushing her away to prevent his vampire from biting her. So sometimes he wanted to kiss her and other times he didn't.

Pull it together, man!

"I'm complicated," he offered. "Sorry about last night. I should have been there to protect you, no matter what."

"Don't be sorry. You couldn't have known I'd need protection. And you know, I think I like complicated."

He smiled at that declaration. If the chick wanted complicated, he was the poster boy for that.

Zen crunched a piece of toast. "So let me get this straight, you can't bite me. That's cool. But when you're attracted to me it's your faery that reigns?"

"Not all the time. I can be normal. As normal as a guy like me is. I can kiss a woman, have sex with her, without wanting to bite her. It's when I'm in faery shape and am mating with a woman that my vampire wants to join in. Something about having my wings out heightens my vamp's craving for blood. That's never cool."

"Yet you were in plain old human shape when making out with me last night."

"I'm never plain or human." He chuckled, thinking that had sounded narcissistic. "If you have to label me as something, I'm vampire. And the vamp likes to make out with a pretty woman as much as any other man would."

"What about your faery?"

"Sex on steroids," he muttered, then grinned. He wasn't bragging, that was just how it worked. "So I'm a case. I did tell you to stay away from me."

"Everything I learn about you only makes me want to learn more. You're brave. Honorable. Handsome. Contradictory. We're alike in many ways. But while I strive to remember, I sense there is some part of you that wants to forget."

"Forget what?"

"You tell me. It's to do with demons—I know that much."

"Maybe you don't know that."

"I'm pretty sure I do. But if you're not cool with talking about it then I'll have to be cool with ignoring you're trying to hide it." She patted his arm. "So you wanted to know what I'm doing today? Nothing. At least not that I can think of."

"I was planning on stopping by my father's place this afternoon," Blade offered. "I want to show him the halo, see if he can modify it for me. He's a sword smith. Makes amazing swords and weapons."

"Can I come along?"

He nodded. "I'd like that."

Malakai Saint-Pierre wore his muscles like armor, and was gruffly handsome. Blade resembled him in pale skin tone, dark hair and height, but the father was a bit broader across the shoulders—if that was possible. Kai was a full werewolf, as Blade had explained to Zen on the drive over. Now she noticed him sniffing the air before her as Blade introduced them. Had to be a wolf thing.

He had a sure, almost painful grip, but when he saw her wince, he apologized and then slapped his son on the shoulder. "What do you have for me?"

"Something surprising."

"Come out into the work shed, you two. Let's have a look."

Zen clasped Blade's hand. She squeezed, more for her reassurance than his. Kai noted the clasp and grinned widely at his son.

"It's not fancy," Kai said to her as they strolled along the back of the house and into the shed. The rough-hewn log work shed was surprisingly bright thanks to exposure windows set into the vaulted ceiling. "But it's where I do all my work."

Scents of charcoal and burned steel mixed with the earth floor and an acidic chemical scent Zen couldn't place. She wandered up to the log wall where half a dozen swords hung from leather straps. The polished steel blades gleamed. Some featured elaborately etched blades; others offered a sleek swash of deadly beauty. She almost touched, but decided she shouldn't without first asking.

"You made all these?" she asked. "You possess amazing skill."

"My dad can make steel sing," Blade said proudly. "So here's what I've got."

Kai hissed at sight of the halo held in his son's hand. "Is that…?"

Blade nodded. "Slayed the bastard who owned it the other night. It was after Zen. Actually, she did the slaying."

"But you distracted the angel," Zen added with a wink to her man.

Kai delivered her a curious onceover. She shivered at the touch of his gaze. "Why are angels after you? My son told me you lost your memory. Are you an angel?"

"I don't know. I have a halo, too. Have had it with me since after the accident that boggled my memory. Does that make me an angel? Or maybe I found it somewhere and it's just a trinket?"

"Interesting. You talk to a witch?" Kai asked Blade.

"Dez hadn't any idea what she could be. Though she did think she was in the process of becoming."

"What does that mean?" the werewolf asked.

"Haven't a clue."

Both men glanced at Zen. She toyed with the rhinestones around her neck, suddenly aware of the overwhelming power a man's stare could deliver. Times two. It was…kind of nice. Made her stand a little straighter.

"Let's take a look." Kai held out his hand and Blade gave him the halo.

The imposing werewolf inspected the circular weapon, tapped it against the wood-and-steel-block table where he must fashion his weapons and put it around his wrist as if a bangle, then popped it off with a flick of his hand and caught it expertly. "Mind if I pound on this a bit?"

"Go for it," Blade said. "I was thinking you could modify it for me. Make it more blade like."

"Halos are the toughest substance to show up in the mortal realm. I doubt any tools I have will even dent it. But I'll give it a go. Maybe a little of your mother's faery dust worked in might soften it up? This could be sweet!"

"Thanks, Dad. Mom isn't home?"

"Nope, but she made some killer red-velvet cake this

morning. It's in the fridge. You two better go have some. Nice meeting you, Zen. And, Blade?"

"Yes?"

"Serve your woman some cake and then come back out, okay?"

The house was a gorgeous cabin-like structure. The open-floor design featured a vast living area and kitchen on the lower level. The second level consisted of an enclosed room with a king-size bed, and an open living area, one wall of which was entirely windows that stretched up to a peak at the pinnacle of the two-story ceiling. The view was lush and green, and a stream bubbled not far beyond the patio that hugged the house.

The cabin was a dream escape, Zen thought. Must have been an awesome place to grow up living in the middle of nature. Now, this was her kind of home.

Blade dished up some cake for her, but not himself—though he did lick the knife clean. "That will make you believe in heaven on earth. My mother makes the best sweet stuff. I almost miss moving away from home when I get a taste of her cookies and cakes."

"Better than blood?" she asked.

"Sometimes."

She sampled a forkful of the dense red cake capped with a cream-cheese frosting and decided not to talk because that would only hamper her from eating more, more and more.

"I'm heading out to see what Dad wants. Probably wants to give me his opinion on the new girl."

"Am I your girl?" she muttered through a mouthful of cake. "We're not even friends."

"That's right," he said, and left out the side door.

"Mmm…" Heaven, indeed.

But what would be more heavenly? To actually be Blade's girl. And to convince the man that there were more interesting things to do than merely kissing her. She wouldn't ask for his bite again. But she really wanted to get back to where they had been the other night when they'd been making out on the couch, and he had licked her nipples. Just thinking about it made her toes curl.

Memory? Who cared about what she couldn't remember? She was making delicious new memories with a man who had begun to hold and kiss her in her dreams.

Now, how to convince him to take a chance on her in real life?

"She's trouble," Kai said. He gave the halo a good whack with his ball peen hammer. Not even a dent. "Angel? That's not good for your vamp, son. Your faery might like to dally with her, but if you whip out the fangs…" His father shook his head.

"I don't think she's angel. Or if she is, if she actually fell to earth, I don't believe she's angel anymore. Though her blood does initially bleed blue."

Kai hissed. "Keep your fangs away from that woman's neck."

"I will. But I sense other things about her. Or so Dez put the idea into my head."

"Like what?"

"Faery."

Kai set the hammer down and turned to his son, arms crossed and head tilted. "She got wings?"

"If she does, she doesn't remember how to bring

them out. And she's got some interesting markings on her arms. Sort of like Kelyn's, but not. They glow."

Kai nodded. Thought about it. "So why are demons after her? And what is with this new club at the edge of town? I've never heard of it. And I usually have a pretty good eye out for all paranormal activity in the area."

"Really, Dad? You're not even pack principal anymore. You've retired."

Kai puffed up his chest. "Are you saying I'm losing my edge?"

Blade shook his head. His dad would always have the edge, but he was more focused on making a good life with his wife right now than pack politics or even the paranormal goings-on in Tangle Lake.

"I didn't know about the club, either," Blade reassured Kai. "It's some creepy old mansion that looks as if it's been sitting on that property for centuries. Which makes no sense whatsoever because I'm sure all of us have been in the area where it sits, probably snowmobiling in the wintertime. And it had this portal in the middle of the dance floor that was sucking Zen toward it."

Kai blew out his breath. "Portals are not cool. If it's a demon hotspot it might suck her into Daemonia."

Blade hadn't considered Daemonia. Thinking about that place gave him a shiver. His parents had told him about it during their Teen Talk. It was the Place of All Demons. No place for any vampire, wolf or faery to go. They'd much prefer he smoke or start drinking than consider visiting Daemonia.

Kai asked, "You think this chick is worth the trouble?"

Blade ran a hand through his hair, but didn't meet his father's eyes.

"I get it. You're afraid if you let yourself care about her this will go down like the last one. What was her name?"

Blade bowed his head and turned a shoulder away from his father. "Octavia."

The last one. Why wouldn't his family stop mentioning her? There was no way he could ever forget until everyone else did.

"That wasn't your fault, Blade. You didn't know Octavia was a *mimicus* demon. And you sure as hell couldn't have known her denizen would let her die."

They could have saved her with intervention from a witch, even demonic magic. A simple spell. But Ryckt, the denizen leader, had allowed Octavia to fade—to death. Blade didn't want to stir into that muck again. He marched toward the door.

"I know you seek forgiveness, son," his father called. "You're the only one who can do that for yourself!"

Blade veered toward the stream that paralleled the back of the house. He stopped on a mossy stone that edged the crisp, gurgling water. Even the fresh, verdant scent couldn't lessen his anxiety. His shoulders felt as tight as his jaw. And his heart squeezed in his chest.

Had he known they would let her die he would have done something. What, he didn't know. He had been so out of it after the torture. But—hell. She didn't have to die!

When he heard Zen's soft voice, Blade cringed. She stood right behind him. Shit.

"I won't ask," she said softly. And she embraced him from behind and tilted her head against his back. "Let me in, Blade. I promise I won't look too deep. I just... I need someone to anchor me to this realm."

He clasped her hand against his chest. He could do that for her, the anchoring part. But the letting her in part was what made him clench his teeth.

"Whatever you've done that makes you feel as though you are better off to push people away," she said, "doesn't matter to me. I'm starting fresh. You can start fresh with me. Deal?"

It would matter to her if she knew his dark truth. It mattered to every family member who still cringed whenever his past was mentioned. He had been responsible for a woman's death. Because of his bite.

"I'm lost," Zen whispered. "But standing close to you makes me feel found. Or at least, safe."

"I can't protect you forever, Zen. So long as I remain clueless about what you are and why so many are coming after you, I can't completely protect you."

"Maybe you should put the halo over my head? I know the mythology. If I am really an angel that'll give me my earthbound soul."

True. It would also make her human.

"And make you mortal. Do you want that? What if you fell to this realm for a reason? With a purpose? Let's keep looking. We'll figure you out."

He turned and she kissed him, and this time he didn't push her away. Because maybe he could protect her. And yes, it did something to his aching heart when he held her close. And he liked that feeling. It was a dangerous path to tread, but he'd never feared danger before.

Losing his heart to Zen could be the worst thing for him, but the best thing for his future.

Chapter 15

Blade dropped Zen off at The Red Rooster. He told her he had something to do with Stryke. He said he'd pick her up later if she wanted to get a bite to eat.

Of course she did. She was never not hungry. That red-velvet cake had only stoked her craving for more food.

Waving him off, she turned in time to see the Mini Cooper pull into the parking lot. Trouble hopped out and handed her the keys.

"Thanks." She tucked the keys into her skirt pocket. "Now how will you get back to your truck, which must be out on that country road?"

"Kelyn drove me out to your car. He'll swing by here in a few minutes and pick me up. Everything's cool. You and Blade getting along?"

"Yes."

"That's good. I thought for sure he'd never want to see you again after the demon affair at the club."

Zen slung the backpack over her shoulder and met Trouble's dark gaze, which was just as high up as Blade's was. "What is it with Blade and demons? Something really terrible must have happened because he always clams up when I ask him about it."

Trouble leaned forward, sticking his face right before hers. He smelled great, like pine trees and fresh-cut wood. "You really want to know?"

Zen nodded.

"Well—"

"Wait!" She put up her hands between them. "Forget it. If Blade wants me to know, he'll tell me. It wouldn't be right to go behind his back and ask about something if he wants to keep it private."

Trouble whistled. "I like you. Even if you do turn out to be demon, I'll have your back."

"I think I can handle myself."

"Really? 'Cause if we hadn't rescued you from the Demon Dance Hall you would be Hades knows where right now."

She rubbed her arm and shrugged. "Fair enough. Just tell me one thing about Blade."

Trouble shrugged his massive shoulders back and puffed up his chest, then shot out, "Maybe."

"Was it a woman? Someone who hurt him?"

She wanted to know, and then she didn't. She didn't have a right to know. Again, Blade would tell her if he wanted her to have that knowledge.

"No," she quickly said. "Forget it."

Trouble smirked. "Wasn't going to tell you anyway. But so you know, you are barking up the right tree. See you later, Zen." He strode off toward the big iron rooster and gave its tail a slap as he passed.

"A woman hurt him," she muttered. "So it's heartbreak that keeps him from being open with me. How to help him get beyond something so devastating?"

The man needed space. And a reasonable means to trust her, if he was going to fess up and tell her something so deeply personal. So she'd give him space. She could do that. If any nasty demons came after her she'd just whip out the halo and...

"Where is the halo?"

Unzipping the backpack she shuffled through it and found the halo nestled in a hoodie jacket. Taking it out, she decided she would have to keep it on her at all times. If it could take out an angel, it sure as heck could take out a demon.

"Watch out, bad guys." She swung the blade defensively in a close arc before her. "I am armed and ready."

The statement felt empowering. But really? She'd accidentally slain the angel, and that was only because it had been distracted by Blade. What if she was alone and trapped by an angel or demon?

Zen gulped down a meek squeak. She sure hoped Blade stuck to his promise to protect her.

"It's like a beacon," the demon said. He was visiting the mortal realm as first hand to his commander, who sat across the table from him. He set the coffee cup down and broke off a big bite of the sugared donut the café advertised as "heart attacks." "We can track her when she's got that halo in hand."

"But so can the angels," Kesabel said. He rapped pointed fingernails on his coffee cup and sneered at the coating of sugar that painted his cohort's lips white. "And we don't want them to get to her before we do."

"We were so close last night." The lackey demon sucked the sugar from his fingertips. "Until the vampire and the werewolf crashed the party."

"That idiot vampire thinks he's got to protect her."

"Someone needs to have words with him."

Kesabel nodded. "Done."

* * *

At the back of the garage where once a farmer had herded dairy cattle in and out to be milked twice daily, Blade leaned over the steel worktable his father had designed for him. He worked on cars as a hobby, but he wasn't a die-hard car fanatic who fixed them up and polished and shined and then parked them at shows for display. He liked a good, solid car and preferred not to buy new. Recycling was the way he'd been raised. He did the same with the weapons he stocked in the small arsenal here in the cool shadows of the garage. He rescued rusted blades from antiques shows and flea markets, took them home and polished and honed them. He liked blades, and it wasn't because of his name. When in combat, being up close and able to feel his opponent's breath on his face was the most challenging and satisfying way to win the fight.

He didn't own a gun. They were too loud, and really, it was too easy to kill with them. If a man were committed to defense, to protecting himself and others, he had better be willing to stand before that threat and give it good and fair fight. A bullet was too impersonal. A coward's weapon.

He drew his fingertips over the one blade he wouldn't leave home without. The bowie knife his father had forged for him when he was a teen. As well…he reached high for the salt dagger that hung above the assorted weaponry. It was fragile, but the hardened salt that had been compressed into the cheese-grater-like base of steel was an effective weapon against demons. Daisy Blu's husband, Beck, had given it to him; it was from his late father, Severo's, arsenal.

And now he'd added an angel halo to his necessity weapons. Or he would if his dad was able to modify it.

So he had told the mysterious Sim he was going to help him annihilate the demons in Tangle Lake. They had threatened Zen. And that was a good enough reason for him to go after the next demon he laid eyes on. And the next. And so on, until he was confident the threat had been eliminated.

He sniffed the bowie knife and then licked it. Traces of demon blood still clung to the polished steel. Fangs descending, he grinned wickedly. He was growing stronger with every demon he killed. It wasn't as though he needed more strength. Only, the gaining of said strength fed his faery's vicious desire for power. As well, strength bolstered his mission. He'd need muscles of steel if he were to fight more angels.

He wondered who Sim was and what his beef was with demons.

Didn't matter. There were no wrongs about this situation. Humans were protected from demons. He got to slay demons. And in the process Zen was also protected. Everybody won.

And because he was feeling so confident, Blade tugged out his cell phone and called Zen at the inn. "I'll pick you up in an hour," he said after suggesting dinner at a local restaurant, and clicked off.

Time to start treating that remarkable woman like the lady she was. And in keeping her close, he'd also be able to protect her.

Dinner at an Italian family-owned place called Mansetti's was followed by a movie. Which Zen had been very excited about. She'd never seen a movie before. Not that she recalled. Afterward, she strolled with Blade, hand in hand, out to his truck, which he'd parked around back in the theater lot far from other patrons.

"That was awesome," she said. "But I still don't think it's possible to shoot a man so many times and he'd continue to rise up, shake it off and go after the hero."

"That's why they call it a fantasy action/adventure flick. He did eventually die after they sliced off his head."

"Yeah, but his body still twitched." Zen thrust her arms out before her in a zombie imitation and twitched her limbs. "I will never die! Fear me!"

Blade's laughter was a startling surprise. She dropped her arms, and wrapped them around his neck. "Do that again."

"What?"

"Laugh."

He grinned and shook his head. "You're a strange one."

"If I told you I thought your laughter was sexy would you do it again?"

"I don't do sexy on command." He chuckled softly and playfully pushed her away. Zen beamed at him. "That wasn't on purpose!" he called as he strode to the truck.

"Doesn't matter." She skipped to meet him at the passenger door. "You've already gone and done it."

"And what have I done?"

He teased the ends of her hair. Such an absent-minded move. His guard was down. She liked that. "You are seducing me with your charm."

"I…don't have a charming bone in my body."

"Oh, I think this one is." She ran a finger down his

arm and stopped at the wrist, where he flexed his powerful fingers. "This one, too." She tapped his shoulder. "It's not your classic charm, to be sure."

"Like you would know, Amnesia Girl. Hop in." He held the truck door open and helped her up with a hand to her hip.

"Can I drive?"

"No one touches the steering wheel," he called as he swung around the hood, then opened his door and slid in, "or the radio. Driver rules."

"Sidekick shuts his cakehole?"

Blade tilted a curious gaze on her. "Where'd you hear that?"

"I don't know. Should I have heard it somewhere?"

"It's a quote from a popular TV show that features monster hunters."

"Huh. Must have picked it up when I walked the world."

Blade turned completely on the seat. His stare was so intense, she felt a shiver ripple through her system. "What?" she said in a panic.

"That's the first time you've ever said that. Actually acknowledged it. That you walked the world."

"So?"

"Angels walk the world after their fall to take in knowledge."

"I knew that. Because…huh." She sat back, considering the implications. "Because I walked the world. That's what I was doing before the bus hit me. I know it as truth."

"You getting back your memory?"

"I don't know. A little? But if I am an angel, that doesn't explain why my blood turns black."

Blade turned the key in the ignition, and, still looking at her, shifted into gear. "Explains why you have a halo."

He let his foot off the gas, and Zen screamed.

Chapter 16

Zen's scream startled him so thoroughly Blade slammed his foot on the brake.

Before the truck stood a man, who wasn't a human, but an angel. Blade knew that because the creature's wings stretched out twenty feet or more on either side of his shoulders. They weren't the standard feathered wings, either. These were fashioned from ice. And they weren't melting in the eighty-degree summer heat.

The angel heaved out a breath of frost that iced over the truck's windshield. Blade felt the chill enter his veins. He'd not felt so cold since the polar vortex had dropped temps below negative thirty degrees this past winter.

He heard Zen audibly shiver.

"Stay here," he said to her.

She slapped the halo into his hand. "You'll need this."

Right. His dad still had the one he'd claimed.

The angel slammed a fist onto the hood, denting the metal surface into the engine a good eight inches.

"Beating on inanimate objects isn't impressive," he muttered. "How about you try me?" To Zen he said, "Keep the engine running."

He kicked open the door and hopped out. He lunged

for the angel, but got caught by an icy wing that thwapped him across the chest and flung him away from the truck. His spine landed against a street pole, the overhead light flickering from the impact.

The angel grasped the front of the truck and lifted. The front tires left the ground.

"Why are you after her?" Blade yelled as he pushed from the pole and charged the angel.

He jumped onto the hood, which didn't stop the angel from lifting it, and reached down to grip the bastard by its thick white hair. Ice flowed up Blade's fingers and hardened the veins in his wrist. "Why?"

The angel roared in a deafening blend of animal sounds and screams. Blade gritted his teeth as he struggled to maintain hold on the creature while his fingers felt as if they'd snap off from frostbite. Out of the corner of his eye he saw the clear ice wing sweep toward him. He slashed the angel's hand with the halo and on the follow-through managed to slice the wing in half. Ice shattered onto the pavement and the truck hood. The truck wheels dropped to the ground, toppling Blade off-balance.

To his advantage, the wings did not bleed.

Going with the momentum, Blade flipped over the top of the angel's head, slicing the halo over its shoulder and down the back as he did so. He landed the ground behind him and twisted to see the blue blood spill from the cavernous icy wound.

The undamaged wing collided with Blade's back. The force expelled the halo from his grip and pushed him forward to catch his palms against the angel's chest. The creature's skin was like dry ice. His flesh stuck to the thing. So he shifted. The subtle changes to his musculature and body were enough to free him from the icy opponent.

With wings out and in full faery form, Blade pranced around the angel, turning it away from the vehicle and Zen. "What do you want from her?"

Nothing but brain-shattering cacophony spilled from the creature's mouth. Either it hadn't mastered the human tongue or it was focused on annoying the hell out of Blade. The sound was louder than standing next to a stack of speakers at a heavy metal concert— turned up to eleven.

Holding his hands out in placation, Blade walked farther backward, luring the creature forward. Its wounded shoulder spilled copious blood that he kept an eye on. If it touched his skin he'd live, but the instant it permeated his bloodstream he was a goner.

Spying the halo on the tarmac, he swept down a hand and snagged it. A wing whooshed toward him, lifting his hair but not cutting him. Rolling up to stand, Blade eyed the truck. Zen sat inside. Safe.

"You're the second one," he said to the angel, guessing the thing understood him, no matter his language skills. "I will protect her with my life." He stretched his wings out behind him then arrowed backward, making him a narrow target. "Time for you to return to where you came from. But this time? I'm sending you to St. Peter's gate."

The angel lunged for him. An icy wing tip cut through Blade's jeans. Heat seared his skin. Slashing an arm down, he drew the halo upward, cutting the angel's leg and across his chest. The angel's body opened up, blood spilling and a bright light emitting. Blade dodged the gush of blue blood. A wicked growl preceded a brilliant flash. The angel dispersed in a scatter of crystal dust and settled like winter snow upon the ground.

"Yes!" carried out from inside the truck.

Blade shook the icicles off his wings and yowled. The angel's icy touch still hurt like a mother. He slapped a hand over his thigh. No blood. He was safe.

A police siren sounded and he guessed it was a few miles away.

The truck drove up beside him and Zen called out the driver's window, "Get in! The cops! Hurry!"

Trying to shift resulted in a vicious twinge to his system. The lingering shock of cold kept him from shifting. Folding his wings up behind him, Blade managed to fit himself inside the truck cab, but had to pull in the top of his right wing and bend it uncomfortably.

"We'll have to return for the angel dust later," Zen said.

"Don't need it. Only a witch would have use for it."

"Fine." Zen pulled the vehicle out of the parking lot. The truck sputtered and clunked and with a lurching heave forward—sped out into the darkness.

"That was close," she said. "That thing might have turned you to ice. And look at your wing! It's bleeding. I think. It's sparkly."

He hadn't been aware he'd taken damage. Blade pulled up the peak of his right wing and examined the cut, which healed even as he ran his fingers over it. Ichor-tainted blood spilled over the dark wing fabric and dropped onto his lap, staining the denim darkly.

Had any angel blood entered his bloodstream? He didn't feel as if he would explode. Because that was what would happen. One minute the vamp was smiling and going about his business. Angel blood gets into his veins—bam!

Zen eyed him for so long the truck swerved toward the ditch. It was only then he realized his pants had split down the thigh and crotch during the shift. And he wasn't wearing anything beneath the jeans.

"Eyes on the road," he directed her. "Don't take your foot off the gas. The engine might be damaged. The minute this truck stops, I think it'll be for good."

"Right." She turned sharply onto the gravel road that led toward his home.

"I'd put my wings back but I need to stretch them out to furl them back up. Gotta wait until we get home. Sorry."

"For what? Saving my life? Again! Dude, you can put those wings anywhere you like. And uh…those pants are going to fall off when you stand up is my guess. I can't wait."

"I just dodged death and you're excited to see me drop trou?"

She shrugged, and while she kept her eyes on the road, Blade took in her broad smile. He forgot about the danger. That smile would undo him.

Hell, it already had.

Zen handled the truck well. And as Blade had suspected, when she stepped on the brake to park, the vehicle heaved to a clattering death.

"Sorry," she said.

"Not your fault. I think it had something to do with the angel." He shivered. "And all that ice. I can still feel it on my skin. It's creepy."

"I'll run inside and get you a towel."

While Zen ran up to the house, Blade stepped out of the truck. Though it was a sultry evening, he shivered again. The angel's touch lingered on his skin, in his very veins. He clutched the jeans' waistband to his stomach, but it wasn't doing much good. The crotch was ripped open.

He smirked. Zen wasn't the sort he wanted to attract in this manner. Because those *sorts* were one-night stands. On the other hand, she'd let him know that she liked to tease him and push their intimate boundaries. And those boundaries of his were fast softening.

Striding up to the barn, he cupped a hand over his crotch when Zen reemerged with a towel. She tossed it at him and turned to face the door.

He wrapped it about his hips, dropping the tattered jeans, but suspected it wouldn't be long before his cock got the better of him and tented the towel. Zen led the way up the stairs, her hips shifting and hair spilling like a sexy veil across her shoulders. She did have some gorgeous curves, and those curves distracted. At the top of the stairs, she turned and caught him in a kiss before he could land on the top step.

"Thank you again. Ooh, you're shivering. You need to put some clothes on."

"Here I thought you wanted to see them fall off me."

"More than anything. But I don't want it to happen at the expense of your health."

"I'm not shivering because I'm cold." Clad in just the towel, Blade wandered into the kitchen, while keeping his back away from Zen's curious gaze, and ran himself a glass of water from the faucet. "The angel's touch iced under my skin." He drank the water then shivered boldly. "You want some?"

"I do want something." She fidgeted with the ends of her hair, then smiled as she tried to avoid looking at him. Classic subtle flirtation moves. Combined with, he suspected, a healthy dose of nerves. "So here we are."

"Yep." He felt a sneaky desire to toy with her discomfort, so he leaned against the counter, hand on his hip. "Here we are. I'd say that date was a disaster, wouldn't you?"

"Not the majority of it. It was just the last part that was harrowing. And that did end well. The villain died the first time. All in all, I had a good time. And you know, I've never seen a naked man before."

"That you know of."

"That I remember. So, uh…could I…" She eyed his towel.

"Seriously?"

She nodded eagerly. Clasped together her beringed fingers in expectation.

"I don't—" She reached for the towel and Blade grabbed it before she could tug it from his hips. "Whoa! Boundaries, Zen."

"Yes, but I'm curious. Your muscles are so—" she spread her hands before him, taking in his abs and pecs "—solid. You're just so strong. And perfect. And—it makes my heart flutter and other parts of me get really warm."

He arched a brow. Did she actually not recognize when she was turned on? This chick did not cease to surprise him.

"And what is eyeing my main stick going to do for you?" he asked.

"I want to see all of you."

"You've seen more of me than you should. Wings?"

"They are gorgeous. And besides, you saw me with my shirt off the other night."

"And you are ogling me with my shirt off right now."

Would she attempt to finagle him out of the towel? He wanted to see if she could.

"Looking at you makes me want to take my clothes off," she confessed. "And press my body against yours. And kiss you. And—oh! I know that I know about this stuff, but I don't think I've experienced it. Does that make sense?"

"Nothing about you makes sense, Zen. You're weird."

Her smile dropped.

"And I like that," he quickly added. "So you want to get your experience with me? Is that all I am?" He crossed his arms. "A means to add a notch to your bed-post?"

"I don't understand that. Do I even own a bedpost?"

"Then, you obviously don't know as much as you think you know."

"Apparently not. Okay, let me try a different tact."

He smirked. Never had a woman's attempt at seduction been so awkward. And yet it was a turn-on to watch her fumble and find her way to more confident ground. Kind of like a flower opening her petals to take in the sun. And where the hell had that notion come from? He did not relate women to flowers.

Did he?

"I...admire you," Zen said. "I mean, we've only just met. And it is apparent to both of us that whatever it is that I am is going to be dangerous to your health. And yet all you want to do is protect me. That's so noble. And sexy."

He brushed a swish of copper hair over her shoulder and stroked his palm up her neck to cup her jaw. "I like you, Zen."

"Even though I'm weird?"

"Especially because you're weird. And if we're going to do confessions, I admit that I struggle inside my head far more than any physical struggles I've had with angels or demons. I've got to stop that. Take life moment to moment. Like right now, I want to kiss you."

She beamed up at him, bouncing on her toes. "Then, let's kiss."

That was easy. He leaned down to kiss her and she sighed into his breaths. And Blade forgot to question the right or wrong of the situation and just let it happen. He wrapped a hand across her back and pulled her against his bare chest. She had kissed before, or maybe it was that they kissed so well together. This kiss felt easy. Sure. Not dangerous.

Her fingers played over his biceps, and the shivers he'd felt earlier vanquished in the warm wake of her touch. He could kiss her all evening and never come up for air.

"You're not resisting," she whispered against his mouth. "That feels good. You're pulling me close to you. You are so strong and hard when I touch you. Your skin is…"

"Pale next to yours," he said on a chuckle. "So pretty." He tapped the marks on the inside of her elbow. "Take your shirt off, Zen."

She pulled the shirt over her head so quickly he thought she might give herself whiplash. And there she stood, without a bra, her caramel breasts high and full and with darker nipples. Blade could taste them already. And he didn't think to question his tactics as he grew more aroused.

She pressed her hips closer, purring an approving noise into his mouth.

"Can angels have sex?" she asked.

"I don't know. But I thought we were going with you not being an angel. At least, not anymore. That becoming thing Dez mentioned?"

"Right. Then, maybe I should give the sex thing a try?"

Yeah. This was getting too deep too fast. Right? But he was encouraging her. And the feel of her hand running down his abs and so close…

He gripped her wrist. "I think with you, slow would be a good idea."

She pouted.

Damn it, why was he so conflicted about this?

Then she sniffed. "You smell so good. I think you're warming up. At least…" She glanced down to the towel. "Some part of you is."

She was not going to let up. Nor did he want her to. This thing with Zen was different than his usual encounters with women who were intent on one thing. Much as she was also that intent, he sensed a playfulness in her that he'd never had the opportunity to experience with other women.

"I want you, Zen," he honestly declared. "I just don't want you to feel—"

"Rushed? Oh, no, I don't feel that way at all. Blade, I want to have sex with you. I mean, like…a lot." She hugged him. "We're not moving too quickly. Oh." Her fingers stroked across his back curiously.

He knew what she was doing and cringed.

"What is that?" She peered up at him. "Feels like a scar. Lots of them. Can I look?"

That she had asked and hadn't brazenly ducked under his arm to gawk meant the world to Blade. It was the part of him that reminded him he had wronged a woman. The part he wanted to forget. And yet, he couldn't move forward with Zen and continue to hide.

He nodded. "I don't want to talk about the reason for the scars tonight, but you can look."

She kissed him, bowed her forehead to his lips, then slipped around behind him and spread her hands across his back. At her soft, exploratory touch, Blade sucked in a hiss. Eighteen scars in all. A one-night stand had counted them for him one evening. She'd been too drunk to care what they had come from and had accepted his lie about a farming accident.

In truth, every one of them had come from a demon talon.

"This makes me sad," she said quietly. "Aren't vampires supposed to heal fast?"

"Demon talons have poison in them. Counteracts the healing process."

"Demons," she whispered. He'd not intended to tell her that. It was too easy to relax with Zen.

And then the gentlest kiss landed on one of those scars, and he shivered. His muscles tightened and his heart trembled. It wasn't from the lingering chill of an unholy angel, but rather the promise of something he feared more than the pain. Connection. Goddess, but it reduced him to something he wasn't familiar with.

Something that felt better than he could ever imagine.

"I will treat you with care," Zen said. "Because you deserve it."

A kiss to one of the scars branded him with innocent kindness. And then another, and then she moved around in front of him, took his hand and led him into the bedroom.

They fell onto the bed in a tumble of sighs and kisses, strokes and moans. Zen's skin, fire under his palms, coaxed him closer, deeper, toward something so innocent. Untouchable.

Yet he held her now, and wasn't about to let go.

Gliding his tongue along her arm, he aimed toward the cream-colored markings, slipping a wet trail over the arabesques, and then toward her shoulder. He kissed her there. And there. And at the base of her jaw, and then her open mouth. She gasped into him, exhaling sweet breath. Giving to him.

"Zen," he whispered. A prayer. A sonnet to her beauty. Simply a name. Not even her name. But it fit her. And him.

Her hand glided down his abs and landed over his crotch. She cooed and nudged up her hip. "That feels interesting."

He would give her interesting. He tugged the towel loose and she eagerly tore it away from his hips. Before he could resume kissing her, she'd grabbed hold of his cock.

"Wow, it's so hard and hot."

He growled and bowed his head to her breast. "That feels good when you give it a squeeze. Mmm, and that firm stroking. Oh, Zen…"

She took to the exploratory touching with a zest that didn't surprise Blade at all. She was a curious woman. And for that, he would not complain.

As she continued to squeeze and stretch and stroke

him, he kissed her breasts and teased her nipples with his tongue. She hadn't developed a rhythm but she didn't need to. Her awkward play was actually making him harder and increasing his breaths. She squirmed and hummed a satisfied tone. A supple explorer lay beside him. It felt so different from any encounter with a woman he'd had previously. This felt real.

"I trust you, Blade."

Though he'd heard it before, that statement meant a lot to him coming from a woman who had no solid grasp on her life. She needed to trust someone. And she trusted him. So he would treat her as the precious entity she was.

Feathering his fingers down her breast and tweaking her nipple to the accompaniment of her grateful moan, he then glided his fingertips over her stomach and parted her legs. She was warm and wet. So ready for him. Her hands bracketed his head, luring him to her breasts. He kissed them both, suckling them while he fingered her teasingly.

"So many sensations," she said on a gasp.

"You overwhelmed?" he asked.

She shook her head. "My heart is racing. Every part of me tingles in the coolest way. Your kisses feel like the best thing ever. And what you're doing with your fingers… Don't stop, Blade. Please, don't stop."

"I won't. I want to be inside you, Zen. You ready for that?"

She gripped the head of his cock and guided him between her legs. "Yes."

He entered her slowly, steadily. The tight squeeze of her made it difficult not to come immediately, but he was determined to give her pleasure first before he came and then just wanted to roll over and fall asleep.

She murmured next to his ear that he was so remarkable. Fingers clutching at his shoulders and back, she tilted back her head as his thrusts grew faster, deeper. She hadn't cried out, as if a virgin, but that meant little. All women were different. There was no real way to know if she had done this before.

Didn't matter. She was here in his arms, and he had been gifted her trust.

"Oh…" Zen gasped, her hands dropping away from him as her body shuddered. "That's…" The orgasm shivered her body minutely beneath him. A smile curled onto her lips.

And Blade felt as if an angel had just fallen into his life.

Chapter 17

Zen woke in the black bedroom, which was more a slate gray thanks to the morning light beaming through the window. The forest was close, and a mosaic of leaves shifted in the soft breeze. She pulled the sheet up to her neck and tucked her legs against the heat lying beside her. And then she realized she was lying next to Blade and stretched down her legs so she could snuggle along the length of him.

And some other length suddenly bobbed against her belly.

She murmured in satisfaction. "I like that guy."

"He likes you" came a voice from under the sheet. He tugged it down and leaned in to kiss her through the hair spilled over his face. She swept it away to reveal one gray eye. "Morning. Would you mind pulling the shade? Vamps aren't keen on bright light so early in the day."

"Of course." She slipped out of bed and pulled the shade, reducing the room to a subtle darkness save for a glimmer of light sneaking in on either side of the shade. "Better?"

"Much. Come back to me."

She slid into bed, and he pulled her up against his

body, then moved on top of her, supporting himself with his elbows and a knee. Pressing kisses to her breasts, he lingered in tasting her, feeling her, holding his ear against her chest to listen to her heartbeats.

"Do I sound normal?" she asked.

"I hope not. There's something so wrong about normal. On the other hand, normal is in the eye of the beholder, yes?"

"Like being an amnesia chick?"

"Yep. For me being vampire with wings is normal. My brothers find being werewolf normal. So who is to say what your normal is?"

"I do know not remembering isn't normal."

"If you are or were an angel, maybe the not-remembering part is all part of the plan?"

She screwed up her lips in thought. "Vampires and werewolves sound a lot easier to me. If your father is werewolf, and I think you mentioned your mother is faery, how did you manage the vampire part?"

"My grandfather. He is married to a werewolf. They had twins, Kambriel and Malakai. Kam's a vamp. Dad's the wolf. Grandpa's bloodsucking genes just happened to show up in me."

"Do you regret not being werewolf like your siblings?"

"No. I've known nothing else. And I've never been made to feel I was different. Besides, Kelyn is full faery. If there's a weirdo in our family, it's my little brother." He chuckled and nuzzled his face between her breasts for a kiss. "But you know I like weirdoes."

"You're a weirdo, too," Zen said. "You're quiet and dark. It's because of these, isn't it?" She ran her fingers over the scars on his back that wrapped around to his sides. "Tell me about them. Please?"

She felt his fingers glide between her legs. "Later," he murmured. "Right now I want to delve into you."

He moved down on the bed, kissing her stomach, her hip, her thighs, until he kissed her deeply between her moist folds.

Zen squirmed and reached down to thread her fingers through his silken hair. She wasn't quite sure what he was doing with his tongue, but she didn't require an explanation. It was marvelous.

Blade watched Zen wander to the window to pull up the shade. Those waves of copper hair glinted like metal when the sun embraced her silhouette, as if she was some kind of goddess.

Or an angel.

"She was a demon," he suddenly said.

Sitting up on the bed, he smoothed a hand over the wrinkled sheet draped across his lap. The sun wasn't too bright on this north side of the barn. His skin wouldn't burn unless he endured prolonged exposure to direct rays. And the faery part of him provided added protection that most vamps didn't have and without which would see them running for the shade long before he did.

Zen spun around. "She?"

"The woman from my past who is the reason why I like to keep my distance from other women. The reason for these scars on my back."

"Oh." She planted a kiss on his forehead. Stroking his hair over a shoulder, she smiled warmly upon him.

"You've kind of shot that need for distance to hell with us, eh?"

He kissed the top of her breast. "It was worth the risk."

"Risk? Right. You thought I could be demon. Or worse, an angel."

"I still don't know what you are."

"But she was demon. This woman from your past? And…things did not go well with her, I take it?"

He shoved down the sheets and swung his legs over the side of the bed. Patting the bed, he waited for her to sit beside him. The heat of her body was as blessed as spring rain. Every part of him shivered and joined together to embrace the goodness he'd been gifted by Zen's presence.

And because of that, he owed her his truth. She deserved to know him. Good, bad and so terrible.

"Her name was Octavia. I met her in the springtime. Midnight, at a local drive-in movie theater that was still open. It shows classics once a month and the whole town attends. She was wearing a yellow dress and flashed me a fanged smile. I thought she was vampire. She even gave off the telltale shimmer that we vamps feel when we touch another of our kind."

"What's that feel like?" she asked, hugging against his side.

"It's sort of a tickle with an electric-shock kick. But not as strong as when you walk across a carpet and touch metal. It's a *knowing*, is the best way to put it."

She placed her hand on his thigh and, tilting her head aside his shoulder, silently entreated him to continue.

"We had an affair," he said. "Brief. Heated. I fell fast for her. That happens with me. If I like a woman, there's usually no going back."

He peered into Zen's bright azure eyes and saw worlds beyond his comprehension. And he liked it there. Lost in her world. He didn't desire to go back now that he had ventured in.

Yeah, so he fell hard and fast. He was a wimp when it came to love.

"I had no idea she was toying with me. Gaining my trust. Grooming me for something unspeakable."

The spill of her hair over his skin lightened his darkening mood. Yet at the same time, it reminded him that he held a woman, and women tended to be tricky. But how to trick him when she didn't even know herself?

"I wanted to bond with her. Vampires do that by sharing the bite and blood. It's a way of taking a mate. For life."

He let that settle in. Because yes, he'd thought to love her that much. Had thought he could spend the rest of his life with her. Once, love had been a marvelous thing to him. Something to value, to desire.

"She was my first real love. Or so I thought. So I bit her. If she had been merely vampire she would have responded with a bite. We'd not bitten each other before. And in fact, when I'd brought it up she had always said she wanted to save it for the bonding. Which is why I knew she would accept my bite. Anyway…"

He pressed his hands to his knees and exhaled, taking a moment to fortify his courage. Did the scars burn? No, it was his imagination. But memory burned deep into his being.

"My faery wanted to get in on the action as well, so my wings unfurled. And in that moment, with my fangs embedded in her neck, she let out a blood-curdling howl and shifted into her demonic shape. That was the first time I suspected she was half demon. I didn't even consider she could be completely demon. I was stunned. Felt betrayed. But still, I wanted to love her, to believe she'd merely forgotten to tell me her truth.

"But then she started to spasm and react to the bite. Because while vampires can bite demons and come away with nothing more than a nasty mouthful of black blood, vampires who are also part faery really work a number on demons. Faery ichor can poison demons. And she got a good mouthful of my faery saliva. She screamed that she was *mimicus*, a breed of demon that is capable of mimicking other breeds.

"I freaked out. I didn't know what to do. So I took her home. Waiting for her was her entire denizen. They were oddly pleased to see me, and didn't give Octavia much attention. And…they were wearing protective armor. It didn't occur to me until later what it would protect them from. They moved in on me swiftly. While I was stricken by what I had done to her, I learned that she had been toying with me. A demon trying to lure a vampire into the denizen so they could have their way with me. But she had no idea what the rest of her denizen knew—that I was part faery.

"What happened next I could have never anticipated."

He spread his fingers over Zen's hand, clasping it tightly against his chest. Heartbeats raced and his skin was clammy. An inhale; gasped breath. Difficult not to fall back into that feeling of danger even though he knew it was long past.

"They tortured me. I don't know how long. Days? Weeks? Felt like forever. And that armor I'd wondered over? It protected the demons from my ichor-tainted blood. All the while, the leader kept bringing Octavia out to show me that she was slowly dying. That hurt me more than any talon to my heart could have. The denizen could have saved her. Could have used demonic magic to force the faery taint from her system, or even witch magic, but they didn't. They let her suffer. And I couldn't do anything to help her because at times I was stretched out on a rack being clawed and beaten and burned."

Zen shivered against him.

"At other times I was free to fend off the dozens of monsters who came at me tearing at my skin and muscles and digging their talons in deep."

She spread a hand over his back. "These are from that torture."

He nodded. "The scars mean nothing. What haunts me is that I couldn't help her. That she was a sacrifice merely for the denizen's twisted penchant for torturing others. No woman should be treated that way. Just left to die. And she wouldn't have died had I not bitten her. She received a small amount of faery taint, which was why it took her so long to die. It was my fault. And, Zen…" He breathed in deeply. "I loved her."

She hugged him so tightly he felt her heartbeats match the pace of his own. Rib to rib, skin to skin. Pulse to pulse. It was too wondrous. Did he deserve this woman?

"I'm sorry, Blade. You shouldn't have had to face that. But if she was lying to you…"

"Yes, she was tricking me, toying with me. It hurts my heart to admit that. But still, it was no reason to allow her to die."

"You're right. You are an honorable man. You wouldn't wish pain on anyone."

Yes, well. She did not know he wanted to slay all the demons now. And the more painful their demise the better.

She hugged him and just let him be still. The silence did not feel heavy or awkward. His breathing was calm yet his heartbeats ran. He'd just revealed a part of himself he had kept locked and sealed. That he had trusted her enough to reveal that was immense. She would honor his trust.

"What can I do?" she asked. "To make this easier for you to bear?"

"Just listening is good. I…don't normally do this. Spill my guts. But I thought you should know. She was demon, Zen. And with us being uncertain what, exactly, you are…"

"I understand. You don't want to make the leap to complete trust with me. You can't. I respect that."

"I trust you. I just don't know what you are. And… you should also know I made a deal with a stranger to kill the demons in the area."

"What?"

"He came to me in the Darkwood not long before I met you. Said the demons are rising, increasing their numbers. He asked me to annihilate them. At first I refused. But after slaying the demons who would have gone after you, I agreed to help. Innocent humans could be harmed. They all need to die, Zen."

She pulled away and turned to sit facing him. She ran a shaky hand over her hair. "I, uh, don't know what to say to that."

"I'm sorry."

And if she was a demon? His declaration that all demons needed to die went against his conviction to save the one demon who had tricked him into the torture into the first place.

If he had saved her, then how could he conceive of slaying so many others?

"I don't feel as if I am demon," Zen felt it necessary to state. "But then, I don't feel as if I am anything in particular." She spied the bowie knife lying on the floor beside Blade's combat boots and lunged to grab it. "Cut me," she said, handing him the blade. "I want to check again."

He took the knife and she held out her palm to him. "Don't worry. I'll heal."

Without a word, he drew the knife tip across her skin. Black blood bubbled up, then spilled in clear, glinting streams down the side of her hand before hitting the black bed sheet.

"No more blue," she said in awe.

"But still black," he offered.

"But then it turned clear. That's ichor, isn't it?"

He nodded. "It could be anything."

"Becoming." She whispered the word the witch had used. "What do you think I will become?"

He clasped her hand and kissed the back of it. "My ally," he said.

"Not in the fight against demons. I don't think... I don't want to be a part of that destruction. But I can stand by your side."

"How about you simply be my friend?"

"Really? You're willing to let me be a friend?"

"Actually, I think we've gone beyond that. What with the sex."

She glided a hand down his back. "You are an amazing lover, Blade. And to be honest, I think that was my first time."

He tilted a look at her. "Could have been. No regrets?"

"Never. I'd love to do it again. Anytime you're willing."

"Is that so?"

She nodded.

Blade twisted and pushed her back against the pillows. "How about a good-morning shag?"

"Does shag mean sex?"

"It does."

"I'm in."

Chapter 18

Zen got out of the shower first and called out that she was going to make breakfast for him today. Or maybe she'd said she was going to get the things ready for him to make breakfast. Blade wasn't sure she had the talent for cooking. Did she remember how? Had she ever cooked?

He turned off the shower. Probably better not to linger in case she did attempt to master the stove. Grabbing a towel, he patted his hair and stepped onto the tiled floor.

Immense relief had relaxed his very being after telling Zen his history with demons. With one demon in particular. He could never forgive himself for biting Octavia. He blamed his vampire for the bite and he blamed his faery for delivering the deadly poison. But really? He was responsible for himself, all of himself. That included vampire and faery. And if one got out of line, it was his responsibility to kick it back in line.

Thing was, the vampire was so strong. Yet it was his faery that craved the demon blood. He had to keep his winged desires in check. That was easy enough. He wasn't sure he'd ever fall so deeply again that he'd feel compelled to mate with a woman and bite her. And until Zen knew what she was he could have sex with her, befriend her—hell, he could even fall in love. But that didn't have to mean forever.

Fall in love? No. He'd meant it when he'd offered his brother condolences after he'd admitted to being in love with his wife. Love was…tough.

But since when had he resisted a challenge?

Smirking and shaking his head, he finished drying off. In the bedroom he slipped on jeans. Raking his fingers through his hair was sufficient. From the smell that wafted in from the kitchen something was up.

A cloud of smoke hung over the stove. Blade hustled by a fleeing Oogie and commandeered the spatula from Zen.

"Sorry," she said. "I didn't think eggs could burn."

"It's okay. I can rescue them. Why don't you get the juice and toast on the table?"

"How did you become such a master chef?" she asked as she plopped two pieces of bread into the toaster. She wore one of his longer T-shirts and nothing else. The neckline spilled over one shoulder, attracting his eye. And his kiss. She met his gaze after that kiss and he winked at her.

"Cooking breakfast hardly qualifies me as a master. My mom used to let us help her in the kitchen when we were little. We all picked up a talent. I think by the time we were in our teens Mom had trained us so well we could cook the entire day's meals and she didn't have to lift a finger."

"Smart mom. You said she is faery?"

"Yes, and so is my brother Kelyn."

"When you shifted last night behind the theater, besides the obvious wings, your body changed subtly."

"That was my faery shape. Same me, just…bulkier."

"That's interesting. I would expect a faery to be slender and, well, fae."

"They come in all shape and sizes. Just like humans."

She hugged him around the waist and kissed his biceps. He didn't mind the closeness. She liked closeness. He could live with that. And she smelled so good, despite the lingering burn scent. Freshly showered and like a spring blossom.

"Can you bring your wings out without shifting?" she asked.

"I can, but rarely do."

"Because it's a sex thing?"

He chuckled. "You really like sex, don't you?"

"I don't understand why anyone wouldn't like it. Anything wrong with wanting to learn all I can about it?" she asked playfully as her fingers slipped beneath his "Do you want to eat or have sex?"

Her bright eyes flashed up at him. "Do you really have to ask?"

He turned off the burner, setting the eggs, which were a lost cause, aside. He swung around, catching Zen at the waist and set her down on the counter beside the sink. She pulled off the T-shirt, rendering her naked, and he kissed her breasts.

"Mmm, that's one of my favorites," she said. "You can do that as much as you like." She wrapped her legs about his bare torso.

"Is it always this awesome when people have sex?" she asked, gliding her fingers down his wet hair. "Why aren't people constantly doing this? I mean, who has time to eat or sleep when you can kiss and touch and, oh…I like that."

He suckled her nipple and teased at the skin with the tip of his fang. It was a brief glide of tooth over flesh, nothing promising, because he couldn't promise the bite. Much as he desired it. Her blood had been black and ichor laced last night. But there was no guarantee some angel blood did not linger.

"I'll show you what I'd prefer over eggs for breakfast," he whispered in her ear, then glided down to part her legs and kiss her copper thatch.

Zen chirped a surprised sound, then settled into the feeling. She lay back across the counter and allowed him to put her legs over his shoulders. Eventually her head tilted into the sink, so he moved her down onto the floor.

Half an hour later, he picked her up from the floor and carried her into the bedroom so they could finally get dressed.

"Why don't I give you a ride into town," he suggested. "You can pick up your car and pay off the room bill."

"Why? Don't I need the room anymore?"

He shrugged. "If you want to, you can stay here for a while. I'll have a talk with Oogie. Let him know you're cool."

"I'd like that. I can do some more shopping while in town, as well. I really enjoy shopping."

"I'll drop you off, then we'll meet later at Panera for the breakfast we ignored earlier. Deal?"

"Deal."

After he'd dropped Zen off at the inn, Blade drove into the filling station and topped off the gas tank. Then he stopped in at the local hardware store. Stryke had emailed a list of tools for him to pick up. Though they had hired a construction firm to build the compound, Stryke was also working on a porch for the main house. Said Blyss liked to sit out there on a swinging bench in the summer. And he wanted a place for the baby to play without toddling too far into the yard.

Stryke would probably be an overprotective father. Blade thought it would be wiser to let the infant run. Unless Stryke carried some latent faery or vampire in him, his child would be born werewolf. Its instincts would be to run free.

But what did he know about child rearing?

Blade wondered if a half-breed man could ever have a child with a woman of unknown nature. Then he caught himself and shook his head at such erratic thoughts. Children were not for him. He could barely get the love thing right.

Hadn't he fallen in love too quickly with the demoness Octavia? He didn't want to analyze it. He'd spent far too much time lamenting that decision in the days and weeks following her death.

Right now, he felt as though life nudged him to move forward. To set his past aside, and—though it could never be forgotten—forge a new future. The feeling was light, and as soon as he recognized it, he again shook his head.

Not in the cards for this unforgivable bastard.

Especially an unforgivable bastard who was currently on a crusade to assassinate every living demon he laid eyes on—as well as the undead ones. Yeah, there were breeds that were classified as undead.

Strolling past a coffee shop, he paused. The rich scent of dark roast curled into his nostrils and drew him in. He ordered a venti black, no cream, and then headed around the corner, down the alleyway. He had parked three blocks down from the hardware store. The town was small, which meant little to no parking, and it was Blade's habit to choose an out-of-the-way spot. One never knew when a demon—or angel—might leap out from nowhere. Best to contain any encounters and keep them from public eyesight as much as possible.

Striding through a shadow cast by a church steeple— he wasn't baptized, so holy objects and images had no power over him—Blade was suddenly ripped from his strides. His back slammed against a brick wall. Coffee splattered the concrete.

He reacted by swinging a punch toward the blond man's narrow face, but his fist stopped an inch from nose. Impact did not happen, and yet his knuckles crunched as if he'd just punched a steel wall.

The man dropped him and stepped back. Splaying his fingers up near his face revealed the dark markings on his skin. "Runes to ward me against whatever the hell you are, *hic niger est*."

"Who are you?" Blade asked of the creature who'd said he had a dark heart.

"Ah? You don't care *what* I am?"

"You're demon." Blade spat at the ground near the man's booted feet. He was as tall as he but slim, and his short blond hair was slicked back tightly against his scalp, the severe coif revealing the nubs of horns above each ear. "You've got two seconds before I kill you."

"Give it a go. Unlike the other demons you've slain thus far, I have come to this realm protected."

Blade afforded a more studied look over the runes marked in crossed black lines all over the demon's fingers, hands and neck. Below his ears ran a trail of the marks, as well. The demon's eyes flickered red, then resumed a fathomless black iris.

The demon offered his hand to shake. "Kesabel, Lord of the Casipheans. And you are Blade Saint-Pierre."

"What do you want?" Blade asked, ignoring the offer to shake.

Again the demon gripped him by the throat and slammed him to the wall. Blade's feet momentarily left the ground. He aimed a fist for the demon's gut but his knuckles crunched against an invisible steel barrier.

"Quit killing us," the demon hissed. "We are not the bad guys."

"Yeah? Then, why are you trying to kill Zen?"

"Is that what she told you?"

"She didn't have to tell me anything. I saw the trio you sent after her."

"They were sent to persuade her toward the portal. For some reason she has been able to resist our efforts. A major fuckup in the plan, let me tell you."

"What plan? To murder an innocent woman?"

The demon dropped Blade's throat. "We're on her side." Spreading out his arms, he declared royally, "She is our queen."

Chapter 19

Blade considered asking the demon to repeat himself. But there was no need. His hearing was excellent.

Zen was their *queen*? Whose queen? If she was any kind of paranormal breed, she was an angel. Though, there was the case of her blue blood turning black. Which was no longer blue but now black and then clear.

"Yes, I can see your confusion," the demon Kesabel offered. He stabbed the air. "Allow me to explain how the fallen angel you've hooked up with was supposed to fall all the way to Daemonia, yet, for some reason, did not."

"You're lying."

The demon spread his arms out. "I have no reason to."

"It is the demonic nature to speak mistruths. Always. You are trying to get me on your side so you can get your hands on Zen."

"I do want to get my hands on her, but I need her alive. The Casiphean queen must be crowned, and that can only occur in Daemonia."

"Casiphean?" Blade had heard the breed name, but that was all. He'd spent more time lamenting his involvement with the *mimicus* to bother learning about any other in the vast profusion of demonic breeds.

Kesabel nodded. "You don't know much about demons, do you?"

"I know I don't like you."

"Yes, well, I am familiar with your troubles regarding a denizen of *mimicus*. Tough bit of luck, eh?"

The scars on Blade's back twinged. "You could say that."

"And now it seems you've a death wish for all our species."

"You could say that, too."

"Isn't really fair, is it? To make all suffer for the sins of so few?"

The demon had no right to place himself above others when it concerned sin. "I thought we were talking about Zen. She is a fallen angel. I'm sure of it. She has her halo."

"Yes, you've guessed correctly about her. Fallen from Above. Yet she was supposed to fall to Daemonia. Why she stopped here on the mortal realm is beyond me. It was destined that she would become our queen. She should have been on board with the plan before falling. All she had to do was—" the demon spread out his arms "—spread her wings and let gravity do the rest."

"She landed here in Tangle Lake," Blade said.

Maybe. If she'd walked the world, as he suspected, then she could have landed anywhere. Tangle Lake may have just been a spot on her route to consume knowledge.

He wasn't trying to fill in details for the demon. He was attempting to piece this together for himself. He didn't trust the demon Kesabel as far as he could spit, but he'd listen. Until the urge struck to slice him in two.

"If you're so keen on welcoming her into your folds as queen," Blade said, "then, why the death threats?"

"Oh, we haven't laid a hand on her. Think about it."

He wasn't going to—but, really? The demons in the house hadn't gone near Zen. Because he had stopped them before they could leave the house. The demons in the club hadn't touched her, either. They had tried to lure her into the portal, though. Beyond that, it had only been *angels* who had attempted to physically harm Zen.

"You were the one who thought it would be a good idea to slay my minions in the house by the field," Kesabel said. "And you and that damned werewolf brother of yours thought it would be fun to slay an entire club filled with my kind. You get some kind of sexual thrill from that, buddy? Taking the lives of innocents?"

Demons were never innocent. But Blade wouldn't give the man the challenge of a protest.

"Right. You're not going to speak when you know I'm in the right," Kesabel said. "You, vampire, like the taste of demon blood. That is known."

Blade flinched at that statement. So his faery half craved demon blood. But it was known? Of course, Sim had said as much to him, as well. What was it with all the riffraff knowing so much about him and what it was that got him off?

"The only time I'm aware that Zenia has ever been in danger is when those damned angels landed," Kesabel provided. "They want to take her out before we can lure her to Daemonia. Or so it appears. Those holier-than-thou assholes are possessive. Even though she's no longer of their lofty caliber, they'd rather kill her than see we Casipheans gain our queen."

"*Lure* her to Daemonia?"

"Yes. You see, it's not as if we can tie her up and take her there. She has to sit on the throne voluntarily. Thus, the portal in the club. It's a straight shot to Daemonia from there. If you'll just allow her to return to the night-club, that'll take care of matters nicely."

That was going to happen never. Unless Zen wanted to be queen. The woman did have amnesia.

"What if she doesn't want to be your queen?"

"Oh, she does. That's the very reason she fell."

"But she doesn't remember that."

"She—what?"

"So you don't know everything." Blade crossed his arms and spread his feet for a commanding stance. "Zen has amnesia. She doesn't know who or what she was or where she came from. You might believe she's your queen, but she doesn't know that."

"Well, that's a bit of tough balls." The demon's temples flared and the tips of the horn nubs briefly glowed red. "I sense we won't have any luck luring her to the throne until she gets her memory back."

"Why would you crown an angel your queen anyway?"

"She is no longer angel. The moment she landed on earth her angelic nature vaporized, so to speak. Though I've never heard of an angel losing their memory from landing in the mortal realm. Most arrive without memory of their angelic rank, but they walk the world to gain knowledge so they can insinuate into this realm."

"She was hit by a bus."

"Is that so?" Kesabel noticeably shuddered. "So she's in memory limbo."

"So is Zen demon?" Blade had to ask.

"She'll not become completely demon until she takes the throne."

Blade hissed. Hell, she was demon. Or would be soon enough.

And he had sworn to slay any demon that crossed his path. This was not good. Worse than not good. It sucked fifty ways to Beneath. But just because the demon talked a feasible story didn't mean he was speaking the truth.

"But until that occurs," Kesabel continued, "she is a sort of nothing, if you will. Much closer to faery, actually, than angel or demon. That's what happens when an angel doesn't quite make it to demon. They become sidhe. Curse those bastard angels! There is a time frame we are working with. Not sure how long it'll require for her faery to completely settle in. I'm pleased you let me in on the amnesia issue, despite the new challenge this presents."

Shit. No points for helping the enemy.

"So," Kesabel said, "I'll be needing you to, A, stop slaying my Casiphean denizen. Our race is dying out. It's why we need the queen in the first place, to repopulate our numbers. And, B, take the girl out for a night of dancing at the club and then ditch her and leave her to bigger and better things."

Repopulate their numbers? Blade didn't want to consider how that one would go down. No matter what Zen remembered, or wanted to do, he could not allow her to be used in such a manner.

Fingers curling into fists at his sides, Blade said, "How about C? None of the above."

The demon thrust Blade against the wall with but a

flick of his wrist. "Don't make me call in the big guns, vampire."

Blade smirked. He liked a challenge. "The bigger the better. Now fuck off. And stay away from Zen. If I see one of you sulfurheads near her, I will slay you."

The demon exhaled heavily and shook his head. "You don't want this war, Saint-Pierre. And yet, it seems you invite trouble around every corner. Perhaps it is your nature. You cannot exist without strife?"

He'd love to live a peaceful life without war. Or demons.

"Bring it," Blade muttered. He wandered off, leaving the demon lurking in the shadows.

"Help!"

Zen looked up from the coffee she was stirring. Outside the café window a woman whose arms were loaded with two toddlers was trying to catch the handle of a stroller, in which lay a baby, as it rolled toward the street. A big black car veered near the curb.

Dashing out from the table and through the café doors, Zen yelled at the driver, but knew that he wouldn't hear her through the car's rolled-up windows. She dodged the mother who was crying and—why didn't she set the kids down?

Without thinking Zen lunged toward the stroller. Its front wheels rolled off the curb. The stroller tilted forward. The sun glinted on the car's chrome bumper, but a foot away from the infant carrier.

She felt the warm body under her palm and curled her fingers about an arm or leg, grasping more baby with her other hand, and snatched it just as the bumper hit the stroller and sent it soaring through the air.

The mother screamed.

Zen tilted her body backward, landing on the concrete sidewalk, the infant clutched against her chest. She fell to her back and pulled up her legs from the street.

"She's got the baby!" someone said.

Above her, two faces appeared. Zen handed up the infant and it was delivered to the distraught mother. Heartbeats thundered. Adrenaline raced. And in the moment the sun flickered in her eyes, Zen's memory burst with a familiar reckoning.

You came here with a purpose. You are from Above.

And she knew what she was.

A hand lifted her by the arm and asked if she was all right. Zen nodded. "Yes, okay." She walked away, even as someone followed her, asking her to stay because she was a hero.

"Anyone would have done it," she muttered and quickened her steps away from the growing crowd around the mother and her children.

"I…" She pressed fingers to her temples. "I remember."

Chapter 20

Blade grabbed the newly purchased tools out of the truck bed and carried them up to Stryke's work shed. His brother wasn't around, which was a good thing. Blade's mind was anywhere but in the moment. It was still back in the alleyway, shoved up against the wall by that arrogant demon.

Kesabel? Did he know someone, anyone, who had knowledge of demons and who might tell him something about the pale intruder? Maybe Dez, who studied diabology, could help him?

None of that mattered right now. Zen was destined to become a demon queen? That was twenty ways wrong. She'd fallen from Above with the intention of being crowned queen.

So why was he trying to stop that from happening?

Because until now he hadn't known it was supposed to go down that way. And now that he did, what would he do? Would it be fair to Zen to force her to become something she had no knowledge of agreeing to? Maybe being crowned the Casiphean queen would bring back her memory?

Only one thing mattered. Zen was destined to become demon. And that trumped all.

He'd opened his home and his life to a woman who was demon. Or who was supposed to become demon. But according to Kesabel, if she remained in this realm for much longer she could instead become faery.

He set the skill saw on a workbench and decided against leaving Stryke a note. His brother would figure things out when he saw the tools. Hopping back into the rusty old white Ford he'd driven because his usual ride did indeed need a new radiator, Blade shifted into gear, but didn't take his foot off the brake pedal. "Ah, hell, I forgot."

He was supposed to meet Zen at Panera. And... He glanced at the dashboard clock. He was an hour late.

He tugged out his cell phone, then remembered she didn't have a phone. Nor did she know her real name. Neither did she know her wicked destiny.

Gripping the steering wheel he squeezed.

Could he tell her? Had he a right to tell her? What if he kept this information to himself? He could continue to slay any demon that went near Zen and take out the occasional angel, as well. She'd never have to know.

As long as she never got back her memory.

"Stupid," he muttered, and shifted into gear, letting the truck roll down the gravel road. The two of them had started something. A relationship of sorts. Maybe? He'd been firm about not being friends with her. Look what had come of that.

It was a relationship. And that bond demanded truth and trust. "I have to tell her."

And then it would be up to Zen to decide which direction her future would move—toward continuing the relationship with him, or toward Daemonia.

Blade knew what he wanted her to decide. He didn't

want to hope, either, but somewhere along the line he'd fallen for the woman. Fangs, wings and heart.

Pulling into the garage beneath the loft, Blade was relieved to see Zen's Mini parked outside. Of course, he had invited her to stay with him. She had nowhere else to go.

He'd invited a demon queen to stay with him. What. The. Hell?

And she would probably be angry. He had stood her up for lunch.

So the best way to do this, he decided as he strode up the stairs, was to blurt out everything he had to say right away. Distract her from his mistake of being late. Make it all about her. Because it was.

This situation had become all about her in all the wrong ways.

He couldn't think about it that way. She deserved compassion and understanding. And probably a place to sit and a shoulder to cry on after he revealed her truth. He could do that. He wanted to do that. Because Zen meant something to him. And yet the thought to push her away was strong.

He smelled something savory as he topped the stairs and Oogie scampered up to curl about his ankle. She was cooking again? This could not end well.

Bending to give the attention-starved feline a scratch at the base of his spine, Blade scooped up the purring cat and wandered toward the kitchen. Zen pulled a couple bowls out of the microwave oven. Oogie didn't even flinch when he entered the kitchen. Had the two come to some kind of understanding?

She spied him. "Oh, hi! I'm so sorry, but I missed our date."

"Uh, you did?"

Oogie squirmed in his grasp so he let the now-nervous cat drop to the floor to race out of the room. Did the cat know what she really was? Oogie liked demons less than Blade did. Hell, Oogie had known all along. What an idiot he had been not to pay more attention to his pet's discomfort around her.

"So we missed our date. But you brought home supper?" he asked.

"As an apology. I was so busy shopping—I really like shopping. And I got this!" She shifted her hip forward to display the rhinestone-encrusted belt wrapped around her pink sundress. The woman did love to sparkle. "Anyway, the time slipped away from me. It's baked potato soup with bacon and cheese. Doesn't that sound delicious? And I didn't cook it. It's from the restaurant, so it's safe. Oh! Guess what?"

"I, uh…"

She wasn't angry. She was just her usual, gorgeous, bright self. Completely unaware. And always trying to please him, of all things.

"Zen, we need to talk. I learned something today—"

"So did I." She set the bowls on the counter and took his hand. "I rescued a baby."

"You—what?" This conversation was all over the place. Blade needed to give her the truth about herself. Before he chickened out and decided to keep it to himself. "Listen, Zen, there's something you should know."

"Exactly." She beamed up at him, her eyes as bright as rhinestones. "I *do* know. Blade, after I rescued the baby, I experienced this weird zinging jolt to my head. And then…"

"And then?"

"I remembered." She grabbed his hands and bounced with giddy glee. "I know who I am."

Chapter 21

Her eyes were emerald, Blade realized. Not kaleidoscope, as would be an angel's eyes. Nor were they red, as would be a demon's eyes. Not even violet, indicative of the sidhe. And she stood…straighter. With more poise than he had noted up to this point. She exuded well-being and a certain strength. Confidence. Not to mention the effusive joy that spilled from her like sunshine.

She had come into herself. Because she had remembered. And Blade found himself walking up to her to be close, a part of her excitement, and yet, at the same time, his heart cringed and dropped.

She knew.

Would she walk away from him now? Go on to become a demon queen? The thought was revolting to him. But was it more because of the idea of losing someone who was a species he hated or whom he was starting to care about?

She took his hands and was literally bouncing on her toes. "I fell," she said. "And I am meant to be the Casiphean queen."

Yep, she knew it all. Damn. He'd lost this one. But had she ever been his? Did it matter to him?

Yes. Damn it, yes. She'd touched his scars. She'd kissed them. Had accepted him.

"So you know that you were once an angel?" he asked.

She nodded. "I fell with a purpose. Or so I assume. I know who I was and that I fell to become a queen, but there's some fuzzy stuff in there, too. It'll probably come back to me slowly. Or who knows? Maybe it'll pop back into my head if I have another harrowing moment like the one with the baby."

"The baby?"

"I saved a baby from being hit by a car. I think, in that moment, with my heart pumping and my body out of sorts, is when it all returned. Anyway, I know there is a denizen of demons awaiting their queen."

"And…you're eager to join them?"

"Well." She squeezed his hand and settled her enthusiasm. "I know how you feel about demons. I'm so sorry to give you this news."

"No, that's okay." It was far from okay, but he wasn't going to spoil her good mood. He had no right. "My only goal was to help you get your memory back. Now you have it. What happens next…" No, he couldn't tell her what he wanted to happen next. "You gotta do what you gotta do."

"And so do you. Which is slaying demons. Does that mean you're going to slay me now?"

"Don't be ridiculous." He crossed his arms over his chest. Yeah, put up a shield. Easier that way. "You still bleeding ichor as well as the black stuff?"

"Not sure. Do you want to check again?"

"No, that's uh…"

Words felt wrong. He could never harm her. But

could she really walk away from him and put on a demon crown like a pretty accessory? Never looking back at what could have been?

What could have been with him. Ah, hell, he'd gone and started caring for this woman. Just like before.

And just like before, she was demon.

But at least this time he had advance warning of her nature. Not that it would do his hurting heart any good. The damage had been done.

She'd touched him.

"Blade." She stroked his hair and caressed his cheek. He almost pulled away, but then he realized if he did, he might be pulling away from the last touch she would ever give him. "What we've started? I like it. The sex. The sharing and companionship. The trust."

Trust was everything. And now he could not trust her.

Or could he?

"But I've always had it in the back of my mind that you would never commit to me," she continued. "Because you couldn't be sure what I was."

"And now I know."

"And it's not your favorite species in the world. Well. I'm not demon yet. Right now I'm sort of in the middle. Becoming, like the witch said. I could become faery if I stayed here on the mortal realm."

"But you won't do that because you have a goal. A destiny."

"Yes. Destiny." She sighed. Her giddy smile did not escape his notice. But she saw him looking at her and pulled on a straight face. "You're upset. Do you... Blade, do you care about me?"

If he lied he'd lose her. If he told the truth, his heart would break. He didn't like either option.

She bracketed his head, slipping her fingers through his hair, and kissed him. Urgently. Deeply. Forever. And it felt as though he was falling alongside an angel swiftly plummeting from Above. Her wings enveloped him and he felt safe—yet leery. He didn't want either of them to land. Could he stop this fall and keep her in a free fall forever?

He wrapped his hands around her back and pulled her in. What luck that the second time he should find someone to care about she turned out to be another demon. Did the gods have something against him? Was he never meant to be happy?

Don't think about it. Take this kiss. Remember it. Never forget the intensity of it. The soft regard of it. The knowing that it was more right than any kiss he'd ever had before.

Take the fall.

Because Zen made him realize that it didn't matter what you were but who you were. What went on in your thoughts, and how you responded to the actions of others. To arrogantly assume that all demons should die simply because one group of them had hurt him? How dare he? He wasn't making the world a better place. He was harming it. Demon by demon.

Blade stood back, still holding Zen's head between his hands. He pressed his forehead to hers. He wanted to ask her, to beg her to stay. To be his. To be the demon he could welcome without judgment.

To be his woman.

But something kept that want from leaping free.

She pulled his hands from her head, and as she lowered them, he reluctantly dropped their connection. "I'm heading to the club tonight," she said. "You know, the place with the portal."

Whoa. She was moving fast. And with a determination that felt similar to when he'd been going after demons.

"There's just one thing," she said, and she turned to pick up the halo from the couch. "I'm not sure why I held on to this. Like I said, some things are fuzzy. But it'll be a nice souvenir, I guess. I'll see if I can take it with me."

So it was as easy as that for her? Memory returned. Back to her mission. Leave the vampire standing in the lurch.

Of course it had to be that easy.

"What's wrong, Blade?"

"I, uh…" Sighing out his apprehension, Blade pulled back his shoulders and blurted out what had to be said, "I talked to Kesabel earlier today."

"Kesabel?"

"You don't know that name?" Shouldn't she know the leader of the demon denizen she was to eventually help repopulate? Although, he wasn't sure if Kesabel was the leader. He had named himself lord of the Casipheans. Whatever that meant. "He's demon. The Casiphean agent come to this realm to ensure you complete your journey to Daemonia."

"Oh. So you knew? Why didn't you say anything?"

"I was going to, but you and your happy bouncing feet beat me to it."

She nodded. Bounced once more. "It's pretty cool, isn't it?"

No. Not cool at all.

"You betcha. Cool. Are you sure about this, Zen? I mean, you don't even know these demons. And to become their queen... That's a big commitment."

"Oh, listen to you, the master of avoiding commitment."

That snarky response slapped Blade across the face as if her hand had done it. He touched his cheek, because the feeling was that palpable. "I suppose you did want this. It's why you fell."

She nodded. "I can't say why I want this, but if I made the fall it must have been for good reason. So you want some soup?"

Soup? What the— On to a new tangent when he was still drowning in the reality of her truth? Blade shoved his hands into his jeans' pockets. "I'm not hungry. But thanks for thinking of me."

"Then, I should probably get going. Things to do before I leave. I was going to donate the car to a homeless shelter. Would that be okay?"

She had really thought this through. "Great idea." He forced on a smile.

"Then, I'll be seeing you!"

She grabbed the backpack by the fridge and headed toward the stairs. Blade couldn't bring himself to call out to her, to ask her to reconsider. To stay. To stop the fall to Daemonia.

She had a mission. He had no right to stop her.

And he had made the fall—only to crash, wings splayed and heart completely shattered.

Zen drove mindlessly toward town. The birch trees lining the gravel road shushed by like slats on a fence and revealed open field at the stop where she turned left and drove toward Tangle Lake.

She'd had to leave Blade's place quickly. And without lingering in that incredible kiss. A kiss that had felt like falling. A good kind of falling. But to stay and draw out her exit would have killed her.

Why had she had to remember that she was waited for by an entire demon race? That they needed her to take her place as their queen? To marry and repopulate a dying breed. She'd not told Blade that part. He wouldn't have taken it lightly.

"I'm a queen?" she muttered. And then with the pride it instilled within her, she announced, "I'm a queen. That's cool. Right? Queens get crowns. I could so rock a crown."

Her fingers curved tightly about the steering wheel as anxiety reared up. "Why?" she asked. She didn't want to lead a denizen of demons. Or an entire race. She didn't need the crown. She just wanted to stand in Blade's arms and know he loved her.

But she'd had to leave. Because he'd never said he loved her.

The man—vampire, faery—had just been helping her to get her memory back. A man who had been hurt in the past because he had loved a demoness. There was no way she could expect him to accept her truth now.

She had lost him.

As much as she'd wanted to stay, leaving had been her only option.

She touched her mouth, trying to remember the irrepressible heat of his kiss. Too quickly it faded. She couldn't remember his mouth against hers. She needed that feeling back!

Slowing at a stop sign at the entry to town, she shifted into Park and bowed her head against the steering wheel.

"I don't want to do this."

But she had been destined to this. By falling she had taken on the task, had agreed to this monumental undertaking. She mustn't disappoint the Casipheans. For if she did, might she risk their anger and a rage of demons storming this mortal realm?

If Blade thought he could take out the few demons that tread this earth now, he'd never be able to handle an entire rage. She had to do this. To save Blade.

Chapter 22

A shout from outside the barn alerted Blade. He rested his elbows on the battered hood of the truck. There was no saving this heap. The angel had obliterated the radiator and the surrounding engine and he bet Beck would tell him he needed to install a whole new engine. He had a few vehicles to choose from to drive, so he'd junk this one. The rusted white Ford had started to leak oil when he'd returned home earlier so he'd drive the Mustang for a while.

The shout came again and he recognized it as his father's voice.

"In here!" Blade called. He flexed his fingers in and out of fists. He wasn't in the mood to talk to anyone.

Zen had run away from him. She hadn't been able to get away from him fast enough. Away, and then on to Daemonia. Where she would be crowned a queen. That had to count for something.

And really, he knew not all demons were evil. He just didn't like them as a species. And he had every right to that opinion.

But he needed to talk to Sim. This was no longer his war. Blade couldn't, in good conscience, slay the next demon he saw. Not if it was Zen.

"What the hell happened to the truck?" Kai asked as he strolled into the evening shadows of the garage. His father wore a T-shirt, suede jeans and was barefoot. The lack of footwear was a wolf thing that Blade had picked up as a child.

"Had a disagreement with an angel." He wiped the grease from his hands on a cloth, then tossed it aside to the open toolbox. "What's up, Dad?"

"I do believe I've outdone myself."

Kai pulled a sword from behind his back and handed it, hilt up, to Blade. "All it took was some of your mother's faery dust, and I was able to manipulate the metal. Still don't know what kind of metal it is, but it's strong and true. This blade needs but to whisper across flesh to draw a deep cut."

The sword blade was about a foot and a half long, and it was wide, honed to cut along each edge. It gleamed and seemed to sing as Blade turned it side to side to look it over. The hilt was simple, wrapped in black leather and impressed with the Saint-Pierre monogram. Yet where the blade joined the hilt words had been impressed in a language Blade did not understand.

"Sidhe writing?"

"It means *warrior*," Kai offered. "Your mother thought it appropriate for you. Can't say that I ever wish for you to be in a situation where you'd need such a weapon, but if so, then you will be well armed. You like it?"

"It's amazing, Dad." He swung the sword, testing the weight. It was light, and yet as he curved through the thrust, the weapon carried a definite direction, a focus. Wielding this he could take out a line of demons with but a sweep of his hand. Or one pissed-off angel. "Thank you."

"My pleasure. It'll probably kill angels. Uh, you don't think there are any more angels walking around Tangle Lake, do you?"

"Not sure." Because if they were determined to stop Zen from making it to Daemonia, now would be the time to kick it into high gear and invade. Did Kesabel know about the angels who were after his queen? "Zen got her memory back."

"Yeah? So what's up with her?"

"She's a fallen angel who was supposed to fall all the way to Daemonia to become the Casiphean queen."

Kai was rarely speechless, but that announcement hit its mark. His dad leaned a palm on the truck bed and raked fingers through his shoulder-length hair.

"She remembered falling, and that she has a mission," Blade explained. "She was hit by the bus, so some memories are a little fuzzy."

"Yikes. So why didn't she fall all the way to Daemonia? Why stop on this realm? I can't imagine the bus stopped such a momentous fall."

"That's the question. And—" Blade swung the sword before him in an exact cut through the air "—she's still got her halo."

"I thought the halo fell away from the angel during the fall?" Kai said.

"Exactly. So she must have been holding it."

And then it hit him like a demon fist colliding with his heart. Blade's jaw dropped open. Nothing felt more true to him. Nothing.

"Because she didn't want to go all the way to Daemonia," he muttered.

"What?" Kai asked.

"Dad, I think having the halo in hand kept her here

on this realm. Has to be," he said, working the options through. "She didn't want to become their queen."

"But why not?"

He met his dad's wondering gaze. "I have no idea. But I don't have time to wonder. I've got to save Zen before she makes a huge mistake. Will you lock up for me?"

Blade grabbed the keys for the 1964 Mustang he'd fixed last year but which was still waiting for a coat of paint. He slid in behind the steering wheel.

"Need me to come along?" Kai called as Blade backed out of the garage.

He could use backup. But he wasn't about to put his father in danger. His mother would never forgive him. "I've got this, Dad! If you see Trouble, tell him I went back to the club."

Because if Trouble showed, then he'd have all the help he needed.

"I'll give him a call!" Kai said, waving him off. "Is she worth it?"

Blade backed the Mustang down the gravel driveway. Worth it? Hell yes.

Zen entered the mansion with a confidence that virtually floated her across the marble floor. The dancing crowd silenced at the sight of her. They were people. And demons. Or maybe demons that wore a human disguise. All eyes were red. And it didn't disturb her.

Because they were *her* people.

Or that was what she told herself. She didn't really have a people at the moment. She wasn't fully demon. Nor was she fully angel. She could become…

Could she toss the crown aside and become something else?

She paused at the edge of the dance floor that now flickered to darkness as the music was pulled to a halt. A few dancers looked around like "what happened?" until they noticed her standing there in a simple yellow dress that fluttered to below her knees. Were they all stuck in this nightclub endlessly dancing in wait to lure her toward the portal?

The thought creeped her out. Why not just walk up and ask, "Will you join us? Be our queen?"

The demons on the dance floor separated to form an open aisle for her that led up to the pulsating red oval of—now she was close enough to see it—fire. A fire that blazed yet didn't seem to give off heat.

The doorway to her destiny. The beginning of her life as a queen who would repopulate the Casiphean denizens and bring—well, she was fuzzy on the details.

Just like she was still unclear on how she'd landed in Tangle Lake. Angels never failed in their course. So why had she?

The clank of the halo, secured at the thin rhinestone chain she'd belted around her waist, alerted her. She shouldn't have brought it along. The Casipheans would view it as something that belonged to their enemy.

Really? If she had originated as the enemy, why now did she intend to walk through the portal to become their queen? Another question that didn't make sense. But she was missing all the information that would put the pieces together and show her the complete picture.

Zen didn't want to turn and look over her shoulder for him.

But she did.

Why she thought Blade would be standing there in the center of the aisle, arms held out to receive her was a question she could not answer. And shouldn't answer. She had a duty. All those standing in silence around her waited for her to accept that calling.

She turned toward the portal, trying to avoid eye contact, but it was impossible not to. Red eyes looked hopeful. Even pleading. Some thrust back their shoulders in defiance, while the ones standing next to them clasped their hands, settling their ire.

Zen set her gaze straight ahead for the portal even as a vile shriek echoed up from the ranks at the back of the nightclub. Demons all around her mobilized. Feet scuffled and the ripple of wings unfurled. While a few remained at her side, bowing, encouraging her to walk forward into the flames, she was aware of so many others who shifted into their demonic forms and soared away.

As if in defense.

Swinging the halo blade obliterated the vanguard of demons charging Blade. Black blood spattered his face and shoulders. He licked it off his lips. The faery in him grinned. *Oh, yeah, that hit the spot.* His fangs descended, eager for a longer, deeper drink.

He didn't hesitate on the upswing, returning the blade across the throats and chests of the next assault. From behind, he was attacked. Claws cut through his shirt and skin. Teeth gnawed at his boot. He kicked aimlessly, and managed to unloose the ravenous threat.

Ahead, the flaming portal glowed. And silhouetted before it stood Zen, looking small and alone, lost in a greater plan that he feared might swallow her up. She couldn't step through that portal until she knew what he had guessed. He had to at least try to make her hear him.

Taking a fist to his jaw, he growled at the perpetrator. He grabbed him by the shoulder and sank his fangs into the sinuous black-fleshed neck. Lusciously bitter demon blood oozed over his palate. It tasted so good. Because of the ichor running through his system, and in his saliva, the demon yowled from the burning bite and scrambled off, clutching its neck. It wouldn't survive long.

"Zen!" His shout was lost in the melee of crazed demons who wanted to ensure their queen made it to the throne. "Zen!"

She was so close. Blade took a knee-bending hit to the back of his legs. Felt as if he'd been plowed into by a truck. He wobbled, grasping at the closest thing—a demon's bald and slimy head—to break his fall. An inhale filled his lungs with sulfur. His faery pleaded for release. And just as he began to unfurl his wings, the next injury he took was a deep cut to his chest that spilled out his blood, dazzled with ichor. The attacker retreated from the sting of the ichor. It could eat away a demon's skin in seconds.

Now thoroughly angered, Blade unfurled his wings. The serrated edges cut through demon throats and appendages and sent some fleeing, while others dived for him, only to be slashed away by a precise sweep of wing.

Ahead, a wall of demons began to form, literally, demons climbing atop one another's shoulders and linking arms before the dance floor to block him from getting near Zen.

Blade charged the wall. Wings lifting him into a soar,

he glided to the top of the demonic wall and slashed the halo sword. He managed to bring down three from the top row, which then toppled them all.

And behind them Zen turned to see Blade land on the dance floor twenty feet away from where she stood. He spread his wings wide to prevent the demons from getting near her, but felt the enemy beat against his wings repeatedly. He couldn't hold them off much longer.

"You held the halo tight so you wouldn't land in Daemonia!" he yelled. "You don't want this, Zen. Don't go!"

She unlatched the halo secured at her hip and looked at it. A crew of demons that flanked her gestured for her to walk toward the portal. Of course, they couldn't touch her, or even push her through. As Kesabel had explained, she had to enter Daemonia of her free will.

"Think about it!" he called. A demon landed on his shoulders and fangs sank into his skull above the ear. Blade reached up and ripped the intruder away, flinging it toward an oncoming pack of its brethren. "Come with me!"

"I…" She clutched the halo with both hands. "I don't know!"

Blade rushed for her, grabbing her by the shoulders. He coiled his wings around them to give them a momentary shield. Her heartbeats were palpable against his palms. Frightened blue irises sought his eyes. Secluding her within his wings, he spoke from his heart. "Zen, you have a choice to step through that portal and become queen. Or…"

"Or?" Her fingers clutched his shirt. Desperation glowed in her eyes.

His heart prodded him toward truth. Surrender. Want. "You choose me."

The brightness he so admired returned to her eyes. Zen exhaled a heavy gasp. "I wasn't aware you were an option."

"I am."

The demons shrieked an awful chorus of mayhem. As soon as Zen's hand landed in Blade's, he knew what she'd decided.

"I choose you," she said.

"Let's get out of here." He pulled her across the dance floor littered with slippery demon blood and some of his own, for sure.

Once outside, they were followed by the denizen but not attacked. They couldn't risk harming their queen. The sky blackened, the moon blinking out as the rage pursued from the sky. Blade pushed Zen in through the driver's side of the Mustang and slid in after her. He risked the rage following him home, but what was worse was the strange cloud looming out from the top of the spooky mansion-cum-nightclub.

"What is that?" he muttered as he backed up, plowing over a couple demons in the process. "Zen, are you okay?"

She studied the halo in her hand. Nodding, she didn't reply.

The cloud moved toward them. He slammed on the gas pedal and barreled down the country road. "Zen?"

She remained silent, turning the halo over in her grasp. Stunned? Under some kind of demonic power?

"Zen!" He shook her by the shoulder and she startled out of it.

"I'm good," she said. "Just need to process."

He smiled at that. She was always good and in need of processing. God, he loved her. He actually loved her.

"I think they're pulling back," he said, observing the sky in the rearview mirror. "What the hell? It's as though they don't want to get too close to you unless it's before that fiery portal."

A mile away from the nightmare he realized the rage had given up on tracking him. But the thick black cloud, as big as a football field, loomed directly overhead. It wasn't composed of demons, and didn't look like bats or even insects. It was a mist, cloud-like.

Some kind of demonic tracking system? Whatever it was, it wouldn't be able to fly over his property, for he'd warded the skies above for many miles.

All that mattered was that Zen sat next to him. She had chosen him. But what was she thinking now? She hadn't stopped turning the halo over and over. It was as if she were enraptured by it. A remnant of her fall. A reminder of her destiny. Was she reconsidering?

She could be.

A trickle of anxiety tightened his grip on the steering wheel and he couldn't force himself to look at the beautiful woman beside him. How long did he have before she left him again in pursuit of a crown? Had he done the right thing?

Hell. This love stuff was a lot harder than it had been before. He'd made the wrong move.

Blade parked the Mustang inside the garage, got out, slammed the door and strode up to the barn. He took the stairs two at a time, disappearing from Zen's view before she got the car door open and slid out onto the dirt garage floor. Angry? He seemed so. A man who had just battled dozens of demons to rescue her had a right to anger.

But had it been a rescue?

She turned the halo over, remembering what he'd shouted to her. She'd held tight to this when falling so she wouldn't land in Daemonia? But why? Why fall with the intent of meeting her destiny as the Casiphean queen, and then—not?

It was late. It was dark down in the garage, and Zen was oddly hungry. She needed to think about this. But at the same time, she'd just walked away from destiny and toward something entirely unplanned.

"Blade."

She glanced up toward the ceiling, where his footsteps were imperceptible. He had offered himself to her as an option. And she had taken that option. So what was up with his sudden need for distance now?

She ran up the stairs to the loft. He stood before the cathedral windows looking out at the waxing moon. The black cloud hovered over the dark forest, but it didn't encroach on his property.

Zen approached slowly. "Thank you," she said, slipping the halo around her wrist to let it dangle. "I think."

The weapon around her wrist felt as if it belonged to her. It did belong to her. But she knew well that when an angel fell from Above the halo fell away. Those angels destined to seek their muse did so, never caring to find the lost halo. Others, well, who knew?

She knew that the halo contained the angel's earthbound soul. To place it atop their head in its original position would restore that soul and make them completely mortal. Human.

It had not fallen away from her. Because...

"I *did* hold on to the halo as I fell," she said with surprise. She wrinkled a brow. She knew that as fact, and yet— "But I'm not sure why. When I figure that out, I'll know whether or not I should return to the portal or run like hell. Blade?"

She touched his shoulder and he flinched. Demon blood spattered his neck. His bare back boasted bloody smears. Yet Zen could see the fresh wounds had healed. Most of them.

He'd taken more scars to save her. He was reliving the one nightmare he'd fiercely tried to never live again. Because of her.

"You have every right to be angry with me," she said quietly. "But I never asked you to rescue me."

He twisted his head around and the darkness in his eyes sucked away her breath.

"Wh-what's wrong? Did I do something to make you so angry?"

He exhaled, his shoulders falling. The sword he held firmly, he tilted out to the side. Streaked with black demon blood, it glinted in the moonlight. He was a warrior to the bone.

"You just left," he said. "Walked away without a goodbye or even bothering to ask if I wanted you to leave."

Because she'd had a destiny to meet. And yet she'd had to force herself to leave him.

Zen bowed her head, glancing over the floorboards. "I didn't think you cared."

He noticeably stiffened. The sword fell to his side.

"You've made it very clear you are not interested in a relationship," she continued, daring to meet his eyes. "You never said you love me."

"I offered myself as a choice!"

"And I took that option! Yet why do I feel it was just a ruse to get me away from the portal?"

"A ruse?"

He turned. Sliding a forefinger down the blade he held, he wiped the black blood from it. He lifted his bloodied fingers to his mouth, and just when Zen thought he'd lick it, he flicked his fingers aside and tossed the halo blade to the floor, as well.

Her heart fluttered, but she wasn't sure if she felt anticipatory or fearful. His eyes were so dark. Had his wings been out surely she would have screamed.

And then he did the most remarkable thing.

Blade dropped to his knees before her. Eyes brightening and fixed to hers, he said, "I love you, Zen. I should have told you. But I didn't want to stand in the way of your destiny."

She brushed his hair over his ear, which glowed bright blue under the moonlight. "Truly?"

He nodded. "I mean it. I love you. You've made my life…lighter. You make me want to leave my past where it is."

"But that means you've fallen in love with a demon queen. That goes against all that you've tried to protect yourself from. And what of your deal with Sim to slay all the demons?"

"It's done. I won't harm another soul unless it first intends you harm."

Still on his knees, he clasped his arms about her hips and pressed his face against her belly. And he didn't say anything, because he didn't need to. Zen ran her fingers through his hair and bowed over him. At this moment he was most vulnerable, and she wanted him to know that he was safe with her. Because she knew who she was. Strong, capable, determined. An angel on a quest to become.

Could she love him when there was something that felt so much greater standing between them? She wanted to. But she didn't want to let him down, if she ultimately descended to Daemonia to take the crown.

But she couldn't tell him that. Not now when it was apparent this man needed her.

And she needed him.

Kneeling before him, she kissed Blade. "I think I've fallen far enough."

He nodded. "Stay here with me. You didn't intend to fall all the way to Daemonia. There's a reason behind your hanging on to the halo. We'll find out what that reason was. I'll help you."

"I'd like that. But what I'd like even more is a kiss." She kissed him. "And a hug." She fell into his hug and he stood, lifting her in his arms. "Take me to bed, Blade."

Chapter 23

"If you can hear me, Sim—and I'm sure you can—we need to talk."

Blade stepped onto the grass behind the barn and scanned the darkness. Zen was inside, sleeping peacefully in her bed after they'd made love. She was his.

For now. And…he would have to be cool with that.

Above, the black cloud had left the sky. Or maybe it was hovering over the Darkwood, out of his vision and looming at the edge of his property, which only cut into a small portion of the forest. He stepped across the grounds, shifting as he did so. He'd left his shirt off and worn a loose pair of jeans in anticipation of the shift. His wings cut the air and soared him up over the Darkwood treetops. No black cloud up here.

Arrowing toward the freshwater stream that cut through the north side of the woods, he this time sent out a mental call to Sim.

He landed at the edge of the stream, his bare feet sinking into the cool water. Bending, he plucked up a small stone and skipped it across the shallow water. A rabbit tucked in the undergrowth scampered out and away, its white tail bobbing.

A scatter of crickets suddenly stopped chirping. Even

the breeze stilled. Something had arrived. It wasn't wolf, demon or even of this realm.

Why hadn't he picked up on that before?

Blade stretched out his wings and turned to face the approaching entity. Halo blade held at the ready, he waited for whatever stalked through the trees. He used the darkness as camouflage, but was aware the moonlight on his wings or hair would give him away in a flash. So be it. Whatever approached must do so knowing exactly what waited for it.

A blue glow preceded the stranger's sure strides.

"Angel," Blade murmured. He swung the blade in a defiant slash before him. "Come at me, other one!"

The angel stepped into view, and Blade saw the blue glow was actually its wings. The shape of feathers was crafted as if with finely wrought blue LEDs, like one of those fast-action photos a person takes while drawing with light. Yet the wings moved as if fashioned from feathers, while Blade knew they were not. Wearing some kind of draped loincloth over its muscled hips, the angel resembled something a medieval artist might have painted.

Perhaps it *was* biblical.

And when its face pierced a ray of moonlight and the odd gill-like scars were revealed, Blade hissed out an oath. "You?"

Sim bowed his head and stretched out his arms as if to accept the accusation, but with a prideful smirk. "You called me?"

The bastard was an angel. Why hadn't he assumed that from the start? Who—or rather, what—would want to extinguish demons? And ultimately Zen.

"Stay away from her!" Blade warned. "She is no longer one of you."

"Until she ceases to breathe this mortal air, the being you call Zen will be a problem." The angel's wing slashed forward. "Just as you have become a problem, vampire. I sense you've given up the quest to slay demons?"

"I won't be a party to the senseless destruction. And now that I know Zen might become demon—"

"She was destined to become demon! And yet she changed that destiny." Sim dashed his wingtip before Blade, the hiss of it as tangible as a steel sword.

Blade jerked his head backward, avoiding the cut of the deadly wing. He swung up the blade, parting the retreating feathers in the odd blue appendage, but not cutting.

The angel hissed. "Where did you get that weapon? It feels angelic."

"Fashioned this from a halo. A halo I got from one of you guys. Picked it out of his crystal ash."

"You must stop killing our kind!"

"Yeah? Why is it both the demons and the angels think asking me to stop killing them is going to work?"

"You are bloodthirsty, half-breed."

Blade straightened his shoulders and his wings spread wide. Not quite as wide as the angel's, but he could do battle with what he had. "Says the guy who wanted me to take out an entire denizen. Hell, a rage of Casipheans. Why couldn't you do it yourself? Aren't angels all-powerful?"

"This mortal realm weakens us."

Blade quirked a brow. The two angels he'd battled

had been strong. Yet they hadn't wielded any super-natural powers beyond strength.

"And our numbers are few," Sim continued. "But I was foolish to ask you, demon slayer, to help me. I had no idea you would get entangled with Synestriel, Keeper of the Second Light."

"Is that Zen's angel name?"

Sim nodded. "She is from my ranks. I, Simaseel, Master of the Ninth Void, sent her on the Fall."

With a sweep of its wings, the angel soared high, and just when he tilted down to dive toward Blade, Blade took to the air to meet his challenger. He dragged the halo blade along the supportive high bone of one of Sim's wings. The angel shrieked in a myriad of voices, and dodged midair. Blue blood dripped over the glow-ing wing.

"She is a traitor!" the angel insisted.

Suspended in the air, Blade maintained his position with slow sweeps of his gossamer black wings. He kept the angel's bleeding wing in focus while he twirled the hilt of the sword and caught it, blade down.

"How is Zen a traitor?" he asked.

The angel's multicolored eyes seemed to spin as if a child's toy, hypnotizing Blade with their radiance. When they'd spoken previously they had been white. A glamour? Most likely. He shook his head and returned his focus to the deadly wings.

"The plan was made before Synestriel fell. We have been watching the Casipheans for eons. It is their time for elimination."

"So you angels take it upon yourself to eliminate en-tire races whenever the mood strikes you?"

"It is ordained."

"Don't give me that bible crap."

"We do not subscribe to the humans' book of biblical stories. We live on truths and follow the destiny of the universe."

"Big talk. Small act. So you wanted to destroy the demons without lifting a finger? Fine. You talked an idiot into helping you. I'm over that now. What does Zen have to do with any of this? Why did she fall?"

"Synestriel agreed to fall to Daemonia to insinuate herself into the Casiphean order. Once crowned their queen she would have utmost control and access to the denizens. She could open Daemonia to our numbers. We would slaughter them before they might growl and hiss and strike back at us."

Blade swallowed. Zen had agreed to participate in genocide? Not all the demons in the world, but an entire breed of them in Daemonia. But that was when she'd been angel. Now that she had landed the mortal realm she had changed. Right?

"This is not your fight," Sim said. Its wings hadn't even to move and the angel maintained its position before Blade above the treetops. "Stand down."

"She doesn't want that anymore."

"This, I have come to know. Why do you think I recruited you to extinguish the demons running rampant on mortal grounds? You are my backup plan. And because of her absence of memory Synestriel has become a liability. She must be destroyed."

Wrong answer. Blade would protect Zen with every ounce of muster he had. Good, bad or otherwise.

It was worth a try. Because, really? He could handle one angel, but if a cavalcade of them came at him, then he was as good as toast. "You know, Zen still doesn't have her memory completely restored. But I don't understand your need to exterminate the demons. Seems to me if you sit back and let the Casipheans lure her into Daemonia, then your work is done. Once she's there, she'll become demon, yes?"

The angel nodded.

"She'll have all that remarkable power to open Daemonia to the angels."

Sim's eyes glowed as blue as his wings. "You suggest we do nothing? Hmm…" The angel folded back its wings and descended to the forest floor.

Blade followed, but kept his wings spread as a sign of aggression. He wasn't letting down his guard around an angel. Even if the blade was capable of killing the creature, the bastard could still do Blade some major harm before dying.

"If she's not got all her memory back," Sim said, "there is no guarantee she will know the plan when she arrives in Daemonia. And she's been on this realm too long. The longer she remains harnessed to human flesh the less capability she has of assuming the demonic form."

"She went to the nightclub last night with the intent of entering the portal to Daemonia. I'd say that's pretty damned determined, wouldn't you?"

"But you stopped her! And I am quite sure you will continue to impede her quest."

"Seems as if your problem is with me, not Zen."

The angel tilted his head sharply. A glint of blue flashed in his kaleidoscope eyes. His sneer could have cut diamonds. "So I'll take you out—"

Blade dodged the sweep of wing that would have sliced his head from his neck had he not moved. Lunging upward, he caught Sim against the chest with a shoulder and pushed him to ground. The angel's wings spread across the mossy rocks and earth. Blade's wings curved forward, pinning the angel's wings down with the sharp tips.

"I'm glad to be your problem," Blade said, wrapping his fingers about Sim's throat. "You want that?"

With his other hand he wielded the halo blade, drawing the tip along the man's outstretched arm, but not hard enough to cut through flesh and release blood. He didn't need to give the angel another weapon against him.

"I will consider your suggestion." And with that, the angel kicked Blade off him and swept away, soaring out of sight over the treetops.

Blade dropped his wings and let out a breath. "That was easier than expected."

But how soon before the angel realized that even if they did leave Zen alone, she wasn't going near the demon portal?

Not if Blade had any say about it.

Zen munched a crisp green apple she'd found in the fridge. She hadn't been able to sleep after noticing Blade had slipped out of bed to go outside. So food it was. She wondered if, as a vampire, he was repulsed when he ate for his faery. Gotta be weird.

But he liked weird. And so did she.

Wandering barefoot in front of the cathedral windows, wearing but the long T-shirt that belonged to her lover, she reveled in the moment. The act of being in his home, eating a sweet, juicy apple. For all other moments would be different, some urgent, some not so urgent. Some gorgeous, some weird. Some would challenge her and…

And it was the challenge she wanted to avoid now. Breathing in, she inhaled the air that designed this mortal realm. And knew that she was no longer one from Above. That realm was no longer her place.

And yet the place she had been destined for, Daemonia, teased in incomprehensible ways. So when it did not—as now—she could enjoy the moment.

When the door opened, she listened as Blade ascended the stairs. He wandered into the kitchen and poured a glass of water, drank it down, exhaled, then padded across the hardwood floor toward her.

From behind, he embraced her, wrapping his hands across her stomach and leaning down to kiss her at the base of her neck. His hair tickled her skin. He smelled like a wild, dark forest. She smiled and offered the half-eaten apple.

"Hungry?"

"Only for you," he said. "I want to hold you now. Forever."

"That's sounds like a choice I'd like to accept."

Zen turned and touched the scar that curled around from the back of his torso, and she bent to kiss the raised flesh. It was a new scar. Because of her.

That was over. She wouldn't again purposely do something that would cause him danger.

"Bring out your wings, lover. I want to have sex with you in faery shape."

"I'm never completely one or the other. If you want the faery, you also get the vampire."

"Would that be so terrible? My blood is no longer blue."

His eyes took her in from head to shoulders and then paused there at her throat. Fangs descended over his lower lip. Zen inhaled a shiver at the incredible sight. The thought of him sinking those into her skin appealed. He would never harm her. And if the bite was a sensual experience, the urge to have him do so would consume her.

"I crave demon blood," he said. It seemed like a confession to her. "It's the faery in me that has the craving, and it makes my vamp go after it like a hound. I don't want to crave yours."

"But if it's mixed with ichor?" She knew that faery ichor was like a drug to vampires. "Can you, a vampire, drink ichor?"

He nodded. "I'm half faery, so ichor is not addictive to me."

"So maybe the demon blood is safe, too? If you crave it?"

"It is safe to me. But, Zen, I don't want something simply because I crave it. It tastes awful. But I feel... stronger after I've drunk it."

"I see. It is a habit, then."

"The only habit I will admit to is wanting to hold you. To kiss you." He leaned forward and kissed her. "To touch your skin." His strokes under her jaw and down her neck caused a shiver of goose bumps to ripple her flesh, as well as tighten her nipples in anticipation.

"Wings," she said softly. "Please? And fangs. Promise I won't ask for the bite."

Her lover's wings unfurled behind him in a glorious spill of crisp autumn scents and winter ice, capped with the luscious hint of spring. Moonlight spilling through the windows shimmered on them. His wings were black and blue and silver, formed in a demonic shape, like something depicted in Doré's etchings of *Dante's Inferno*, and serrated around the edges in gothic peaks and curls. Black filaments dusted the tips and a faint blue arabesque designed curls in the shimmery silver.

Zen reached over his shoulder to touch one, but Blade put up a finger to stop her. "Be careful. You touch my wings, you'd better mean business."

"I'm all about the business, lover."

"Yeah, but the kind of business I'm talking about is an erotic touch."

"I know what happens when a person touches a faery's wings." Because know-so-much chick was in her zone. "I'm in."

Dipping under his arm, Zen stepped around behind him and between his wings. She spread her palms over the soft, yet tellingly strong appendages. They fluttered under her touch. Blade hissed in a gasp, indicating his arousal.

"Hold me," she said.

He wrapped his wings about her, caressing her torso firmly. She raised her arms over her head and tilted her head back against his neck. The sensations of warmth and erotic massage across her skin were irresistible. One of his wing tips pushed up under her shirt and coaxed the garment off over her head. The man was talented with those things.

A wing swept over her breast, her nipple growing instantly rigid. Soft as feathers but warm, so warm, his wings permeated her skin with a kind of anticipatory joy.

"Blade, that's amazing."

The wings swept away and he turned to kiss her,

wrapping his wings forward to again embrace and pull her forward. And he lifted her, cradled by his wings, and held her to him as he dipped his head to lick her breasts.

She gripped the hard, bony upper portions of his wings and felt the gush of life within them. Much like a firm erection in her grasp, the wing was supple yet solid. He growled against her breast, a hungry, wanting plead for more.

She stepped back and lazily took him in. Regal, exquisite, a gorgeous creature of wing and...yes, the fangs were down. Muscles flexed and drew her eye to the skin that felt so soft under her fingertips, yet was hard as stone. And when he grinned, it was the most wickedly appealing invitation she'd ever received.

"Come at me, woman."

Zen actually jumped into his arms, her legs wrapping about his hips. "Show me some of that wing action," she whispered at his ear, then bit the lobe and tugged.

The soft wings, which were not made of feathers but rather a suede-like material, caressed Zen's back, and with Blade's nod, she leaned back into the cradle of them and spread her hands over the strong but soft appendages. Holding her with but his wings allowed Blade to kiss her breasts and glide his hand down to her mons, where he dipped one finger over her clit and slowly massaged the swelling, wet bud.

She clutched at Blade's wings, gripping the edges to anchor herself to the exquisite feeling. He moaned deeply against her chest and lashed his tongue over her nipple. "Touch them. Stroke them," he said.

So she matched the rhythm of his finger between her legs and stroked the fabric of his wings. She could feel the hot blood rushing through them. Blood and ichor? Or was it all ichor since this was the faery part of him?

Who cared? Zen squirmed and shifted her hips, accepting his ministrations and wanting him to go faster, deeper... And then the rush of sensation frenzied through her system.

Chapter 24

So there was a new plan. Zen would lie low, keeping herself off the radars of both the angels and demons. And Blade would stand his ground of no longer killing demons for the sake of killing them.

Right now, in Blade's mind, the angels were the bad guys. Zen was still holding out judgment on the demons, and that was her right. Perhaps the middle ground was the best place to stand, but defense was so ingrained in Blade that this step to setting down arms was big enough.

It was well past noon. They'd lingered in bed making love again with the rising sun, though the shades were pulled. He couldn't get enough of Zen's body, and she seemed to want all of him. Constantly. He was cool with that.

Sharing himself was...easy with Zen. This relationship was not the same as that with Octavia. He wouldn't allow it to be. He'd walked into this one with eyes wide-open, and now that he had the facts—as dire as they were—he would continue to protect and love her. Because he had fallen. And unlike Zen's fall, his had been accidental, and yet, he was pleased about the step into this new, yet strangely familiar territory.

But he had a few errands to run today, and rather than answer his brother's curious questions about why he had forgotten, Blade kissed Zen on the forehead and promised to return in an hour or so with some lunch for her.

He stopped by Stryke's place. The construction crew had arrived and had begun to dig the basement, but they needed a permit to pour concrete footings.

On his way in to town he got a phone call from Michael Donovan, the halo hunter Dez had said she'd track down for him. He was in town for the day, passing through, visiting old friends, and he wanted to talk.

After stopping at the city hall for the permit, Blade drove to the city park. He wandered past the football field where a couple guys were tossing the ball and toward the docks that overlooked the lake. The straightest lake in the state, his sister, Daisy Blu, often said of Tangle Lake. It disturbed her that the town's namesake wasn't tangled. Blade could but snicker over her frustration.

He parked himself under an awning set into a rectangular concrete base where a picnic table had once sat. Work-release crews from an area prison were repairing and repainting the tables this weekend in preparation for the big city shindig that celebrated the summer.

Pulling a pair of sunglasses out of his pocket, he slid them on. The sun's rays didn't touch his skin here, and he could walk in daylight, no problem. But vampires did burn faster than most, and he avoided direct sunlight for more than a few minutes whenever possible.

Tonguing the tips of his fangs, he realized he'd not bitten Zen when they'd been making love. And his wings had been out. She had intimated she'd like a bite, and he'd thought it might be okay. No more blue blood? She should be safe for him.

Maybe.

He still wasn't willing to risk it if even the tiniest bit of angel remained in her. Would she ever be completely angel-free? He hoped so. Because the bite would allow him into a part of her more valuable to a vampire than anything else. Her very soul. They could bond.

He wasn't ready to bond with her. He wouldn't jump so quickly as he had with Octavia. A slow, trusting relationship felt right to him. And he wanted that from Zen.

He wanted a lot from her. And that realization made him sit up straight. He really had fallen in love with her. Idiot. Love was for fools. And never ended well.

"Saint-Pierre?"

Turning, Blade nodded acknowledgment to a man with short dark hair who wore aviator shades. Khaki cargo pants and a crisp white shirt rolled up to the elbows gave him a big-city casual look. He shook his hand and determined he was merely human.

"Michael Donovan," he said. "The witch said you've come upon a couple halos lately?"

Blade drew up the halo sword and held it, tip up, before Donovan. "You talking about this?"

The halo hunter preened over the weapon, even snapped his finger against the blade, then said, "Wow. That used to be a halo. How did you manage to rework it? An angel halo is formed from the most indestructible metal known to man. And angels, for that matter."

"My dad is a sword smith. Add a touch of my mother's faery dust, and voilà."

Michael whistled in appreciation. "May I?"

Blade clasped the hilt tighter. "You going to give me some answers?"

"I'll do my best. I know a lot about angels, but not everything. I've been hunting halos for over a decade. Ran into an angel or two in the process. And just so you know, you can trust me. My girlfriend's a vampire. So I know about all the species."

Blade eyed the man discerningly. He wasn't about to trust him, but should the human attempt anything funny he'd not get farther than two steps before Blade made him understand it wasn't wise to mess with him.

He handed the sword over, hilt pointing toward the halo hunter. Donovan took it and, with an awe-filled sigh, studied the blade, running a finger carefully along the metal, and then balancing the precise weight.

"How many halos do you have?" Blade asked.

"Eighteen. Found them all over the world. When the angel falls the halo falls away."

"Right. Unless the angel holds tight to the halo when falling."

"Why would they do that?" he asked, handing over the sword. "Doesn't make sense. The very purpose of the fall is to maintain their angelic nature so they can stalk the mortal realm. Of course, the halo could serve as a handy weapon, but it could also be put over the angel's head, rendering it merely human as the earthbound soul is returned to the body."

"An angel might hold on to the halo because they didn't want to fall for the original reason intended."

Donovan wobbled his head in an uncertain nod. "Maybe."

"There's another halo in town, unchanged and in

original form. It's in the hands of the angel who fell with it."

"No way. Where is it? I've got to get my hands—" Donovan dropped his shoulders and relaxed his enthusiasm. "Well, you know. I'd like to take a look at it."

"You're not going anywhere near that halo. The owner is partial to it."

"Is this the angel who could be a demon that Dez told me about?"

Blade nodded. "Tell me about angels who fall to become demon."

"Hmm...I do fancy myself a bit of an angelologist as I learn more about them." Michael crossed his arms and considered the question. "There is a race of demons who were once angel. The Casipheans."

"Yes, that's the breed I'm dealing with."

"Okay. The Casipheans fell eons ago and landed directly in Daemonia. They are the only race of demons who possess divinity."

"Divinity?"

"An angelic birthright. And believe me, if I were an angel from Above I'd want to take out the Casipheans because it's not right, you know, a demon walking around with divinity. Divinity is only for the chosen. Or so the angels believe. Yet they are the ones who taint it most."

"Do the Casipheans know this?"

Michael shrugged. "My demonic knowledge isn't top-notch. I only knew that tidbit because I've had a conversation with an angel slayer. The Sinistari are angels who are specifically chosen to slay those angels who hunt their muses. They fall to Beneath, become the Sinistari demon and sit in wait until they are called to slay a Fallen."

"This angel lore is complicated."

"That it is. But just imagine, whether or not the Casipheans know, their divine vibrations are constantly infusing the entirety of Daemonia. It's gotta be interesting in the Place of All Demons. Ha! I bet it drives those bastard angels mad."

Blade quirked a brow. "You don't like angels much?"

"I believe they are far more evil than some demons. Bunch of self-righteous assholes. I am a big fan of the Sinistari."

The angel slayers. Interesting. There was so much Blade did not know about other species and breeds. And there were days he wished to remain oblivious.

But not today. He needed all the information he could get to protect Zen.

"So have you spoken to these angels who seem to be giving you trouble?" Donovan asked.

"One of them recruited me to slay any demon I laid eyes on. I initially refused, but then—I hate demons."

"Everyone has a right to their opinions."

"Simaseel is the angel heading the demon-slaying mission. The angels are trying to infiltrate the Casipheans and annihilate them."

"Makes sense."

It shouldn't, but it did if the angels were jealous that breed of demons possessed divinity. And it was wrong in ways Blade could not begin to understand.

"So how do we stop a cavalcade of angels?" he asked.

"Why? Have you switched sides? Are you fighting for the Casipheans now?"

"No." Stand for the demons? Never. "I just…" He

exhaled and shoved the sword back in the sheath he wore at his hip. "I need to know everything to help her."

"Who her? The angel demon?"

"Zen. Or Synestriel, as Simaseel called her."

"The Keeper of the Second Light," Michael said with a knowing nod. "She created all light that beams from manmade sources."

"Really?"

"Yep. Anything that gives off a glint, sparkle or glow, but which is not naturally generated."

"Like…rhinestones?"

Donovan shrugged. "Yes, I suppose."

"Makes weird sense." And he did like weird. "Zen's blood is no longer blue, so I believe whatever angel she had in her has faded."

"But she was angel for a while?"

Blade nodded. "Simaseel sent her to fall and become the Casiphean queen."

"That's where the infiltration plays in." Donovan leaned against the wood post. "Clever."

"But she—Zen—has amnesia, and is only just beginning to remember her mission. Right now, she's swaying regarding her alliances. I want to push her over to the right side."

"And which side is that?"

"Mine."

"Ah, love."

"I didn't say anything about love, man."

"Yeah, but that's generally the catalyst that makes a man do crazy things. Like stand up for an amnesiac Fallen One when the angels will surely rip him to shreds. And speaking of crazy, you, uh, won't mention my name to any of the involved parties, will you?"

"No reason to."

"Whew. I've been living a relatively quiet life lately. Not sure I'm up for angel battles. I don't mind taking out the occasional vamp, if need be, though."

"What does your girlfriend say about that?"

"Vinny is cool with me doing what is necessary for the two of us to survive. She's been through a lot. I'd protect her with my life."

Blade could relate.

"You sure I can't take a look at the halo your Zen has?"

"Positive."

"Had to try. There is one other thing."

"What's that?"

"I suspect the divinity that's been festering in Daemonia can be used as a weapon against the angels. You know once an angel touches mortal ground it loses power?"

"Sim had mentioned something similar. They still seem damn strong to me. I've fought a couple in the past few days."

"Their strength is depleted, which gives you an idea of just how strong they could be in Above. But what I'm talking about is their ability to move objects with but a gesture, the mind control and general badassness. Angel feet touch mortal ground? So long badassery," Donovan added. "And the Casipheans are überstrong as well— at least with all that divinity coursing within them."

"I don't think they are aware of that hidden talent. How do they use it?"

Michael shrugged. "You got me. But it's something, right?"

"Could be." Rain started to sprinkle the grass, and

Blade held out a palm to catch the droplets. "Thanks, man. I appreciate you taking the time to talk to me."

"No problem. I won't be leaving town until noon tomorrow. So, you know, if you think you might want to do a little more show-and-tell…"

"Give it up, man."

"All right, all right. I'll leave you to your apocalyptic troubles."

"I do have one other thing." Blade pulled out the postcard he'd nicked from Zen's stuff before leaving and handed it to Michael. "You know anything about that?"

"Wow." Michael merely glanced at it, then handed it back to Blade. "Where'd you get that?"

"You know the painting?"

"Of course. It was done by Eden Campbell. She used to be a muse, until a Sinistari demon rescued her from the angel who wanted to impregnate her with a Nephilim baby. Name was Zaqiel. He was an asshole. Eden has been painting angels all her life, without knowing that she was connected to them. That's how it works for a muse. One day it's life as usual. The next, they're being chased by a horny angel. Where did you get that postcard?"

"Zen had this on her. She said it spoke to her, even not knowing what she was."

"Interesting. But you already know how she's connected in this big circle that ever fascinates."

"That I do. Thanks again." Blade strode off, leaving the halo hunter by lake's edge tossing stones into the water.

Chapter 25

While she was drying off from the shower in the bathroom, Zen heard the door shut and Blade's footsteps rushing up the stairs. It was late in the day, but the sweltering heat had compelled her to hop in for a quick and cool rinse.

"In here!" she called, letting the towel drop to the floor as she walked out into the bedroom.

"Wow." He walked in and strolled his gaze up and down her naked skin. "That's a nice way to greet a guy." He thumbed a gesture over his shoulder. "I picked up a salad and sandwich for you. Left it in the fridge."

"Thanks. I am hungry. But it can wait."

She climbed onto the bed and patted the sheet beside her. He sat and she kissed him and pulled off his T-shirt. It wasn't necessary to ask him to take off his jeans; he'd already quickly shoved them down. Afternoon sex was awesome, but with the rain pinging the window—and the man always had the windows open a crack—a humid breeze floated over the bed. She nestled into the black sheets and stroked her fingers along his leg, delighting in the soft dark hairs. No blue here.

He kissed her head and drew her hand up to kiss each

finger. Down her wrist, and up to her elbow, he paused. "These markings are brighter."

"Yes, I noticed that. What do you think?"

"Faery?" he offered with a shrug.

"You know as much as I do." She walked her fingers over his abs and tapped one of his steely pecs. "How did the chat with the halo hunter go?" she asked.

"Interesting. He really wants to get his hands on your halo."

"Did you tell him it was mine?"

"I did."

"I own very few things. I value what I have. I would never give the halo up, even if…"

He sat up against the headboard and ran his fingers through her hair, brushing it from her face. "Keep the halo on you at all times, Zen. Promise me."

"I will. The Casipheans will have to accept it is mine. Does that mean you're worried someone is going to attack me again?"

"The Casipheans still have a chance of luring you to their side."

"I won't go."

"But you just said—"

Zen sighed heavily. "I know. I'm not sure what is right anymore." She stretched out her arm and stroked the marks, which had brightened to white from the original cream. "Why did I fall to become their queen?"

"I can answer that. I spoke to Sim last night before returning and making love to you all night long. That bastard is an angel."

"He is?"

Blade nodded. "Simaseel, Master of—uh, I don't recall. Doesn't matter. You ready for this?"

"It's not good, is it?"

He shrugged. "We all react and move through life according to how we've been raised. Or in your case, created."

Yes, because angels were not born and nurtured from an infant, they were created. Come into being fully mature and ready to do…whatever it was they had been assigned—or perhaps even destined—to do.

"Simaseel knew why I fell, didn't he?"

"Do you remember that name?" he asked. "Simaseel?"

"No. Should I?"

"He said you were in his ranks in the Ninth Void. That he sent you to fall. Called you Synestriel, Keeper of the Second Light."

"Really?" Her posture straightened and she lifted her chin. "That sounds so regal."

"I think it's a reason why you are into the sparkly stuff." He tapped the many rings that glinted on her fingers, then took her hand and kissed the knuckles. "Zen, you were destined to become the Casiphean queen. But it's not for the reason you believe. According to Sim, once inserted within the demonic ranks, you were then to open the gates to Daemonia, allowing the angels to invade and kill off the entire Casiphean race."

Her mouth dropped open. For a moment she was aware that she could not sense her heartbeats. Empty inside, she grasped at her chest. "But that's genocide."

Blade nodded.

"I don't want…"

Was that what she really wanted? Before she'd lost her memory, had her goal been to infiltrate the demons so her former race of angels could destroy them all?

It was hideous to consider. Unthinkable.

Blade clasped her hand. "Zen. Think about it. When you fell you held tight to your halo. You knew, either right before making the fall, or moments after beginning that long descent, that you didn't want to go through with it. Holding on to your halo prevented you from entering Daemonia. It is what stopped you here on the mortal realm. Don't you see? You couldn't go through with it."

Shoulders dropping, she breathed out slowly as she drew a knee up to her chest and propped her chin on it. Her heartbeats resumed a more regular pace. His version sounded good. Not so violent. And much less evil.

Had she been an evil angel? What made her think she could ever move beyond that?

Her lover moved up onto his knees and bent over her, stroking her hair and tilting up her chin to meet his searching gaze. "Zen, you're not that angel anymore."

"Sure, but what am I? What must I become?"

"Whatever you become, you're not going to join the demons. That's not you, either."

"How do you know?" came out in a panicked question. "Maybe…maybe the Casipheans *need* a queen to lead them? To protect them from the imminent angel invasion?"

"They've their own means of defense against the angels. Trust me on that one."

"But—"

"Zen." He kissed her softly. All she wanted was his kisses. The world faded away when their mouths connected. And that was a world she wanted to live in. "The invasion won't happen as long as you keep out of Daemonia. If you want to protect the Casipheans, stay here in the mortal realm." He looked aside and said softly, "With me."

He wanted her to stay? Zen had never felt so needed, so special. So...real. And that she belonged someplace. Could she stay with this beautiful man who embraced her despite his own dark troubles? Of course she could. But would her origins ever remain a brutal reminder to his awful torture by demons?

"I love you, Blade. I mean, I think I do. I'm not sure what love is, but if it's something that makes a person feel certain of their position in the world—right here with you—then that's the definition I'm using."

He stroked her cheek and brushed his mouth over her lips. Oh, that world that only they two could create. She was in for the long haul.

"You are love, Zen. You've been nothing but open and wondering and positive since landing in this realm. You were meant to be here. I think you wanted to be here. Maybe as an angel, agreeing to the plot to eradicate the Casipheans was your means to escape?"

"Could have been. That's the part I'm still blurry on. Oh, but, Blade, how can you allow me into your heart knowing that I had planned to be part of such an annihilation?"

"Because we all do what we must. I agreed to much the same when Sim asked. When we learn more, we do better. I'm no angel, Zen."

"Well, no, you're faery and vampire. Which is exactly how I prefer you."

"Weirdo." He kissed her softly, his nose nuzzling hers. "I won't force you to stay. I just want to keep you here awhile longer, until we figure things out."

"Sounds like a plan. So I don't have to worry about angels anymore?"

"I wouldn't go as far as to get comfy. I'd keep one eye out to the sky. I did give Sim something to think about regarding backing off from you. But when he figures out that was a crock I'm not sure what to expect. What we need to do is give the angels good reason to retreat, and the demons, as well."

"Which is?"

"Haven't a clue. You hungry?"

"I could eat anything you put in front of me."

He smirked and his eyes flitted down to his cock, which was erect.

"Is that so?" Zen tapped the head of the hopeful appendage.

"It has to stop with me," Zen said later as she finished the salad Blade had picked up. They'd had a quickie and then just knowing food waited for her in the fridge, she had dragged herself away from her naked lover for sustenance. "I've been muddling on things, and I recall the moment I agreed to Simaseel to fall and insinuate myself into the Casipheans."

"You do?"

She nodded, and placed her palms together before her, closing her eyes reverently. She nodded again, decided, and opened her eyes, spreading out her palms. "It was a lie, as you suspected. I wanted to be the change. To stand on the side of life."

"But the Casipheans are not without sin."

"Who am I to judge?"

"Well, you do come from divine beginnings. If anyone is allowed to judge—"

"That's not me," she said. And she felt it in every atom of her being. This was what she had fallen for. To save lives. And to stop an annihilation. "I will stand for the Casipheans. Simaseel must be stopped."

She laid a hand over his. She had no right to ask, but she wanted to. Because with him she felt whole, strong and capable. "Join me."

"You're asking me to protect the demons."

"Yes, the very species who tortured you and left you for dead."

"I...don't know if I can do that," he answered. "I can step back. Do them no harm. But protect them?"

"It's a lot to ask. You're right. Let's leave things where they are right now. Me and you. Together. We're together, yes?"

He kissed her and nodded. "For as long as you'll have me."

She would have him forever, if that was possible. Though she was still torn between two worlds. She must help the demons, but would that wrench her lover from her arms?

And he couldn't commit completely to standing at her side in the defense of the Casipheans. Zen couldn't help but feel her heart fall a little to know she may have to stand alone and risk losing the best thing that ever happened to her.

Chapter 26

With Zen in the house flicking through the TV stations in fascination, Blade stalked out behind the barn and beyond the shed.

From the loft window, he had spied something moving in this direction. It wasn't an animal, because they were more stealthy, and anything from the Darkwood was usually cautious of the wards he'd put up surrounding his property.

Had Simaseel returned?

Now, as he tracked the edge of his property, the Darkwood grew up to his left, a black wall of gnarly barked trees with leaves that appeared drained of life even in the middle of summer. The wildlife within the forest moved about without fear. He liked to think that someday he would be as fearless. Because, really, he did fear some things.

Like losing the best thing that had happened to him lately.

She'd asked him to stand in defense of the demons. He couldn't do that. He wasn't that forgiving. But should he be?

The snap of a twig lifted his head. He stopped, turned toward the forest and looked over the row of red eyes that had likely tracked him since he'd left the barn.

He knew this denizen. All too well.

"Ryckt," he said coldly.

"Foul One," the leader of the *mimicus* denizen addressed him.

The demon stood before his ranks. His body was as black as night, his clothing blending in with the foliage—if he wore any—for he was in demon form. Horns curled over and behind his ears, and his elongated face dipped his chin low to a narrow chest. Blade knew well that their limbs appeared emaciated, their black flesh clinging to bone, but they were deceptively strong. And they could take on any form, and go undetected by those of the species they mimicked.

"We are watching you," Ryckt stated.

"Is that so? Never would have guessed," Blade said lightly. Though it took all his bravery to do so. The scars on his body pulled tightly.

This was the denizen who had tortured him while Octavia had slowly died. These were the demons that would play with a man's very soul just to see it quiver. And they would stalk a vampire-faery half-breed because their leader had the twisted desire to see how much torture it could withstand. And to test their armor against the ichor.

"Step forward if you wish to talk," Blade said.

"I know your wards are fierce. I am perfectly capable of conversing with you from where I stand."

Not fierce enough if they had allowed the denizen so close to his home.

"What do you want?" He had the bowie knife stuffed in his waistband, but wished he held the halo blade.

He prayed that Zen stayed inside the barn and did not come out looking for him.

The demon leader shifted from one foot to the other. "You are giving Kesabel a difficult time."

"So he sent you to look after me?"

"Indeed."

"Since when do the royal denizens of Daemonia associate with the lowlife *mimicus* demons who haunt the mortal realm?"

"The Casiphean numbers in this realm dwindle."

Blade smirked. He'd had something to do with that. Though he'd decided he wasn't going to slay another demon, he'd take out this entire denizen right now if they attempted to cross his wards. Because he had a reason to kill them. Slowly.

"She's never going to join their ranks," he said. "Tell Kesabel to give up. The angels are determined to infiltrate their denizen—through Zen—and destroy them all."

"So say you?"

Blade sensed the demon's genuine concern. "So I say. I spoke to Simaseel yesterday. He revealed his plan to me. Best thing for the Casipheans to do? Retreat."

"Our kind never retreat."

"Then, your denizen will be obliterated alongside the Casipheans. Idiot demons."

And Blade turned and walked off, forcing himself not to look over his shoulder.

"The moment she leaves your property she is ours!" Ryckt called.

"You can't force her to enter the portal!" Blade yelled.

"She will do just that if the stakes are high enough."

Blade fisted a rude gesture at the denizen and strode back toward the barn.

* * *

"Who was that?" Zen asked as Blade topped the stairs in the loft. "I glanced out the bathroom window and saw you talking to someone at the edge of the woods. A brother?"

"The *mimicus* denizen."

"Demons?" Her jaw dropped open. That was the denizen who had tortured Blade. "I don't understand. I thought you had wards?"

"I do. Guess I need to have them renewed. Kesabel sicced Ryckt and his denizen on me since I won't hand you over to him."

"But even if you did 'hand me over'—" she made air quotes for those words "—it wouldn't matter. I'm supposed to go willingly into Daemonia."

"They know that. They just want to piss me off."

"Oh." She rubbed a palm down her arm and gave him a sidelong glance. He seemed just a bit too casual about this announcement. "Have they?"

"Yep." He smacked a fist into his palm. "I told them the angels have it out for them, and that they should head for the hills, but I don't think the warning was taken for what it was. I need to talk to Kesabel again. If you are intent on protecting the Casipheans, then we need to get them on our side."

"We don't have a side, Blade. We, or rather I—since you haven't agreed to defend the demons—am the center, trying to keep the peace."

He pushed his fingers through his hair and tilted back his head. Zen could sense his anger and the uneasy acceptance of her goal to make peace between the angels and demons. Of course he couldn't stand by her side, defending the very creatures he hated most. And now the denizen who had tortured him and left permanent scars in his flesh was watching him?

"I want to stand on your side, Zen, but…" He sighed heavily.

"Your heart is true. But you mustn't sacrifice your principles to please me."

"Sounds like the best reason to sacrifice." His smile was genuine. "For you."

If he was serious, she could so get behind his help.

"You don't need to do this." She wrapped her arms around his waist from behind. "I am capable."

"I believe you are capable. And I'm not particularly keen about protecting demons. But I want to stand at your side. If you'll have me." He pulled her around to stand before him. "You're becoming more faery every day. The moment you are fully faery you are no good to either the angels or the demons."

"So we just wait it out?"

"No. I don't like hiding, doing nothing."

"You would not." She tilted up on her toes to kiss him. "But can we wait through the night?"

"Of course. The denizen can't cross my wards. You're safe here."

"And so are you."

"Is that so?" He kissed her. "I do feel safe in your arms. That, no matter what the world tosses my way, I can overcome. Because if you're standing there waiting for me when the dust clears, then everything is right."

"I'll be there. I promise."

"What about being queen? Can you give that up?"

"Oh, hell, yes. Though I will miss the crown."

"You think there's a crown?"

"There had better be. One can hardly be queen without some sparkly headgear."

He kissed her head. "When this is over I'll give you the prettiest, sparkliest crown I can find."

"Promise?"

"You have my word."

They had sex in the shower, and afterward, Zen curled up on the couch with Blade to watch a late-night showing of *Dracula*. She laughed at all the right places. He loved her for that. He was distracted from the black-and-white flick by the flash of headlights on the ceiling.

Now what?

"Who's that?"

"Stay here." Grabbing the halo blade from the kitchen counter, he headed down the stairs and outside.

Trouble hopped out of his truck and strode up to the open garage entrance where Blade stood staring skyward. The massive black cloud had returned. "What the hell is that? Can you ever not attract danger, little brother?"

"I can use your help again," Blade said. "That cloud comes from the nightclub. Must be some form of demonic spy cloud. And you see those red eyes at the edge of the Darkwood?"

Trouble cast his gaze along the forest edge, and he suddenly jumped. "What the hell?"

"The *mimicus* denizen," Blade confirmed. "They're keeping an eye on me."

"That's the ones who fucked you up?"

"Yep."

Trouble punched a fist into his palm. "How do they play into all this?"

"Kesabel hired them."

"Kesabel?"

"The Casiphean leader who wants to make Zen their queen."

Trouble whistled. "This is way beyond my story line, bro. You're going to have to catch me up. I just stopped by for some gas. Was headed to the casino in the next town and realized I needed a fill."

"You can fill up and then come inside for coffee. If I'm right, we're going to have an all-nighter."

"So you're a demon?"

Zen sat up from the couch, where she'd almost dozed during a commercial, and eyed the cocky werewolf who approached. "Trouble, hi. Uh, not demon. Yet."

"That's what Blade tells me. We're heading to the nightclub to take a look around. Guess my casino plans are spoiled..." He plopped onto the couch beside her. "*Dracula*! I love this one. Did my brother tell you we used to tease him about being Dracula when we were kids?"

"And how many times did I let you get away with that?" Blade called as he topped the stairs.

"Once." Trouble winked at Zen. "He beat the shit out of me and I gave it up. No one ever gets my jokes."

Zen pushed the blanket off and sat up straight, stretching out her arms. "If you guys are going to the nightclub, I'm coming along."

"No," Blade called as he disappeared into the bedroom. He reappeared with the bowie knife and stuffed it down the side of his combat boot. The halo sword he shoved in the sheath strapped at his hip. "You're safe if you stay in the barn. I've wards that will keep everything out."

"Those same wards that you said needed refreshing? I don't want to stay alone. Not with demons lurking in the woods. Besides, I could be of help. I do have the halo."

"No," Blade said at the same time that Trouble said, "She could be helpful. If the demons want her, she could play bait."

Blade gaped at his brother.

Zen shrugged and nodded eagerly. "I can do bait. I think."

Trouble winked at Blade. He had to admit he'd rather keep Zen in eyesight even if it meant added danger.

"Fine," he conceded.

Zen slipped on her shoes and bounced.

"But no bait. You do as I say, and keep out of sight when possible. Promise?"

"Whatever you say, boss."

Chapter 27

Trouble drove because he owned the big, bad Dodge half-ton diesel. The abomination was painted olive-green camouflage. Trouble thought the paint job ironic. His brothers snickered about it behind his back. He navigated the truck down the country road toward the club.

Zen sat next to Blade, arm wrapped around his and head tilted onto his shoulder. She was warm and smelled like sex and apples.

He kissed the crown of her head. "You got your halo along?"

"In my backpack. You told me never to go anywhere without it."

"In case of emergency…" He wondered if it was wise to suggest such a thing? There could be no other option if things got hairy. "Put the halo above your head."

He felt her peer up at him but he kept his eyes on the dark country road, peeled for red eyes or moving objects not in human form.

"What if it's too late?" she said in the tiniest voice.

He caught Trouble's glance that seemed to echo, *yeah, what if?* What if the angel within her was gone and wouldn't react to the halo and accept her earth-bound soul?

"I'll have your back," he said. "Promise."

She snuggled even closer to him and he wished they were not driving toward danger, but instead away from it all. Could he steal a moment out of time to simply enjoy being with Zen? They'd shared a few moments of bliss, but that had been between running from demons and angels. Could life ever be normal?

Did he want normal?

"Yes," he murmured. With all his heart and soul he wanted the freedom to exist without having to look over his shoulder all the time.

"Your brother Stryke lives a good life?" she asked.

"Uh…yes?"

"Do you want that?"

"Perfection? No." Had she been privy to his thoughts? Or was it they shared a connection that they mustn't ignore? "I want peace," he said. "Quiet."

"Seems as if you have quiet out on your little plot of land far from the city and your family members."

True. And he had been generally demon-free until Zen had entered his life.

"I've brought you something more," she said. "The question is, will it be too much for you? Will you want to return to the peace you had when this is all over? Demons forced back to Daemonia and angels extinguished?"

"All I want is you, Zen."

"You have me. Now let's see what you do to keep me."

He looked down at her and she beamed up a smile curved beneath violet eyes. Violet? Was she so close to faery, then?

Trouble's grin was so loud that Blade could but smile

in response. So he'd gone sappy. If Trouble said something he'd give him the fistfight he deserved. Only problem was, his brother would enjoy that too much.

"Kelyn's behind us," Trouble announced.

He slowed the vehicle to a stop. Blade rolled down the window. Kelyn, his faery brother, called out to be heard over the idling diesel engine, "Need some help?"

"You bet. Follow us to the nightclub."

"You going to kick more demon ass?" Kelyn yelled.

"With hope, no."

But Blade knew that hope had long been siphoned from his soul.

After the brothers got out, Zen moved over to the driver's seat. They stalked up to the stone staircase before the mansion. There stood a man, or probably the demon Kesabel, waiting for him. Zen hadn't seen Kesabel so she could only guess.

She rolled down the window and the blond brother, Kelyn, was standing by the door. He said, "No matter what happens you stay in the truck. Blade's orders. And roll up the window."

She nodded, but didn't feel like a weakling damsel who needed to be protected by the boys. She was smart enough to know to stay out of the fray, if that should occur. But that didn't mean she wasn't going to jump in should things require another hand. Though she saw no other demons in the darkness surrounding the mansion. And surely their red eyes would reveal them.

She tried to hear what Blade was saying to Kesabel, but the obnoxious rumble of the truck engine made it impossible. Trouble had asked her to keep it idling for a fast getaway, if need be. So she strained to hear through the closed window.

"You brought an army?" Kesabel asked as Blade stopped at the bottom step. The demon, clad in maroon leather armor Blade was all too familiar with, stood two steps up.

"If you consider three men an army," Blade said, "then my numbers won't even blink should you call on yours."

Kesabel chuckled. "You know my fellow Casipheans are few in this realm."

"Right. You had to call out the *mimicus* denizen to help you. I see they lent you some armor. They don't scare me, Kesabel. You're going to have to try harder."

"I'm not attempting to scare. I'm going for the win." He made a show of glancing over Blade's shoulder toward the truck. "I see you brought our queen. If you would be so kind as to escort her into the club, we can get started."

"Started?" Kelyn, who flanked Blade's side, glanced to him.

Blade shook his head at the idiot demon's audacity. "She has no desire to become your queen. Listen, Kesabel, and I say this with sincerity and the genuine desire not to slaughter more of your ranks."

The demon crossed his arms. The small portion of his neck that was exposed revealed many of the dark runes, no doubt, wards against vampires.

"I spoke with Simaseel," Blade said.

"The very angel who sicced you on us. You finally figured that one out?"

Yeah, so he'd been slow on that one.

"The angels sent Zen to infiltrate your denizen. If you invite her through the portal and make her your queen? She'll open Daemonia to Sim's ranks and they will eradicate you."

"Impossible. Angels cannot access Daemonia."

"Yeah? All right, then. Let's give it a go." Blade made a show of turning toward the trucks. He didn't give a signal to his brothers to follow because Kesabel cleared his throat.

As expected.

"Truly?" the demon asked.

Blade nodded. "Sim wants to take you guys out. I assume because you possess divinity."

"A faery tale. Fat lot of good divinity does us in Daemonia."

"You don't actually know how to utilize it, do you? You know, you can fight the angels with divinity."

"Lies told to you by the angel to lure us closer to the brink."

"Actually, it was told to me by a halo hunter. What did he call himself? An angelologist."

"A made-up word for a boastful human who thinks he knows things."

"All righty. If you want to ignore the truth."

"Divinity is but a remnant. Trust me, vampire. Are you or are you not going to allow Synestriel to approach the portal?"

"That's a big not."

Kesabel scratched his head near the horn. "Then, we'll have to give her reason to want to make such a sacrifice." The demon glanced at Trouble, who flanked Blade five feet to the right, and then to Kelyn, who stood to his left.

"There's nothing you can do that will make her come to you."

"How about this?"

Blade saw the demon swing forward his arm, but as he deflected it expertly with a forearm, the demon's other arm shot up with an undercut. He felt the wooden stake enter his chest, plunge between rib bones and tear through heart muscle.

Gripping the wood dowel stuck in his chest, Blade dropped to his knees. Behind him Trouble and Kelyn swore. And Zen's scream was the sound that kept him in this world, alive, but struggling for consciousness.

Chapter 28

Zen ran toward her lover, on his knees before the demon. The brothers hadn't had a chance to stop the inevitable staking. Even Blade hadn't seen it coming in time to retreat. Damned demon!

A skitter in the air averted her gaze upward as she ran. A black cloud swirled toward earth.

"Demons!" Trouble yelled. The eldest brother shifted to werewolf shape in a matter of seconds. His clothing tore and fell away from the incredible growing musculature, and his wolf head and maw tilted back to howl.

From out of the mansion poured the denizen in demon form, talons scything the air and wicked menace clouding the night atmosphere.

Kelyn grasped Zen's arm before she could get to Blade. "You're not safe! Get back in the truck."

"No! He's been staked."

And yet, when most vampires would disintegrate and sift to ash on the ground, Blade had not. He knelt there, gripping the thick wooden dowel as Kesabel looked over him.

"It's what the demons want," Kelyn said. "To get you out in the open."

Zen met her lover's fierce gaze. He yelled something at her, but she couldn't hear for the noise from above.

It wasn't the usual demonic din that accompanied their ranks, but instead was populated with animal sounds of all species. They weren't demons…

"Angels," Kesabel hissed. And to the heavens he shouted, "Thou shall not pass!"

The spoken angel ward was not effective when issued by a demon. Dozens of angels aimed for the ground where the vampire knelt, flanked by a werewolf and a faery.

Zen wielded her halo. She managed to make it to Blade's side. He stood, still clasping the stake.

"Get in the truck," he demanded.

"Nope. Got a battle going on right now. And you look as though you need some help."

"I'm fine."

She studied the stake in his chest. "That's your definition of fine?"

"If I don't yank it out…" He winced. "I'm good."

"Just need to process, eh?"

He nodded and managed a smile.

"Blade!" Kelyn stopped before Blade and Zen, back to them. He wielded a bow and arrow aimed toward the descending angels. "You good?"

Blade nodded to his brother. "Let's do this!"

The werewolf took a hit to the chest from two demons working in tandem. But even as the wolf's back landed on the ground, his arms arced forward, catching his attackers by the necks and crushing their heads together. He flung them aside and leaped into the fray.

Bow and arrows in hand, Kelyn utilized his wings effectively as weapons as he flew over demon heads and clashed with angels. Before placing the arrow to the bow, he sliced through his skin with the arrow tip. Ichor glittered on the sharp point. Sure poison that dropped the demons to the ground and momentarily stunned the angels.

Blade held strong, even though the stake in his heart pulsed and burned like a mother. But he knew to keep it in. Removing it would allow his heart to deflate and burst—sure death. He swung at Kesabel, then realized who it was and pulled the swing just before the halo blade slashed the demon.

Kesabel paused, hands up in surrender. "Take your shot, demon slayer."

"You are not my enemy. Use your divinity," Blade growled. "It's the only way to defeat these bastards!"

"But I don't— I've...staked you. And still you insist..." Kesabel studied his palms. "Really?"

All around the two men the battle raged, angels taking out demons and vice versa. The werewolf and faery had joined forces and stood back-to-back, with Zen at their sides. She wielded her halo expertly, having learned that throwing it toward an opponent would slice through skin and bone, and then the halo would return to her grip. Like a boomerang with unholy intent.

While Kesabel considered the power within him, Blade struck the angel who loomed overhead. The opponent grasped him by the wrist and took flight. Midair, Blade unfurled his wings, but one appendage was struck by a passing angel, and that upset the sword from his grasp. The halo blade fell to earth. Trouble looked up just in time to catch the sword and wield it, leaping over falling demons to go for the angel who shrieked in defiance.

Using his wings as weapons, Blade sliced at the angel

but only succeeded in cutting arms and legs. He couldn't get to any part that would cause death. And really, the only effective weapon for killing these bedamned things was the halo blade or Zen's intact halo.

Fangs descending in anger, he resisted the urge to bite, for that would bring his death. And yet, death sat lodged in his heart. The organ pulsed and pushed blood around the wood column, yet had not given up on him. On life.

On Zen. He had to survive for Zen.

Sure that his brothers would have Zen's back while he was air-bound, Blade twisted in the air, bringing the angel around with him, so he was under him. He slashed his wing across the angel's, and his opponent retaliated with a howl. It was then Blade realized he fought Simaseel. The bastard who had tricked him into taking demon lives. Easy enough to do when he'd been so down on himself over the torture.

No longer. He would rise above his torment. He'd begun by helping out in the community. And he would continue by opening his heart even more. He could live life without always looking over his shoulder.

With a swift angle of wing, Sim turned them both in the air and forced Blade to ground. His spine and hips landed on the fieldstone staircase before the mansion. Blade felt his bones break, his jaw crack and his brain shudder inside his skull.

Sim clutched the stake, intent on yanking it out. "Time to die, vampire."

"You first!" A sweep of the halo blade sliced the stake off right at Blade's chest. It cut his skin, it was so close. But it also shaved off the stake and released Sim's grip on it. The angel hissed, clutching his hand. Blue blood seeped from a slice on his fingers.

Kesabel landed over Blade and offered him a hand, tugging him up to stand. When the angel lunged for them both, Kesabel shoved the sword hilt into Blade's grip. "This belongs to you."

Blade reacted and stabbed, piercing the angel through his glass heart. "Meet you in Beneath, asshole." Sim yowled the horrifying din of the angels. A blue glow crept out at the sword wound. The tinkling sound of glass shattering preceded Sim's abrupt silence. The angel dusted to crystal ash and dropped in a mound at Blade's feet.

"Good riddance," Kesabel said. "Duplicitous asshole."

"Zen was his cohort," Blade said.

"Indeed. Yet I scent a soul in her. She is not the queen for us. I took that from one of your brothers," Kesabel offered, gesturing to the halo sword. "The werewolf was faring well enough with claws and fangs."

Blade slapped a hand over his chest. The wooden stake sat flush with his rib cage and little blood seeped out around it. "You saved my life. What was that for?" he asked the demon.

"I figured out how this divinity thing works. And you know, it does repel the angels. Pisses them off, too, which is the sweet part. Thanks." He clamped a hand on Blade's shoulder. "We may not have a queen, but the Casipheans will survive now that we know how to protect ourselves from our greatest foe."

"So you're going to leave Zen alone?"

Kesabel nodded. "She's more faery now than anything. I'm not convinced she'd even become demon if she did willingly descend to Daemonia. And if it was all a plot to kill us, well, then…"

"Forgive me for the ranks of Casipheans I've killed," Blade said. "I was doing what I thought right. But now I know it wasn't."

"I believe forgiveness is a human weakness," Kesabel offered. "Survival is a valuable trait to possess, especially for a vampire. No forgiveness is necessary. We will find a fitting queen. Some day. I offer you my friendship and a lifelong alliance, if you will accept."

"I do."

"You are a warrior, Blade Saint-Pierre."

Blade slapped his palm into Kesabel's and they shook. And as an angel with fiery wings soared in toward Kesabel's back, Blade leaped over the demon's head and tangled with the predator. A slice of the halo blade took off the angel's head. Blade shoved him away quickly to avoid the blue blood that spewed out.

And as he spun in the air, taking in the grounds below, he saw the angels retreating with the Casipheans tight on their wake. Kesabel commanded his few but powerful forces. Below on the ground stood Kelyn, gossamer violet wings spread wide and bow aimed toward the sky. And with her shoulders pressed against Kelyn's shoulders, Zen held guard at his back. No enemies dared approach the twosome.

Trouble loped across the battlegrounds, sniffing at the fallen dead and dashing his claws through the heaps of angel and demon dust. He did not see the emaciated demon stalking close behind him.

"Ryckt." Blade soared downward toward his nemesis, catching the demon through the shoulder with his pointed wingtip and lifting him from the ground seconds before he would have landed on Trouble.

The demon struggled but remained pierced through, even as he turned to face Blade. Suspended in the air high above the waning battle below, Blade looked into his enemy's red eyes for the first time as an aggressor.

And yet, he could not force himself to end the bastard's life, for his heart had altered.

"She didn't need to die," he said. "Octavia. You used her to lure me to your denizen."

"That I did." Ryckt lashed out his long black tongue and managed to flick it across the wingtip that pierced his shoulder. "You going to crush me now, vampire? This armor is strong and sure."

"Yeah? But it's got a weak point. I'm going to do for you what I should have done long ago."

With a bend of wing, Blade forced the demon toward him and sank his fangs into the thick vein that pulsed on its neck. There was just enough room above the armor to get a good hold. He drank deeply of the horrible blood. His faery writhed with pleasure. But he would take no joy in this win. Spitting upon the wound, he then rubbed it into the open flesh, ensuring his ichor-tainted saliva seeped in.

"No!" Ryckt squirmed and Blade released him, allowing the demon to fall. He didn't make it to the ground in one piece. The burst of demon ash showered the other piles of ash below.

So his heart hadn't altered completely. That had been a debt he needed to pay. Now he could move on.

Casting his gaze over the ground below, Blade focused on one figure in particular. Zen looked up and her eyes met his. He slapped a palm over his heart and winced. He'd forgotten about the stake.

Zen watched as the man who would slay angels for her descended from the sky. His tattered black wings allowed the moonlight to seep through in the holes torn here and there. He looked a dark angel, but he was the furthest thing from a creature from Above.

And she was glad for that.

"All's well," Kelyn announced. He'd stood beside her most of the time Blade had not been able to, taking out the enemy with bow and arrow. The faery was swift, to the degree that she hadn't seen him move most of the time.

Kelyn clasped her hand and the faint violet symbol on his wrist glowed. And in turn, Zen noticed the white marks on her inner elbows glowed.

"Does that mean…?" she said.

"I think you're sidhe," Kelyn said. "Only time will tell." He brushed her cheek and showed her the black smeared on his finger.

"That's not my blood," she said.

"Good. You had me worried. There's Blade."

The vampire landed on the ground behind them. His wings swept the air, stirring up a pile of crystal angel dust in a flurry.

Zen ran to her lover as he stumbled toward her. Hand clasped over his chest, only then did she remember he'd taken a stake to his heart. How could he be alive? Vampires died when staked through the heart. Had she only moments before he might suddenly be reduced to dust?

"No, please no."

Just as her arms touched his, he fell to his knees

before her. Head wobbling, he managed a weak smile up at her. "Love you," he muttered. Then he dropped to his side.

"Blade!"

The werewolf shifted down to his four-legged wolf shape and loped over to his vampire brother's side. He sniffed at the wood stuck in his chest and growled lowly. Kelyn joined Zen and touched Blade's throat over the carotid artery. "He's alive."

"He's got a stake in his chest." Zen stated the obvious. "We have to get it out!"

"No." Kelyn stayed her with a hand to hers. "That's the worst thing you can do. Pulling the stake out will cause the heart to explode. Right now, it's the only thing holding him together, so to speak. Have to leave it in and allow it to push out naturally as he heals."

"That's crazy. He's going to die!"

The wolf barked, echoing his brother's insistence.

"Really?" She touched Blade's cheek. "He's cold."

"He's going to need blood, and lots of it. I'll put him in the truck. Trouble, you drive into town and find blood donors. Zen, you go along with Trouble and he'll—" The brothers exchanged looks. Trouble nodded agreement to some silent command Kelyn had given him. Then the faery said, "I'll take him home. And hold vigil."

Chapter 29

Blade existed in a bleary state of exhaustion and orgasmic high. He was aware of his brothers' presence. They wandered near the couch where he lay, talking about everyday things such as women and who was going to help Stryke with the construction work. Every so often he would smell a human woman's perfume, and she would coo over him. One of his brothers would explain to the nameless woman how he was sick, and as a dying man he wanted one last kiss from a beautiful woman.

He knew what they were doing. It was a sneaky method he'd never engage to get blood. But he needed the blood and was too weak to protest the trickery, so he didn't argue. After about the fifth or sixth woman, he licked the wound on her neck and used his vampiric persuasion to make her believe she'd had a blind date with a man she had liked but wasn't interested in seeing again, as he'd done with those previously. Kelyn drove her back to town.

Trouble was off in the kitchen making something that smelled awful. Meat. Blade did hate the smell of cooked meat.

"Where's Zen?"

"You up and at 'em, bro?" Trouble's head appeared

from over the back of the couch. He was chewing on something Blade didn't want to know about. "Hungry?"

"Not for that crap."

"How you feeling?"

"Alive." He patted his chest. Had the stake moved out of his body about a quarter of an inch? He was sure when Kesabel had sliced it off it had been shaved even with his chest, so much so he'd been skinned. The skin had healed. "How many days has it been?"

"Three. You're holding on, though. Getting stronger with every neck you tap. Kelyn was right. We just keep feeding you blood and your body will heal. Soon enough it'll push that stake right out."

Blade shuffled up to a half sitting position. A dizzy wave washed through his skull. "Where is she?"

Trouble's jaw pulsed. "Uh, I told Zen to leave you be."

"She left?"

Trouble shrugged. "It's best for the both of you, bro. Sure you don't want something? I made deer sausage and kraut."

Blade had to forcibly keep from gagging. "I need Zen. She wouldn't have left town."

"She didn't leave town. Hey! Sit down. You have to rest."

Blade stood, wobbled and caught a hand on the back of the couch. This infirmity was for the birds. He needed to move, to finish what he'd started. "I need to find Zen."

"Dude." Trouble pulled off a pink ruffled apron—where he'd found that, Blade had no idea—and tossed it aside. "Fine. But tell me one thing. Do you love that chick? The one who doesn't know what she is? The one who brought a war between the angels and the demons to your doorstep?"

"Hell yes."

Trouble's smile preceded his feisty punch of fists before him. "Yes! Then let's go find her."

"Just me."

"I don't think so, man. You're wobbly at best. You're going to need more blood. I can hook you up with this chick—"

Blade clutched Trouble's shirt and jerked him to a stunning silence. "Just. Me," he muttered. "You get that nasty smell of meat out of my house before I return."

"Dude, you are no fun when you're dying."

"I'm not dying," he muttered as he wandered down the hallway to clean up.

Zen had denied the Casiphean crown in favor of choosing him. It was the right choice. The only choice. But Blade did not forget the promise he'd made Zen. After showering, he dressed and headed in to Tangle Lake, to Zen's favorite clothing store. It took some fast-talking and a little flirting, but he accomplished his mission.

Now with a black velvet bag in hand, he plodded through the forest, thick with undergrowth and few worn paths. The paths had been tromped down by his father and siblings when they went out for a run in wolf shape.

After Trouble had come clean about Zen's where-abouts he'd revealed he had suggested Zen go to his parents to stay while Blade recovered. And Kelyn had taken her there.

Blade couldn't believe she'd agreed to it. And then

he knew Trouble could be persuasive, if not intimidating. But the last thing he needed right now was distance from the one vital being who gave him life. He was suffering. The stake would take another week or two to completely push out, and that meant lots of blood to invoke the healing process.

It hurt like hell, but he was thankful that Simaseel hadn't ripped it out of his chest. The demon Kesabel had saved him. Guess not all demons were worthy of death. For without the demon's quick action he wouldn't be wandering through the woods, stumbling here and there because he wasn't at full strength, in search of a woman.

Not just any woman. The one woman who made him believe he could do better.

The gurgle of the falls signaled he was near his destination. Behind the falls was a cove of rocks where he and his brothers often rested after swimming up the stream. The water was always cool but refreshing. He was compelled to strip and plunge in, but that could wait. He had to find Zen.

A scurry of rabbits bounced to his right. Overhead, a dazzle of dragonflies, their iridescent wings catching the sun through the tree canopy, bobbled in the air, flying the same direction he was headed. The hiss of a snake clued him in on one slithering beneath the fallen leaves and grasses. And a doe leaped into view before him, glanced his way, then dashed onward, but not as if she needed to flee.

They were—all of them—headed somewhere. Together.

And then Blade felt it, the distinctive vibrations that scurried over his skin and hummed in his veins. His faery alighted within and his furled wings shivered. For moments he forgot the pain of the stake in his heart. A gorgeous perfume lured him forward, near the stream's edge, where, lying on a wet stone, he spied the halo.

She stood there, arms spread out and head tilted back. Facing him, he saw her eyes were closed as she communed with nature. Calling out to all the creatures that arrived the same time as he did. The doe walked up to Zen and sniffed at her fingers. She opened her eyes, and without startling the deer, smiled and whispered something he couldn't hear.

Clad in a floaty white dress that was so sheer he could see her dark nipples, with a start, she noticed him. The doe didn't dash away; instead, it stepped to the stream's edge for a drink.

"Blade."

Dropping the velvet sack near the halo, he approached cautiously, so as not to frighten any of the animals that surrounded Zen as if she was a Disney princess and they were waiting for her to break into song. But once close enough, he rushed into her arms and pulled her in for a hug.

"I needed you," he whispered aside her ear. "Had to find you."

"You've found me."

"What are you doing out here?"

"Your brothers told me to stay away while you healed."

"So you did?" He pulled back and studied her eyes. They were violet, like Kelyn's eyes. And the markings on her arms were bright white. He traced the curving lines inside her elbow. She was faery. "I would have you stay with me. Always."

"I didn't want to interfere in the healing process. And Trouble said there would be women. Lots of them."

Good ole Trouble. Never as much help as he thought he was.

"There weren't that many," he offered. "And I only drank their blood. Needed it to heal."

"And it worked?"

He tugged up his shirt and she pushed it higher to reveal the end of the severed stake sticking out of his chest. "Still more to go."

"You should be home. Resting. Drinking blood."

"Zen, seeing you makes me stronger. Don't ask me to leave." He twined his fingers in hers. "Please, let me stay and look at you."

"Look at me?"

"You are gorgeous. You've become, haven't you?"

She nodded. "Yes. Full faery now. You like?"

"I like you no matter what."

"I'm still waiting for a kiss. It has been days. I should think—"

He kissed her. Soundly. Firmly. Deeply. He kissed her so she would know that she was his and he hers. He kissed her to let her feel his pulse and know he was alive. He kissed her to taste her sweetness and know her strength. For she was strong and powerful.

And she was his.

"That's better. I won't ask you to leave. Ever," she said. "In fact, I want to show you something. But only if you promise to sit down on that rock there by the bunny. You are more pale than usual and you're swaying."

"Fair enough." When he landed on the rock, Blade realized he needed the rest more than he could have imagined because his head swam, as did his brain.

Yeah, more blood was a necessity. He should have found a donor before searching for Zen. "What do you want to show me?"

"I've been spending my days out here in the forest just sort of…becoming."

He lifted a brow. "And?"

"This is what I've become."

Bowing her head, the breeze listed through her copper hair. The rabbit sitting next to Blade sat up on its hind legs, as did the pair of squirrels on the other side of him. A red fox poked its nose through a frond of greenery and sniffed the air. A lush scent of flowers filled the atmosphere, accompanied by the ozone aroma of rain. It was a heady scent that seeped into Blade's being. Zen's innate perfume. He placed a hand over his heart. The wound had stopped aching.

With a sweep, her wings unfurled behind her. They were quartered as if a dragonfly's wings, and though clear they shimmered a coppery sheen to match her hair. They fluttered and then snapped out behind her and began to flap, lifting Zen from the ground.

Legs bending, then straightening as if a ballerina doing a plié, she giggled and clasped her hands to her mouth as she looked down at him. "Aren't they cool?"

He stood, following her as she floated up about ten feet from the ground. "You are the most gorgeous woman I've laid eyes on, Zen. And you sparkle."

"I know! Faery dust. That's the coolest part!"

"Can I join you?"

"Please!"

He tugged off his shirt and his wings snapped out. That startled the animals, but only for a few moments, and they sneaked back to witness as he soared up to hug Zen.

"I'm completely faery now," she said. "Your mother said so. My eyes have been this color for days. What do you think?"

"I think I'm in love."

He pulled her into his embrace, and his tattered wings curled around hers, twining within one another as they hovered above the forest floor. The dragonflies circled them, and birds fluttered close by.

"You feel that?" he asked.

"Oh, yeah. When our wings touch that's ten kinds of all right. We could have sex like this, floating in the air, clinging to one another with our wings."

"I think we should."

She placed her hand over the stake. "But first you have to heal." She circled the wood, and in her wake a glittering of faery dust coated his skin. "You can bite me, yes? My ichor won't harm your vampire?"

"It won't, thanks to the ichor that runs through my veins."

"Then, bite me, lover. Take my blood for your strength. And to make me yours."

He didn't vacillate with the consequences, because damn the consequences. He'd waited too long for this.

Blade sank his teeth into Zen's neck, drawing out the sweet, warm ichor and drinking from her deeply. No blood tainted her ichor, neither the dark taste of demon blood nor the deadly blue angel stuff. She moaned and her body hugged to his, her breasts conforming against his chest. Their wings flapped slowly, turning them minutely. Zen's faery dust spilled onto the water below, sparkling in the sun.

And as he drew her life into his body, he felt the immense power infuse him. His muscles spasmed and Zen grasped on to his arms, but he kept his lips against her neck, drinking of her. Marrying himself to her in the unspoken act of shared life.

She was *his* queen.

And the ache in his chest burned suddenly. He grunted. Zen sighed up from the exquisite pleasure of his bite and met his gaze. "What is it?"

"I think your ichor is healing me." He looked down.

She gasped as they watched the stake ease its way out of his chest. The skin around it tightened as the stake narrowed to the point, and when it was out it fell to the water below. Blade's skin knit and healed completely. He felt his bones repair and the muscles about his heart sew into strong fabric.

She kissed the bare spot where once the deadly stake had been. "Did I do that?"

He smirked and wiped a smear of ichor from his lip. "You sure did. That's some powerful ichor in your veins. Born of the angels and forged by the demons. You, Zen, are exquisite."

"You're pretty awesome yourself. Can you love a faery?"

"I already do. Can you love a vampire faery?"

"Best gift I've ever received."

"That reminds me...I brought a gift for you."

"Really? You mean I get something more than your love?"

"It's on the ground by your halo." He clasped her across the back and they descended to the soft, moss-frosted earth. Handing her the velvet bag, he waited for her reaction.

"Oh, my mercy!" She pulled out the crown, which was the cheap display-model tiara from the clothing store she had tried to buy with little luck. Sun glinted in the rhinestones. It was gaudy, but suited for her.

"Would you trade a halo for that?" he asked.

She toed the halo toward his foot, ignoring it for the prize in her hands. "You have to ask? You can give it to the halo hunter. Just let me try on this gorgeous crown."

"You are my queen," he said as he placed it on her head and kissed her.

"Take me home with you," she said. "And never let me go."

"I promise to hold you always."

* * * * *

*I hope you enjoyed Blade and Zen's story! If you're
interested in reading about the others featured in
THE VAMPIRE'S FALL,
here are the details:*

*Blu and Creed's story is
HER VAMPIRE HUSBAND*

*Malakai and Rissa's story is
MALAKAI*

*Daisy Blu and Beck's story is
GHOST WOLF*

*Stryke and Blyss's story is
MOONLIGHT & DIAMONDS*

*Dez and Ivan's story is
THE DEVIL TO PAY*

*Michael and Vinny's story is
HALO HUNTER*

*You can find all these stories in digital format
at your favorite online retailer.*

REQUEST YOUR FREE BOOKS!
2 FREE NOVELS PLUS 2 FREE GIFTS!

⊕ HARLEQUIN®

INTRIGUE

BREATHTAKING ROMANTIC SUSPENSE

YES! Please send me 2 FREE Harlequin® Intrigue novels and my 2 FREE gifts (gifts are worth about $10). After receiving them, if I don't wish to receive any more books, I can return the shipping statement marked "cancel." If I don't cancel, I will receive 6 brand-new novels every month and be billed just $4.74 per book in the U.S. or $5.49 per book in Canada. That's a savings of at least 12% off the cover price! It's quite a bargain! Shipping and handling is just 50¢ per book in the U.S. and 75¢ per book in Canada.* I understand that accepting the 2 free books and gifts places me under no obligation to buy anything. I can always return a shipment and cancel at any time. Even if I never buy another book, the two free books and gifts are mine to keep forever.

182/382 HDN GH3D

Name	(PLEASE PRINT)

Address	Apt. #

City	State/Prov.	Zip/Postal Code

Signature (if under 18, a parent or guardian must sign)

Mail to the Reader Service:
IN U.S.A.: P.O. Box 1867, Buffalo, NY 14240-1867
IN CANADA: P.O. Box 609, Fort Erie, Ontario L2A 5X3
Are you a subscriber to Harlequin® Intrigue books
and want to receive the larger-print edition?
Call 1-800-873-8635 or visit www.ReaderService.com.

* Terms and prices subject to change without notice. Prices do not include applicable taxes. Sales tax applicable in N.Y. Canadian residents will be charged applicable taxes. Offer not valid in Quebec. This offer is limited to one order per household. Not valid for current subscribers to Harlequin Intrigue books. All orders subject to credit approval. Credit or debit balances in a customer's account(s) may be offset by any other outstanding balance owed by or to the customer. Please allow 4 to 6 weeks for delivery. Offer available while quantities last.

Your Privacy—The Reader Service is committed to protecting your privacy. Our Privacy Policy is available online at www.ReaderService.com or upon request from the Reader Service.

We make a portion of our mailing list available to reputable third parties that offer products we believe may interest you. If you prefer that we not exchange your name with third parties, or if you wish to clarify or modify your communication preferences, please visit us at www.ReaderService.com/consumerschoice or write to us at Reader Service Preference Service, P.O. Box 9062, Buffalo, NY 14240-9062. Include your complete name and address.

HI15

REQUEST YOUR FREE BOOKS!
2 FREE NOVELS PLUS 2 FREE GIFTS!

ROMANTIC suspense

Sparked by danger, fueled by passion

YES! Please send me 2 FREE Harlequin® Romantic Suspense novels and my 2 FREE gifts (gifts are worth about $10). After receiving them, if I don't wish to receive any more books, I can return the shipping statement marked "cancel." If I don't cancel, I will receive 4 brand-new novels every month and be billed just $4.74 per book in the U.S. or $5.49 per book in Canada. That's a savings of at least 12% off the cover price! It's quite a bargain! Shipping and handling is just 50¢ per book in the U.S. and 75¢ per book in Canada.* I understand that accepting the 2 free books and gifts places me under no obligation to buy anything. I can always return a shipment and cancel at any time. Even if I never buy another book, the two free books and gifts are mine to keep forever.

240/340 HDN GH3P

Name	(PLEASE PRINT)	
Address		Apt. #
City	State/Prov.	Zip/Postal Code

Signature (if under 18, a parent or guardian must sign)

Mail to the **Reader Service**:
IN U.S.A.: P.O. Box 1867, Buffalo, NY 14240-1867
IN CANADA: P.O. Box 609, Fort Erie, Ontario L2A 5X3

Want to try two free books from another line?
Call 1-800-873-8635 or visit www.ReaderService.com.

* Terms and prices subject to change without notice. Prices do not include applicable taxes. Sales tax applicable in N.Y. Canadian residents will be charged applicable taxes. Offer not valid in Quebec. This offer is limited to one order per household. Not valid for current subscribers to Harlequin Romantic Suspense books. All orders subject to credit approval. Credit or debit balances in a customer's account(s) may be offset by any other outstanding balance owed by or to the customer. Please allow 4 to 6 weeks for delivery. Offer available while quantities last.

Your Privacy—The Reader Service is committed to protecting your privacy. Our Privacy Policy is available online at www.ReaderService.com or upon request from the Reader Service.

We make a portion of our mailing list available to reputable third parties that offer products we believe may interest you. If you prefer that we not exchange your name with third parties, or if you wish to clarify or modify your communication preferences, please visit us at www.ReaderService.com/consumerschoice or write to us at Reader Service Preference Service, P.O. Box 9062, Buffalo, NY 14240-9062. Include your complete name and address.

HRS11